"A very funny tale."
— *Tampa Tribune*

"Hits the mark . . . Fun."
—Associated Press

"Clever . . . mischievous."
— *Booklist*

"Crisp, knowing, Washington satire."
— *Vanity Fair*

"Gallops along . . . full of tasty nuggets."
— *Orlando Sentinel*

Praise for SUPREME COURTSHIP

"Spins through a political world only slightly more insane, but a whole lot funnier, than the one we face every day."
—*Chicago Sun-Times*

"Laugh-out-loud humorous."
—*Sunday Oregonian*

"I loved it . . . read it and enjoy. Christopher Buckley is the nation's best humor novelist."
—*Christian Science Monitor*

"Buckley has fun with the court's fractious politics and even more fun riffing on the strange creatures and customs of its marble halls . . . And he's admirably fair-minded, skewering politically correct crusaders on one page and holy-rolling bigots on the next. His villains are Washington's ideologues, left and right, whose principles always boil down to self-regard . . . bit by bit [his novels are] building up into a significant social portrait, the beginnings of a vast Comédie-Washingtonienne . . . At a time of high political absurdity, Buckley remains our sharpest guide to the capital, and a more serious one than we may suppose."
—*New York Times Book Review*

more . . .

"Fast-moving, breezy . . . a wry, behind-the-scenes tale of Washington politics."

—*Seattle Post-Intelligencer*

"So funny . . . Buckley has given us yet another maliciously funny tale. The dialogue sparkles . . . read SUPREME COURTSHIP for the laughs—and for the inside view of what really goes on in Washington. One of Judge Pepper's admirers praises her with words that could also apply to all of Buckley's capital satires. 'It's not every day we get candor of this quality in Washington.'"

—*St. Louis Post-Dispatch*

"The author has not lost his knack for playing serious situations for laughs . . . One of the book's telling points is that he never mentions which political parties these folks represent, and you realize it doesn't much matter. When you are sketching a political cartoon, donkeys and elephants alike are juicy targets."

—*Hartford Courant*

"Full of wry observations on the follies of Washington high life. What makes it laugh-out-loud funny is Buckley's sense of how little you have to exaggerate to make Washington seem absurd."

—*New York Daily News*

"Buckley slashes with the same rapier wit exhibited in last year's hysterically funny *Boomsday* . . . The laughs are fast and furious in this satire . . . His plot is clever . . . More importantly, the book is just plain funny."

—*Louisville Courier-Journal*

more . . .

"Takes reality and gives it a half turn . . . entertaining and funny . . . Buckley does not disappoint."
—*Weekend Australian*

"Merry, escapist . . . funny and entertaining."
—*Booklist*

"Buckley is in sharp satirical form with this novel."
—*Myrtle Beach Sun-News*

"Fun to read . . . Buckley has a way of reducing Washington pomposity to its most base and humorous elements."
—*Newark Star-Ledger*

"Funny . . . Buckley's rules of satirical engagement seem to be: Work quickly and swing at everything that moves."
—*Richmond Times-Dispatch*

"Satirist Christopher Buckley is back skewering politicians in this laugh-out-loud funny romp."
—*Tulare Advance-Register* (CA)

"Buckley's deft hand at humor and knowledge of 'inside the beltway' politics deserves any court's unanimous approval."
—*Tampa Tribune*

SUPREME COURTSHIP

SUPREME COURTSHIP

A NOVEL

CHRISTOPHER BUCKLEY

NEW YORK 12 BOSTON

TWELVE

Twelve
Hachette Book Group
237 Park Avenue
New York, NY 10017

Visit our website at www.HachetteBookGroup.com

Twelve is an imprint of Grand Central Publishing.
The Twelve name and logo are trademarks of Hachette Book Group, Inc.

Book design by Fearn Cutler de Vicq
Printed in the United States of America

Originally published in hardcover by Twelve.

First Trade Edition: September 2009
10 9 8 7 6 5 4 3 2 1

The Library of Congress has cataloged the hardcover edition as follows:
Buckley, Christopher
  Supreme courtship / Christopher Buckley.—1st ed.
    p. cm.
  ISBN: 978-0-446-57982-7
    1. United States. Supreme Court—Fiction. 2. Judges—Fiction. 3. Television personalities—Fiction. 4. Washington (DC) —Fiction. 5. Political fiction. I. Title.
  PS3552.U3394S87 2008
  813'.54—dc22   2008007788

ISBN: 978-0-446-69798-9 (pbk.)

For Jolie Hunt
BGITU

CHAPTER 1

Supreme Court Associate Justice J. Mortimer Brinnin's deteriorating mental condition had been the subject of talk for some months now, but when he showed up for oral argument with his ears wrapped in aluminum foil, the consensus was that the time had finally come for him to retire. Thank God, his fellow justices agreed—unanimously, for once—cameras weren't allowed in the Court.

Brinnin was a distinguished jurist who had cast some of the most consequential votes of his day. But the sun had now (emphatically) set on that day. His mind, once capable of quoting entire opinions as far back as the nineteenth century, in toto and verbatim, was now succumbing to medication (for persistent sciatica) and increasingly copious evening martinis. He had taken to summoning his clerks in the middle of the night to tell them that there were moray eels in the toilet. On another occasion, also at three a.m., he met them at the front door holding a bag of kitchen garbage and instructed them that they must get it to Omaha—without delay. (Justice Brinnin had grown up there.) It was when Justice Brinnin became convinced that the ghost of Oliver Wendell Holmes Jr. was whispering in his ears trying to influence his vote that he reached for the aluminum foil.

Chief Justice Declan Hardwether, who was himself going

through a rough patch at the time, found the situation embarrassing. He was not by nature a confrontational man and so was at pains what to do. None of the other justices, who were, at any rate, hardly speaking to one another, wanted to intervene. So the CJ turned to the den-motherly Justice Paige Plympton.

"You've got to do something," he pleaded, "before he shows up dressed like the Tin Man, singing 'Somewhere Over the Rainbow.'"

Justice Plympton dealt with the situation with her usual grace and gentle persuasiveness. And when that didn't work, she assembled Justice Brinnin's children in a conference call intervention.

In due course, the Marshal of the Court hand-delivered Justice Brinnin's letter of resignation to the White House. The news was duly announced. Nothing raises the national temperature more than a VACANCY sign hanging from the colonnaded front of the Supreme Court.

PRESIDENT VANDERDAMP was not at the time riding a tidal wave of popularity. His approval ratings were, in fact, abysmal, though his press secretary was always quick to stress that they were in "the *high* twenties."

Donald P. Vanderdamp had been elected two and a half years ago in a three-way race that included a hedge-fund billionaire who spent $350 million of his own money. Vanderdamp squeaked across the finish line with two electoral votes to spare. He had run on a platform of "changing the way Washington does business."

Everyone who runs for president says they are going to change the way Washington does business. The surprise was that Donald P. Vanderdamp, former Eagle Scout, naval officer, mayor, governor, affable, decent, churchgoing, family-oriented, golden retriever–owning midwesterner, actually meant it. He was sixty-four years old and, as one waspish pundit put it, "fast approaching retirement age, and not a minute too soon." He was physically unremarkable in an Eisenhowerish sort of way: balding, trim, pleasant-looking but with the quietly commanding look of, say, an airline pilot or high school principal. Some people fill a room. Not Donald P. Vanderdamp. His blandness—what another pundit had called his "ineffable Donald-ness"—had served him well over the years. It invited underestimation. People tittered at his great passion and hobby—bowling.

Faced with a national debt mind-boggling even by Washington standards, Donald P. Vanderdamp had rolled up his shirtsleeves on his first day in office, unscrewed the cap of the presidential veto pen, and gone to work. He wrote *No* on every spending bill that the Congress sent to his desk.

He was determined to bring order to the nation's books. So far, he had vetoed 185 spending bills, acquiring the nickname "Don Veto." It was an incongruent term, given his total lack of Italianate qualities. Donald P. Vanderdamp was paradigmatically nonethnic, as middle American as sliced white bread. (Excellent with peanut butter and jelly but not much else.) But as Don Veto he had evolved into the sworn enemy of the majority of the United States Congress, whose members understand that their main job, their highest calling, their truest democratic function, is to take money from other states and funnel it to their own. What greater homage to the Founding Fathers and the men who froze at Valley Forge could there be than a civic center in Tulsa paid for by the taxpayers of Massachusetts?

Nominating someone to the Supreme Court can be hard enough for a popular president. For one at the opposite end of the likability spectrum, it presents a daunting challenge, as well as a delicious opportunity for the chief bouncer at the rope line in front of the Supreme Court entryway: the chairman of the Senate Judiciary Committee.

The current occupant of that powerful chair was a man named Dexter Mitchell, senator from the great state of Connecticut. Dexter Mitchell despised Donald P. Vanderdamp, though he was always careful, in his public statements, to say that he had "the greatest respect" for him. He despised him for a variety— or as they say in Washington, "multiplicity"—of reasons. He despised him because he had vetoed S. 322, a bill Mitchell had sponsored that would have required every helicopter rotor blade in the U.S. military to be made in his home state of Connecticut. And he despised Donald P. Vanderdamp for ignoring his suggestion that he appoint *him* to fill the Brinnin vacancy on the high court. (More about that in due course.)

President Vanderdamp's first nominee to succeed Brinnin was a distinguished appellate judge named Cooney. Enormous care had gone into his selection, knowing that Senator Mitchell's Judiciary Committee was preparing an auto-da-fé that would have made the Spanish Inquisition blush. Cooney was a jurist of impeccable credentials. Indeed, he seemed to have been put on earth precisely for the purpose of one day becoming a justice of the United States Supreme Court.

Senator Mitchell's Judiciary Committee staff investigators were known on Capitol Hill as the Wraith Riders, after the relentless, spectral, horse-mounted pursuers of hobbits in *The Lord of the Rings*. It was said in hushed tones on Capitol Hill that the Wraith Riders could find something on anyone: could make it look like Mother Teresa had run a whorehouse in Calcutta; that St. Thomas More had been having it off with Catherine of Aragon; or that Dr. Albert Schweitzer had conducted ghastly live medical experiments on helpless, unanesthetized African children on behalf of Belgian drug companies.

However, faced with the blemishless Judge Cooney, the Wraith

Riders were left to whinny there was nothing with which to hang him, not even an unpaid parking ticket. He was an exemplar of every judicial virtue. Not one of his decisions had been overturned by a higher court. As for his personal life, he was so reasonable and wise that he made Socrates sound like a raving, bipolar crank.

Dig deeper, Senator Mitchell told the Wraith Riders. Or dig your own graves. Off they rode, shrieking.

And so, on day two of the Cooney hearings, Senator Mitchell, smiling pleasantly as usual, began: "Judge Cooney, you are, I take it, familiar with the film *To Kill a Mockingbird*?"

Judge Cooney answered yes, he was pretty sure he'd seen it, back in grade school.

"Is there anything about that you'd care to . . . *tell* the Committee?"

Judge Cooney looked perplexed. Tell? He wasn't quite sure he understood the question.

Senator Mitchell held up a piece of paper as if mere physical contact with it might forever contaminate his fingers.

"Do you recognize this document?"

Not from this distance, Judge Cooney replied, now thoroughly perplexed.

"Then let me refresh your memory," Senator Mitchell said. The vast audience watching the proceedings held its breath, wondering what radioactive material Senator Mitchell had unearthed to incriminate this spotless nominee. It turned out to be a review of the movie that the twelve-year-old Cooney had written for *The Beaverboard*, his elementary school newspaper. "'*Though the picture is overall OK*,'" Senator Mitchell quoted, "'*it's also kind of boring in other parts.*'"

Senator Mitchell looked up, took off his glasses, paused as if fighting back tears, nodded philosophically, and said, "Tell us, Judge, which parts of *To Kill a Mockingbird* did you find quote-unquote boring?"

In his concluding statement several grueling days later, Senator Mitchell said in a more-in-sadness-than-in-anger tone that he could "not in good conscience bring myself to vote for someone who might well show up at the Court on the first Monday of October wearing not black judicial robes but the white uniform of the Ku Klux Klan."

And that was the end of Judge Cooney. The chairman of the Judiciary Committee issued a statement politely inviting the White House to "send us a nominee we can all agree on."

PRESIDENT DONALD P. VANDERDAMP repressed the temptation to storm up Pennsylvania Avenue and insert Senator Mitchell's microphone in an orifice not specifically designed for such purposes, swallowed what was left of his pride, and instructed his staff to find another Supreme Court nominee, preferably one who hadn't written movie reviews for his elementary school newspaper. In due course, he put forward nomineee number two, a New York State Court of Appeals judge named Burrows.

Judge Burrows had credentials that would entitle him to the E-ZPass lane at the Pearly Gates. Again, the Wraith Riders returned from their exhumations shrieking helplessly. Burrows's after-hours hobby—his *hobby*—was providing pro bono legal counseling to inmates at the state penitentiary. He had lost a leg ejecting from his F-4 fighter plane over Vietnam. None of his rulings had been overturned. His wife was a Vietnamese refugee. They had adopted two Rwandan orphans.

Senator Mitchell, studying his dossier, furrowed his brow. *No, this would not be easy.* The Wraith Riders whinnied forth again and this time did not return with empty claws. A woman had been located who had dated Burrows when he was a midshipman at the U.S. Naval Academy. Senator Mitchell smiled and dispensed lumps of sugar to the Riders.

"Judge Burrows," Senator Mitchell said, "does the name [such and such] mean anything to you?"

Judge Burrows calmly but coolly returned the senator's gaze and said that he hardly thought that had anything to do with anything.

"Perhaps we should be the—pardon the expression—judges of that," Senator Mitchell just as coolly replied. After a few more questions he had grudgingly elicited that Judge Burrows had indeed dated Ms. Such-and-Such back then; further, that at one point she thought she might have become pregnant.

Again the room hushed.

"Judge Burrows," he said, "and I really do hate having to ask these questions, but it is my job . . . is it true that you tried to talk Ms. Sinclair out of having an abortion?"

No, Judge Burrows replied. Not at all. But he had offered to do the honorable thing and marry her and raise the child. And then it turned out that she wasn't pregnant after all.

The next day Senator Mitchell announced that he could not, in good conscience, vote to approve someone so "maniacally" opposed to a woman's right to choose, as enshrined in *Roe v. Wade*.

And so ended Judge Burrows's brief Supreme Court career.

That afternoon the normally placid-faced President Donald P. Vanderdamp strode to the helicopter on the South Lawn of the White House looking, as one reporter commented, "like he was ready to bite the head off a live chicken." He did not throw the crowd his customary wave. Even the presidential golden retriever, Dwight, a friendly, pattable hound, looked eager to sink his fangs into the nearest shin.

MORE THAN SEVERAL HISTORIANS of the Vanderdamp presidency have speculated that the events that followed might very well not have taken place if the President had not chanced to turn on the television late that Friday night at Camp David, the presidential retreat. But turn it on he did. Rarely has channel-surfing been so consequential.

In an oral history on deposit at the Vanderdamp Presidential Library in Wapakoneta, Ohio, President Vanderdamp relates that he was simply trying to find the Bowling Channel that night. He was not a guileful person, so there is no reason not to believe him. Apart from the news shows and the bowling, he was not a big watcher of television, preferring crossword puzzles and murder mysteries. He claims never to have watched *Courtroom Six* before or ever to have heard of it, though it was one of TV's top ten–rated shows.

At any rate, that Friday night found the President at his retreat in the Cactoctin Mountains, alone in bed with a bowl of Graeter's black raspberry chip ice cream—an Ohioan delicacy—and the faithful hound, Dwight. The First Lady was being honored for raising awareness of a disease at a dinner in New York. Fuming over the Burrows fiasco while clicking his way through the cable channels in search of a decent bowling tournament, the President happened upon *Courtroom Six*. The rest is, as they say, history.

The episode he came upon was the one involving the ex-wife who, seeking revenge on her ex-husband for what she considered an inequitable distribution of assets, had snuck into his wine cellar while he was away and opened hundreds of bottles of prized Bordeaux wines—by hand, one by one—replacing the wine with diet grape juice; then recorking and resealing them. It's one of *Courtroom Six*'s more well-known cases. As the wife is being sworn in by the clerk, she raises a hand ostentatiously encased in an orthopedic brace.

"May I ask," Judge Cartwright, presiding, asks, "what's the deal with the hand?"

"Carpal tunnel, Your Honor."

Judge Cartwright, barely suppressing a grin, says, "The jury will disregard the defendant's remark."

"Objection," says the prosecutor. "Grounds, Your Honor?"

"I don't know." Judge Cartwright shrugs. "But I'll think of something."

President Vanderdamp's finger, poised on the channel button to keep on flicking, stayed. He found himself, along with millions of other Americans, entertained and captivated. He watched the entire show. He found himself quite taken by the charm and sassy style—to say nothing of the good looks—of Judge Pepper Cartwright.

"Pepper?" the President said aloud to himself, musing. "What sort of name is that for a judge?"

Dwight lifted his head off the pillow next to the President's and cocked an ear in hopes of discerning syllabic similarity between the words being spoken and "biscuit."

President Vanderdamp was not an imperious—much less imperial—president, one to summon the staff at late hours with urgent requests. When he walked Dwight on the White House grounds, he cleaned up after him himself. He had once ordered a (richly deserved) B-2 bomb strike in the middle of night, mainly because he did not want to disturb his elderly secretary of defense, who had just had another prostate operation and needed his sleep.

Now he reached for the presidential laptop, a computer of truly dazzling capability, and Googled Judge Pepper Cartwright and *Courtroom Six*. He stayed up well past his normal bedtime.

THE NEXT MORNING at breakfast he asked the steward, "Jackson, have you ever seen a TV show called *Courtroom Six*?"

"Yes, sir."

"What do you think of it?"

"Watch it every chance I get, sir."

"What do you think of the judge—Judge Pepper?"

"Oh," Jackson smiled, not servant to president, but man to man, "I like her a whole lot, sir. She's a smart lady. She hands it out good. And she's awful . . ."

"Go ahead, Jackson."

Jackson grinned. "Awful easy on the eyes."

"Thank you, Jackson."

"Another waffle, sir? Griddle's still hot."

"Yes," the President said. "I think I will. But Jackson—not a word to the First Lady."

"Oh, *no*, sir."

CHAPTER 2

Good show," said Buddy Bixby, creator and producer of *Courtroom Six*, and spouse to its star.

They were in Pepper's dressing room, generally referred to jocularly as her "chambers," following the taping.

"What was so awful about it?" Pepper said, removing her judicial robes, revealing a bra, pantyhose, and high heels. It was a sight to induce infarction in the most hardened of male arteries, but in a husband of six years, barely a glance.

"I said it was a good show," Buddy said. "What am I supposed to say?"

"'Good' is what you say when you thought it was roadkill. When you really think it was good, you do that producer macho trash talk. *'Great fucking show.' 'Outta the fucking ballpark.'*"

"It was a great fucking show. It took my fucking breath away."

"You're the only person I know who can say that while sounding like you're suppressing a yawn." Pepper yanked a Baby Wipe from the box and began removing makeup. "What's eating you, anyway?"

"We're getting killed against *Law & Order*."

Pepper sighed. "We're not getting killed against *Law & Order*. We're doing fine."

"We're down a half point." Buddy treated any dip in *Courtroom Six*'s ratings as a state of emergency. "By what definition is that 'fine'?"

"What's got into you? You're more nervous than a long-tailed cat on a porchful of rocking chairs."

"These sentences you're handing out . . ."

"What about them?"

"You're letting the women off kind of easy, don't you think?"

"No. What else did you want to talk about?"

"The bitch poured $150,000 worth of fine French wine down the drain! And you sentence her to six hours of *anger management therapy*?"

Pepper tossed a Baby Wipe into the wastebasket. "What did you have in mind? Lethal injection? Hanging?"

"What about making her drink the grape juice? *That* would have been something. Poetic justice. Instead of anger management therapy." Buddy shook his head. "I'm glad you're not in charge of the war on terror. The terrorists would be at spas having manicures."

Pepper brushed her hair and tried to tune out her husband's normal postshow hand-wringing and critiques. The better things went, the more he needed to worry that some calamity was imminent, a once-charming trait now a bit tedious. Buddy did care about *Courtroom Six*. It was his class act—"class" being a somewhat relative term, considering his other shows: *Jumpers*, a reality show based on security camera footage of people who jump off bridges; *G.O.* (the medical abbreviation for "grotesquely obese"); and now a show called *Yeehad*, a "comedy" about five patriotic Southerners who decide to travel to Mecca to blow up Islam's most sacred shrine, the Q'aaba. Buddy had eight shows running. According to *Forbes*, they were earning him $74 million a year. But *Courtroom Six* was the jewel in the crown.

"I'm just saying that there would appear to be a noticeable feminist . . . *thing* going on with these sentences you're handing down."

"I thought we'd had that discussion."

"Excuse me for pointing out something the *entire world* is talking about. I'm just saying—if it *please* the court—that you've been letting these women off easy. But if it's a guy, you go at him like he's a fucking piñata."

"Buddy, honey," Pepper said, "the ex-husband, whose Bordeaux wine you regard like it's holy water, was tighter than bark on a tree with the alimony and the child support. I'm not going to cry me a river on account of his '82 Petrus." She sniffed. "Been me, I'd have busted the bottles over his head. One by one."

"I rest my case," Buddy said triumphantly.

"Well, you go rest your case. *This* girl is going to go rest her tail."

She shimmied into her jeans and lizard-skin cowboy boots. Simple white blouse, raised collar, turquoise stud earrings, suede jacket, and over-the-shoulder handbag: she looked like a woman who knew her way on a New York City sidewalk. In the handbag was a .38 caliber Smith & Wesson LadySmith revolver, a gift from her grandfather. She was licensed to carry.

"Could I just say one thing?" Buddy said.

"No, darlin'. But I have a feeling you're going to, anyway."

"Do you know how many of our viewers are male?"

"No, sweetheart. I leave those details to you. I'm just a simple girl from Plano."

"Yeah, yeah. Well, then, my little cactus bud, you might be interested to know that we're down six percent among male viewers."

Pepper said, "Well, damn. I guess there's nothing left to do but throw myself off the Brooklyn Bridge. If nothing else, it'll give you a season finale for *Jumpers*."

Bill said pleadingly, "But—don't you *care?*"

"I care that I'm going to be late for my mani-pedi."

"Why have we had such success—historically speaking— among male viewers?"

"Presumably on account of my Solomonic dispensation of justice."

"A major factor, no question. But another factor?"

Pepper was headed for the door.

"Excuse me," Buddy said, "am I *boring* you?"

"Yes. Seriously so."

"Then let me get right to the point." Buddy lowered his voice, as if he were revealing a classified secret. "The sponsors are not happy."

Pepper rolled her eyes.

"Fine," Buddy said. "Shoot the messenger if it makes you feel better. As for Hummer and Budweiser? I would not describe them as happy campers."

"Buddy. *Buddy.* We're the number seven show on TV. I just do not *see* the problemo."

"The problemo? I'll tell you the *problemo.* The problemo is that I care-o."

"All right," said Pepper, slinging her bag back over her shoul-der, "if it'll get me out of here, I promise—I *swear*—next female defendant, no matter how innocent she is, that bitch is going to Guantánamo for some serious attitude adjustment."

Buddy smiled. "Thank you, Your Honor."

PEPPER CARTWRIGHT and Buddy Bixby, respectively of Plano, Texas, and New Rochelle, New York, were from very different worlds but had happened to find each other seven years before in a courtroom—an actual courtroom, that is—Courtroom 6 in Los Angeles Superior Court.

Buddy was at the time a midlevel (which is to say, not high level) local TV news producer, fast approaching fifty. His career had consisted of a series of almosts. He had almost gotten footage of Squeaky Fromme attempting to shoot President Gerald Ford; had almost gotten an on-camera interview with the reclusive billionaire Howard Hughes; had almost bought Microsoft at six dollars a share; almost gotten the big job back in New York.

He'd been asked to be the speaker at his twenty-fifth college reunion, a prospect that greatly pleased him, until the class secretary, whom Buddy had cordially detested for twenty-nine years, called back a few days later blithely to say never mind, he'd just heard back from the first person he'd asked, parenthethes, *No offense, but sort of a bigger catch than you, ha-ha, so anyway, see you there, big guy.*

Asshole.

Lying in bed that night, eating a giant bag of Cheetos while staring existentially at the ceiling, Buddy imagined the headstone on his grave: "Here Lies Buddy Bixby. Almost."

One day at work, looking to fill a "soft" feature slot for the weekend program, one of the reporters mentioned there was this judge down at Superior Court: "H.O.T. Hot. Made me want to go out and commit a crime."

Buddy went down to court to check out the judicial dish. The sign on door of Courtroom 6 announced: JUDGE PEPPER CARTWRIGHT, PRESIDING. He thought, Pepper Cartwright— what the hell kind of name is that? Walking in, he saw a woman in her midthirties, tall, lush brown hair, cool blue eyes, high cheekbones, and deep dimples. She smiled but had a no-nonsense look to her. She wore glasses, which she kept taking off and putting back on. She'd chew on the stem in a pensive gesture. She had an accent which at first he thought Southern but quickly nailed as Texan. Sassy, flippant, sexy. All that was missing was a cowboy hat.

It was an assault case. Felony assault. The defendant looked well dressed for a felonious assaulter. He had three lawyers at his table.

The assaultee was on the stand, being cross-examined by one of the defense lawyers.

"Mr. *En-ri-quez*," the lawyer was saying, trying to make the surname sound criminal in itself, "you have testified that my client, Mr. Burson, quote-unquote threatened you. Would you define the verb 'threaten' for the court?"

"Objection," said the DA wearily.

"Sustained," said Judge Cartwright. "Cut it out, Counselor."

"Your Honor, I'm merely trying to—"

"If you're unsure of the meaning of the word 'threaten' I'll have the court clerk provide you with a copy of Webster's dictionary. You'll find it under *T*, right before *time*-waster."

"Your honor, I know what 'threaten' means. I'm merely trying to establish whether Mr. Enriquez knows what—"

"Come on, Counselor. Giddyup here. I've seen glaciers move quicker than you."

Several jurors laughed. One of other defense attorneys smiled, until his client noticed, whereupon he reassumed an attitude of expensive consternation.

Mr. Enriquez, Buddy inferred, was a kiddie-league soccer referee. The defendant was evidently the father of an eight-year-old player. He had apparently disagreed with several of Mr. Enriquez's calls against his daughter's team and, after the game, had—allegedly—tried to run Mr. Enriquez over with his Mercedes in the parking lot.

A squabble broke out over whether the cost of the defendant's Mercedes was admissible. The defense had kept objecting to the DA's repeated references to the "hundred-thousand-dollar weapon."

"Mr. Setrakian," said Judge Cartwright to the DA, "are you

trying to make a socioeconomic point here? If I may analogize, a ten-dollar Saturday Night Special handgun is just as lethal as a $100,000 engraved London-made shotgun. Or are you striving to make some other kind of point here?"

"Your Honor," said the DA, who seemed to be enjoying himself immensely—everyone in court seemed to be, even the jurors—"I am merely trying to establish that a weapon, in this case a $100,000 Mercedes E Class—"

"Objection," two of the defendant's attorneys said simultaneously.

"One objection per client, if you don't mind," said the judge. "Now see here, Mr. Setrakian," she returned to the DA, "you have majestically established that the defendant's car cost a bucket of money. I very much doubt if this point you've been making as subtly as a sledgehammer has been lost on any juror who's managed to say awake."

"Your Honor," the DA said, grinning, "you're being very severe with me today."

"I'm sorry, Mr. Setrakian," Judge Cartwright said, cheeks dimpling as she put her glasses back on. " 'I must be cruel only to be kind. Thus bad begins, and worse remains behind.' Proceed, please. Proceed. Let's try to finish up before the next ice age."

After adjournment, Buddy sought out Judge Pepper's chambers. He presented his media credentials and was admitted. Judge Pepper was standing behind her desk. Buddy stood and stared.

"You here to see me about something," she said, "or just browsin'?"

"No. Sorry," Buddy said, still staring.

"What can I do for you, sir?"

"What you said back there to the DA. 'I must be cruel in order to be nice . . .' What was that about?"

Judge Cartwright stared back curiously. "That would be Shakespeare."

"Shakespeare?" Buddy said. "No shit?"

"Yes, shit." Judge Cartwright cocked her head. "You all right, sir?"

"Oh, yeah," Buddy said. "Great."

CHAPTER 3

White House Chief of Staff Hayden Cork was as usual in his office early on a Saturday morning, while the rest of the world slept in, played tennis, and lingered over the papers and coffee. He was putting together the final touches on the file for President Vanderdamp in this, their (sigh) third effort to fill the (damn) Brinnin vacancy.

Though he was exhausted and enervated by the Cooney and Burrows debacles, the adrenaline was pulsing in Hayden Cork's veins. His engine normally ran cool, but there's no more heady kind of head-hunting than picking a nominee for the Supreme Court of the United States. For a president, nothing short of war, perhaps, is more consequential than putting a justice on the Court—a fact generally pointed out every four years by whoever is running second in the polls.

Before flying off yesterday to Camp David in a simmering rage, Vanderdamp had instructed Hayden to have a name ready for him first thing Monday morning.

"See if Mother Teresa is available," he said acidulously.

"I believe she's dead, sir."

"Then try the Pope."

"I have a thought," Hayden said cautiously. "But I don't think you're going to like it."

"Go on."

"Dexter Mitchell."

The President's normally placid Ohioan face curdled.

"Mitchell?" he said. "After what he did to Cooney and Burrows? Never mind to us. Hayden, have you taken leave of your senses?"

"Walk with me, sir. As we know all too well," Cork said, shifting in his chair, "he wants the job himself."

"Yes," said the President. "I recall. That visit he paid me. Not an experience I'd care to repeat."

"No, sir." It was a painful memory. "But if I may, it might earn us some points on the Hill. God knows we could use a little goodwill up there. And it would be a real, boy oh boy, stunneroo. Take everyone by surprise."

"Hayden," the President said. "Listen to me very closely. I'll say this once more and never again. Write it down. Dexter Mitchell will not sit on the Supreme Court while I am President. Did you get all that down? Read it back to me."

"I understand, sir." It was now or never. "But it was Graydon's idea."

Hayden Cork knew that the mere mention of the august syllables would give the President pause. "His thinking is that since most of the senators on Mitchell's own committee can't stand him, they'd be grateful to you for getting rid of him."

"By making him one of the nine most powerful people in the country? In the universe? That's one heck of a way to get rid of someone."

"Okay, there's that, but our immediate problem, frankly, sir, is a Congress that . . . Sir, let's face it, we're not very popular up there."

"I don't care about that, Hayden. I am trying to accomplish things here."

"I *understand* that, sir. I'm merely *saying* that *Graydon* thinks it would be the smart move. Those were in fact his exact words. That it would be the smart move."

The President stared at his chief of staff. "Sounds as though you two had a good long chinwag about all this," the President said.

"He is your most trusted senior adviser, sir. Or would you prefer I not discuss the welfare of your presidency with him?"

"I'd like a name from you by close of business Monday. I don't mean to ruin another weekend, Hayden. I know you've been working full-out. But just get me a name. This circus has gone on long enough."

"Yes, Mr. President."

THERE WERE SEVEN NAMES in Hayden's dossier this sunny Saturday morning: two (venerable) state Supreme Court justices, a (more or less venerable) senator, three appellate judges (pretty venerable), a state attorney general (venerable enough), and the dean of the Yale Law School (predictably but by no means excitingly venerable).

Another way of putting it was: two women, one African-American, two Jews, one Hispanic, and—Hayden smiled. His inner chief of staff let out a little war whoop of joy—*an Indian*.

Native American, Hayden corrected himself: the very first ever to be named to the high court. Yes, he was sure Vanderdamp would go for him. Vanderdamp was as American as a Jell-O mold. How more American could you get than someone named Russell Runningwater? He could hardly wait to see Dexter Mitchell's face when he learned the news. *Let's see you try to bury* this *heart at Wounded Knee, you son of a bitch*. Hayden beamed. Outside, birds chirped. The sun shone on dewy emerald grass. Butterflies—nature's own screen savers—flitted about.

Hayden's phone rang. "The President, Mr. Cork, for you."

Excellent, Hayden thought. He sat up straight in his chair, a habit even after two and a half years and how many thousands of presidential phone calls.

"Good morning, Hayden."

"Good morning, sir."

"And what are you doing in the office on a Saturday?" It was a little routine they had.

"Attending to the people's business, sir."

"Good, good. And how sails the ship of state?"

"Steadily, sir, steadily."

He sounded relaxed. Camp David usually had that effect. The private bowling alley. The sandpaper grit in yesterday's conversation was gone.

Hayden was not one to waste presidential weekend time on persiflage. "I've got those names for you. And the one at the top of the list is one I think you're going to like. I guarantee it'll give our friend Senator Mitchell a case of third-degree heartburn."

"What do you know about a Judge Pepper Cartwright?" the President said.

Odd question. "The television personality?"

"She has a show called *Courtroom Six.*"

"I don't watch TV. Other than the news shows. Would you like some information on her?"

"No, no. I want to *see* her."

"Is there a particular episode that you'd like me to locate for you?"

"No, Hayden. I want to see *her.* Judge Cartwright. In the flesh. I want to meet with her. Right away."

"Very well, sir," Hayden said, mystified. "I'm sure she'll be flattered."

"Oh," the President chuckled softly, "I expect she will be. Call her right away."

"Yes, sir. And what should I tell her is the purpose of the meeting?"

"Well, I'd be a little coy about that over the phone."

"Coy, sir? I'm not sure I follow."

"You haven't had your second cup of coffee, Hayden," the President said. "I want to talk to her about the Brinnin seat."

Hayden Cork's universe stood still.

"I'm not trying to be obtuse, sir," Hayden stammered. "But I'm not sure I'm . . . tracking here."

"The Court, Hayden."

Hayden Cork tried to speak. His tongue refused to obey the signals being transmitted from the brain. All he could say was, "Not the Brinnin seat, sir. Surely . . ."

"Why? Is there another opening? Did a justice croak in the night?"

"Not to my . . . No, sir."

"All right, then. Call her. Call her right now. Get her up to Camp David—today. Tomorrow at the latest. Be easier, a whole lot easier, to talk to her up here than back at the office with the whole darned press corps listening at the keyhole. Vultures."

Say something, Hayden thought, like a man struggling against an enveloping coma. *Do not let him terminate the conversation. Do not let him hang up.*

"Sir . . . have you . . . discussed this with Mr. Clenndennynn?"

Graydon Clenndennynn: wisest of the Washington wise men, grayest of its eminences, adviser to seven—or was it eight?—presidents. Former Attorney General. Former Secretary of State. Former Secretary of the Exterior. Former Ambassador to France. Former everything. First among equals in the Vanderdamp kitchen cabinet. The man, it was rumored, with more *n*'s in his name than anyone else in Washington.

"Hayden," the President said. "I know what I'm doing."

Panic—panic of the pulse-pounding, skin-dampening,

sphincter-tightening type—gripped Hayden Cork like a boa constrictor. How many times had those awful words—"I know what I'm doing"—been uttered throughout history as prelude to disaster? The night before Waterloo in Napoleon's tent? In the Reichschancellery before invading Soviet Russia? Before the "cakewalk" known as Operation Iraqi Freedom?

"Mr. President," Hayden croaked, "I really must—"

"Thank you, Hayden. Good-bye, Hayden."

"But—"

"*Thank* you, Hayden."

"Sir—Mr. President? Hello?"

Hayden Cork cradled the phone. Outside, the sun was shining, birds were chirping, bumblebees bumbled, but there was no springtime now in his heart; only winter, and a harsh wind shrieking through leaf-stripped trees.

His temples throbbed. He hesitated, then picked up the phone and gasped to the White House operator, "Get me Graydon Clenndennynn."

Less than fifteen minutes later, Cork's phone rang. Graydon Clenndennynn did not personally carry a cell phone; his minions did. He was in his eighties now, and of an eminence that scorned such modern devices.

"Yes, Hayden," he said without annoyance, but with formality that signaled this was not the time for leisurely philosophical discussion.

"Where are you?"

"Beijing."

"Damn," Hayden said.

"At dinner," Clenndennynn continued, "with the deputy chairman. What's the emergency?"

Graydon Clenndennynn did not object to being interrupted in the middle of meetings with world leaders, as long as it was the White House calling. Nor, to tell the truth, was he above certain self-enhancing acts of legerdemain. Once, to impress a Russian foreign minister, he arranged to have himself called in the middle of their meeting, so that he could tell the interrupting aide, "Tell the President I'll just have to call him back." The minister was duly impressed—until the Russian security services reported to him that the call had originated from Graydon Clenndennynn's own Washington office.

"You need to get back here," Hayden said. "You need to get back here right away. I'll send a plane."

Clenndennynn said, sounding alarmed, "Is there—has the President been—"

"No, no, *no*, he's fine. No, he's not fine. He's gone off the deep end. He's completely and totally lost it."

"Hayden," said Clenndennynn, "I'm keeping the second most powerful man in China waiting. Our Peking duck is mummifying. Tell me in a simple, English sentence: what is the precise nature of this emergency?"

Hayden summarized the situation.

There was a long pause at the other end, followed by a baritone "Hmm," a preliminary note on a large organ signaling the key of the hymn about to be played.

"I'll be back in Washington on Tuesday," Clenndennynn said. "Stall."

"He told me to get her up to Camp David—today."

"Hayden. Short of nuclear warheads that have already been launched, there is no situation that cannot be met head-on with inaction."

"What am I supposed do?" Hayden said.

"Tell him anything. That she's realizing a lifelong ambition and climbing Mount Kilimanjaro. Temporize, Hayden. *Temporize*. I must go."

Graydon Clenndennynn handed the cell phone to his aide

and rejoined the deputy chairman and duck. Six thousand miles away, Hayden Cork exhaled and leaned back in his black leather chair. His intestines were still in a knot but at least the kettle-drum throbbing in his temples had subsided. Graydon would figure something out. The President would listen to him. All would be well.

AN HOUR LATER, having uncharacteristically not heard back from his chief of staff, President Vanderdamp decided to place the call to Judge Pepper Cartwright himself.

He was not a man who stood on formality. He still carried cash, unlike some presidents who went four or eight years with empty pockets. He got Judge Cartwright's unlisted number in New York from the White House operator, and dialed it himself. He liked to do that. The truth was he got a kick out of saying, "Hello, it's Donald Vanderdamp. The President. Am I calling at a bad time?"

IN NEW YORK, in a penthouse atop a building that looked out over Central Park, the phone rang.

Pepper Cartwright opened her eyes, looked warily at the beside clock. *8:49.* On a Saturday? She looked over at Buddy. Sound asleep. He'd come in after she'd gone to bed. As usual. This marriage needed to sit down and have a little talk about things.

She looked at the caller ID display. *NSF THURMONT.* What in hell was NSF Thurmont? She closed her eyes and listened.

"Hello. It's Donald Vanderdamp—the President—calling for Judge Cartwright." Pepper opened one eye and looked at the machine. "Would she be kind enough to call me back at

202-456-1414. Thanks very much. If it's not inconvenient, perhaps she could call back at her earliest—"

Pepper picked up. "Hello? Who is this?"

"Judge Cartwright? Screening your calls. Can't say as I blame you. I know it's early, but I really would like to speak with you. . . ."

He talked on as Pepper thumbed a Google search on her BlackBerry with her other hand. *NSF Thurmont . . .*

The first match came up: "Camp David—Wikipedia, the free encylopedia."

"Jesus Christ," Pepper said, sitting bolt upright.

"Beg pardon?" said the President.

FOUR HOURS LATER she was in a U.S. Army helicopter descending onto the helipad of Naval Support Facility Thurmont, better known as Camp David, in the Cactoctin Mountains of Maryland, sixty miles north of Washington.

Through the window she saw aides waiting by a golf cart. She looked at her watch. Normally at about this time she might be meeting the girls for a Bloody Mary brunch, then squeezing in some Pilates. She wasn't sure what she was doing here. The President wouldn't say exactly what it was over the phone, only that it was "highly confidential."

"Welcome to Camp David, Judge," one of the aides greeted her. "The President is expecting you."

The President is expecting you. She felt fluttery. She climbed into the golf cart, which made her feel somewhat ridiculous, like she was being given a VIP tour of Disney World. The aide, accustomed to nervousness in visitors, said, "My wife watches *Courtroom Six* every chance she gets."

Moments later she found herself in a room that she recognized from news photos. It was paneled in knotty pine. In the news photos it was usually filled with world leaders wearing forced smiles, knowing that they'd been invited here to have their arms twisted while being fed navy hamburgers. Versailles, Camp David was not.

And there, suddenly, he was. The President of the United States. She'd never met one in person. He looked smaller than he did on TV. Bland-but-nice-looking. It was difficult to imagine him commanding huge armies and fleets, much less nuclear missiles. What was that he was wearing? Oh, my God. A silk bowling jacket embroidered: CAMP DAVID BOWLING LEAGUE.

"Judge Cartwright," he said, grinning, shaking her hand. "I am sincerely sorry for interrupting your weekend like this."

"No, that's all right, sir," Pepper said.

"Coffee?"

"No, thank you."

"Well," he said

"Well," Pepper said.

"Do you bowl?"

The first moments of a presidential audience can be nerve-racking. Pepper froze. Had he just asked her if she wanted a bowl of something?

"A bowl, sir? Of . . . ?"

"No," he said, beaming, "*bowling.*"

"Oh. Sure. It's been a while, but . . . yeah. Great. Why not?"

And so she found herself following the leader of the free world down a flight of steps. They were tailed by two silent men of football-player physique with earpieces. The President was saying something. Was he talking to himself, or her? He gave the impression of a man who *might* talk to himself. No, he was apparently talking to her.

"I bring world leaders down here. You can just see them rolling their eyes and thinking, *Oh, my gosh, what a rube this guy is!*" He chuckled. "But then what happens is—they love it. Just love it. Turns them into kids. Bowling isn't that big in other countries. Though I'm working on that. Sometimes you have to drag them away, they're having such a good time. Even the French president. Bet you he went home and told everyone at the Elysée Palace that the President of the United States is a bumpkin. But I will tell you for a fact that he couldn't get enough of it. Now, I like the French. My staff is always telling me I can't say anything nice about them in public. But I don't listen to that. I went to France last year. And when I got there, the very first thing I did was to go lay a wreath on Lafayette's grave—just like Pershing did in 1917. Did you know he's buried under earth from Bunker Hill? I get choked up just thinking about that. Some of the French papers got their noses out of joint and said I was just trying to rub it in that we pulled their bacon out of the fire in World War One. *And* Two, of course. But that's not why I did it. Nosiree, Bob. Wanted to pay my respects—and the respects of this country—to a great man. My staff, well, let me tell you, they had conniptions. But you can't let the staff rule your life. Oh, no," he said, as if savoring some hard-earned private wisdom. "No, no, no."

She now found herself standing in complete blackness. He flicked on a switch and suddenly the room they were in was illuminated to reveal a single-lane bowling alley.

"Ahh," he said, as if being massaged. "This makes all the rest of it worthwhile. Now, what size are you?"

"Size, sir?" What in hell was he talking about now?

"Shoe."

The most powerful man in the world disappeared into a closet and reemerged, holding a pair of ladies bowling shoes, size eight. The shoes were red, white, and blue and had little eagles on the toes.

"I designed them myself," he said, adding, "if you don't mind, please don't share that particular detail. I've got enough problems these days without the press having a grand old snicker about me spending my spare time—not that I have any—designing patriotic bowling shoes."

"Not a word, sir."

"It's so gosh darn nice and quiet down here," he said. "You wouldn't know if the whole world was blowing up. Of course, they'd tell me if it were. They wake me up eighteen times a night to tell me things I'd just as soon not know. But I guess that comes with the plane and the limousine and the free housing. Well, Judge, here we are. Now, would I be correct in thinking that you're saying to yourself, 'What in the name of heck am I doing here and what does he want?'"

"That would be ... yes, sir. It is crossing my mind about now."

The President smiled and said, "I want to nominate you to the Supreme Court."

Pepper stared. "The Supreme Court of ... what, sir?"

"The United States."

The President picked up a bowling ball, lined up his shot with care, and rolled his ball down the lane. It knocked down all but the two pins on either side. "Heartbreaking sight, the split," he said. "Happened to Michaels at the Bayer Classic last week. He just couldn't seem to find the pocket. Don't suppose you ..."

"No, sir, I missed that."

"Heck of a tournament. Seat of the pants stuff. Bob Reppert made six X's *in a row*."

"Must have been quite something."

"Oh, it was."

The President bowled again, knocking down the tenpin.

"Big difference between nine and a spare. And here I was hoping to impress you. Your lane, Judge."

Pepper's first ball went into the gutter. The second one rolled slowly down the lane off center and knocked down all the pins, so slowly they seemed to go down one by one.

"Oh, beautiful, Judge. Beautiful. Sit down for a moment. You saw what happened to my last two nominees to the Court?"

"Yes, sir. I mean, I saw some of the hearings on TV."

"Disgraceful, what they did to those two men."

"It did seem a hair . . . political."

"Senator Mitchell. He doesn't like me much. Well, no one up there does. But they shouldn't have taken it out on those two fine men. But that's all past. They've had their fun. Now it's my turn."

President Donald Vanderdamp suddenly looked less bland to Pepper. A Mephistophelian glint of mischief came into his eyes—incongruous in a man wearing bowling shoes and jacket. "I'm going to send them a nominee that's going to give them a full-blown epileptic fit." He was chortling again. "And the best part is, there's not a darned thing they're going to be able to do about it. Oh, this is going to be rich. Rich."

"Sir," Pepper said, "may I say something?"

"By all means," he said jovially.

"I sure do appreciate your considering me, but I think I'll pass, if you don't mind."

"Oh, no," the President said, matter-of-factly. "It's too late for that. It's all been decided."

"Decided?"

"By me, Judge," he said, the smile disappearing. "Your country needs you. Sorry to sound like a recruiting poster. But that *is* the situation."

It suddenly felt claustrophobic. "I understand if you want to make some kind of point to these senators, sir, but this is my life you're using to make it. And I kind of like it the way it is." She added, "Not to sound ungrateful."

"You don't want to be on the Supreme Court?"

"I didn't say that, sir. I meant—"

"Meant what?"

"Mr. President," Pepper said, "I'm a *TV* judge."

"You were a real judge."

"Well, yes, in Superior Court. But I wouldn't presume to suppose I was qualified to sit on the Supreme Court."

"Judge Cartwright," the President said, trying to sound a bit huffy, "don't you suppose that I've given this just a teensy bit of thought?"

"A teensy, maybe."

"You're perfectly qualified. Why, according to the Constitution, you don't even have to be a lawyer to sit on the Supreme Court."

"That might actually make for a better Court."

"Exactly my point."

"I wasn't being serious, sir."

"I Googled you," the President said. "Sounds almost indecent, doesn't it? Drives my staff *cuckoo* when I get on the Internet. They probably think I'm surfing porn sites and it'll get out. Anyway, I know about you. Texas. Law review at Fordham— great school, that. Top notch but down-to-earth kind of place. Clerked for a federal judge out in California, stint as a prosecutor, Superior Court in LA, then *Courtroom Six.*"

Pepper shifted uncomfortably in her seat. "You Google good, sir."

The President nodded. "I sometimes think we don't need the FBI and CIA, what with all the information that's out there." He frowned thoughtfully. "Now there's a budget saving for you. Fold the FBI and CIA into the Department of Google. Hm. Might give that some thought. But they'll do the routine investigation into you, not to mention the five zillion reporters looking to get a Pulitzer Prize for finding out you smoked pot when you were sixteen. *Did* you smoke pot when you were sixteen?"

"No, sir."

"That's a relief."

"Waited until I was seventeen."

The President stared. Then said, "Well, I suppose these days anyone who didn't was the odd one. Did you—"

"Shoot heroin? No, sir."

"Well, then." The President brightened. "I don't see a problem. However, as you know, the process is not for the faint of heart. Ask Judges Cooney and Burrows. But since you're here and we're on the subject, any major skeletons rattling around in the closet?"

"My closet's so messy there isn't room for skeletons."

"Good answer," the President said.

"They kind of hang around the rest of the house."

"The Ruby business."

"There is that ghost, yes, sir."

"It wasn't hardly your fault, for heaven's sake. You weren't even born in 1963."

"No, but . . ." Pepper sighed. It wasn't her favorite topic. "But under the general heading of Sins of the Fathers. Wasn't really a sin, per se. Maybe not the best judgment. The Warren Commission did clear him. But it was a life-changing event, you might say."

"Tell me. If you would."

Pepper hesitated but, sensing that the President was inviting her to rehearse a story she would at some point most likely be compelled to relate, said:

"Daddy hadn't been on the Dallas police force long, just a few months, really. The Sunday after the President was shot, they gave him the job of standing guard outside the garage entrance to the police headquarters while they were transferring Oswald. So he's doing that and this man walks on by—the Warren Commission actually established that he did just happen to be walking by—sees the commotion, and says to Daddy, 'What's going on down there?' Daddy says, 'They're moving Lee Harvey Oswald, the man who shot President Kennedy.' The man says, 'Gee, really? That sure would be something to tell my grand-kids. Okay if I just take a look?' Daddy being Daddy, a nice, friendly man, basically, says, 'Well, I guess there's no harm.' And the man turned out to be Jack Ruby."

The President nodded thoughtfully.

"Well, you can imagine the going-over he got. But it must have been pretty obvious to everyone—except to those who make a living off conspiracy theories—that he wasn't a part of any plot. He was just Roscoe Cartwright. DPD. Patrolman. But that was the end of his career in law enforcement."

The President nodded.

"He got religion. Lot of people do after something like that. Not that there's anything quite 'like that.' Became a Bible sales-man. He was better at that than standing guard. Made good money. Pretty soon had his own distributorship. I was born, and they bought a little house in Plano, outside Dallas. Momma, she taught high school English. I'm named for a character in Shakespeare. Perdita. Only Daddy thought said it sounded sort of Mexican so I ended up being Pepper. Do you want to hear about ghost number two?"

The President nodded.

"Momma liked to play golf. They'd joined this little country club called—kind of ironic, if you think about it—Heavenly Val-ley Country Club. One Sunday afternoon—I wasn't quite ten—she said, 'Come on, honey pie, let's go play a few holes.' Daddy said, 'Helen, it ain't right to play golf on the Sabbath.' They still call Sunday the Sabbath in that part of the world, least they did then. She said, 'Roscoe Cartwright, I work like the dickens all week long, teaching, volunteering for every civic group in town, and I can't see why the Good Lord would give two hoots and a holler if I play a little golf on my day off.' Daddy went off to sulk in the garage with his power tools, like men do."

President Vanderdamp nodded gravely in agreement.

"We were on the fourth fairway. This thunderstorm came up suddenly. They do, down there. She said, 'You go hide under those trees, honey, I'm just going to take my swing.' And then there was this . . ." Pepper's voice trailed off.

"I'm sorry," the President said.

"She was the twelfth person that year in the U.S. to be killed by lightning on a golf course. I read that in the newspaper, along with a hundred stories saying it wasn't lightning at all, but part of the—don't you know—conspiracy."

"Can't have been easy."

"It's a funny country sometimes, that way. Some people just refuse to accept the obvious. Daddy didn't take it as a conspiracy, though. He took it as prima facie evidence of just where the Almighty stands on the subject of golfing on the Sabbath. He gave a sweet eulogy. Turned out he had kind of a talent for public speaking. Maybe it came from all the Bible study. He quoted from her favorite Shakespeare sonnet. The one that goes

> 'Let me not to the marriage of true minds
> Admit impediments. Love is not love
> Which alters when it alternation finds . . .'

"Anyway, he waited until we got home and then had what they called back then a nervous breakdown. A serious nervous breakdown. So they came, took him off to—they called that in those days either a rest home or the happy farm. I went to live with my granddaddy—Daddy's father—JJ. He's a retired sheriff. He pretty much raised me, really. Sweet old bird, but tough as boots. Ready for ghost number three, sir?"

"Go on," said the President.

"Well, they were big on electroshock therapy at that particular 'rest home.' Daddy came home three months later. For a while there he mostly just sat there drooling and staring at the TV, even when it wasn't on. I overheard JJ telling someone—I remember clear as anything—'They musta put enough electricity through that boy to run a freight train from here to El Paso.' JJ's full of lines like that.

"Anyway, Daddy eventually stopped drooling. He announced to us one night over fried chicken that he had a whole new meaning in life—to give witness to the Word. JJ just rolled his eyes and said, 'Pass the biscuits.' But Daddy was serious. He bought an old warehouse with his savings, fixed it up as a church. Called it the First Sabbath Tabernacle of Plano. For a crucifix, he mounted Momma's golf clubs. They had gotten, well, fused by the lightning. That was," she sighed, "kind of vivid for me.

"He started giving witness to the Word and pretty soon had himself a congregation. This was back when cable TV was starting up and they needed something to fill the air with, so they put him on. His Hour of Power was called *Halleluj'all*—still is. You may have even heard of it. He's the Reverend Roscoe. Pretty soon he was a big deal. His church has twelve thousand pews. He gives a big annual barbecue. The governor comes, all the state politicians. To be honest, I think it's his private jet they like. It's called *Spirit One*. He lends it out.

"Anyway, while Daddy was getting himself famous as a minister, I hung out with JJ. He'd take me down to the courthouse and jail, taught me how to shoot. I'm good with pistols. Guess I shouldn't say that too loud in case your Secret Service folks are listening. But it was JJ insisted I go East to school. He wanted to get me out of Roscoe world. He took a dim view of all that holy rolling stuff. I went to this boarding school in Connecticut. All the girls were named Ashley or Meredith. I was out of my social depth, but the other girls hadn't talked to murderers in jail and most didn't know one end of a pistol from another. And they couldn't blow perfect smoke rings, either. And that's about it. The rest you got from Google. You serious about all this?"

President Vanderdamp, who had been staring intently, said, "Yes. Absolutely. It's an unusual situation, I grant you. But I think you're just what it calls for."

Pepper said, "I have the feeling this is a joke and I'm the only one who isn't in on it."

"I offered the Senate two of the most distinguished jurists in the country and they blew their noses on them."

"And I'm the next hanky?"

"No. You're the next associate justice of the U.S. Supreme Court, if we play our cards right. Don't sell yourself short. You're a TV star. Someone called you the 'Oprah of our judicial system.' People love you." He chuckled. "And I for one can't wait to see the look on Dexter Mitchell's face. He won't know whether to . . ."

"Shit or go crazy?" Pepper said.

"Really, Judge," the President said. "Such language, in front of the President."

Pepper said, "You're the politician, not me. But it seems to me this thing could backfire on you, and you've got a reelection coming up."

The President said, "I'll let you in on a little secret, but it has to remain a secret. Understood?"

"Yes, sir, I can handle that."

"I'm not going to run again."

Pepper stared. "Isn't that unusual?"

"It shouldn't be. I said—going in, and you can look it up on Google—that a president who doesn't spend four years fretting about reelection can accomplish far more than one who does, who spends every second of the day worrying about his approval ratings. As you can see," he smiled, "I have not spent the last two and a half years trying to win popularity contests."

"No," Pepper said. "I suppose not."

"They hate me up there on Capitol Hill. Why? Because I keep vetoing their spending bills. Why, they're so mad at me they're even rounding up votes for a constitutional amendment to limit presidents to a single term. Just to get back at me! Great heaven. It's like passing Prohibition to keep one person from drinking. And meanwhile, of course, stringing up my Supreme Court nominees from lampposts. Well, don't get me started on the subject of the United States Congress. But," he patted Pepper's knee and grinned, "they won't find it so easy to string you up. So, Judge Cartwright. Ready to serve your country?"

"Is there a less ominous way of putting that?"

"It does sound ominous, doesn't it?"

"Could I think about it?"

"Yes. Of course. But I'd appreciate an answer by Monday."

"You couldn't make it Friday, could you? I've got a dilly of a week. We're going into Sweeps Week and . . ." The President was staring at her.

"Young lady," he said, "I come bearing a very considerable gift, not an offer of a lunch date."

"Yes, sir. Sorry, sir. Didn't mean to sound unappreciative. It's just, I have this hard time deciding things."

"You're a judge. Your job is to decide things."

"See, I'm a Libra."

The President stared. "You might want to leave that out at the hearings."

CHAPTER 4

The army deposited Pepper back at the Thirtieth Street heliport by five that afternoon. After the silence of the Camp David bowling alley, the bustle and roar of crepuscular Manhattan felt vibrantly reassuring. She decided to walk the couple of miles back to the apartment, wanting to think things over and postpone the inevitable moment of evasion with Buddy. The President had asked her not to discuss it with anyone.

"Even my husband?"

"Is he discreet?" the President asked.

"He's a former TV newsman."

"Oh, dear. Then especially not your husband. If this thing leaks, it's over before it's even begun. The first time the public hears of this, you need to be sitting next to me in the Oval Office."

Pepper thought about discussing it with Buddy, but his record on discretion was anything but reassuring. And she had a hunch that he was not going to take this news well.

"Where the hell were you?" Buddy said crossly when the click of her heels on marble announced her return. "I must have called you four hundred times. You didn't answer your cell or your BlackBerry. I was going to start calling emergency rooms."

"I know, I know, sorry, baby." She gave him a kiss, which he did not return. "I needed to spend a little quality time with myself. Clear my head. Woke up feeling kind of cobwebby up here." She tapped the side of her head, which at the moment felt anything but clear.

Buddy was looking at her either incredulously or suspiciously. He was sixteen years older than Pepper and at that age when an older husband begins to worry about a younger, attractive wife—who has gone inexplicably AWOL for a day, and returned with an unconvincing explanation.

"But where were you?"

She flung her handbag onto an armchair, looked him straight in the face, and said, "With the President of the United States. At Camp David."

"Camp David," Buddy said. "Really. And how is the President?"

"Fine. He's into bowling. Sends his best. You hungry? I'm starved. Want to go to that tapas joint? Grab some sangria. Fool around?"

"First tell me where you were today. I was fucking frantic, for God's sake."

"Baby, I told you. The phone rang, it was the President. He wanted to see me. They sent this helicopter for me and everything."

"Are you insane?"

"No, starving."

"Pepper. Where. Were. You. All. Today?"

"Camp. David."

"Dammit."

"What?"

"You're serious?"

"As a heart attack."

"Well, okay, then, and what did he want?"

"He's a fan, turns out."

"The President of the United States watches the show?"

"Apparently. Yeah."

"Jesus. Why didn't you take me along?"

"You were asleep, darling."

"Why didn't you wake me?"

"You were out. What time *did* we get in last night, anyway?"

Buddy hesitated slightly too long. "Oh, I don't know. Late."

Pepper said, "For a guy who divides his days into seconds, you sure get vague when it comes time to accounting for the nocturnal hours."

"Whoa with the cross-examination, Your Honor. You're the one who disappeared all day without a trace. All right, all right. Let's get something to eat."

"Not hungry."

"You said you were."

"Well, I guess I filled up. On bullshit," she said, and stalked off to the bedroom.

"Pepper."

"Kiss my ass."

"I thought," Buddy said after her, "we'd been over all that."

"Well, I guess we aren't over 'all that.'"

"All that" being a blind item that had appeared some months past in Page Six*: "Which unjudicious reality TV producer has just hired his fourth young-lovely 'personal assistant' whose duties include more than keeping him supplied with foamy lattes?"

She slammed the bedroom door behind her, and then felt foolish for imprisoning herself while actually hungry. But then

---

* Widely read gossip page in the *New York Post*, credited with introducing the neologism "canoodling" (kissing, generally someone other than one's spouse, in a public venue) into the English language.

a few minutes later she heard the front door slam recipro-cally. She walked to the Barnes & Noble at Lincoln Center and bought two shopping bags of books about the Supreme Court, including numerous autobiographies of justices. (There were a surprising number of them by sitting justices. She had been under the impression that they generally waited until later to sum things up.)

Pepper opted for takeout at Shun Lee and, now looking like an expensive, thoughtful bag lady, lugged her trove back to the apartment and holed up in bed with the books. She read them late into the night. It felt weird and illicit—she kept listening for Buddy—as though she were back at summer camp after lights out, with a flashlight under the blanket reading *Nancy Drew and the Strange Supreme Court Nomination.*

The next morning she found Buddy asleep on the couch. She crawled in beside him and by the time they got up the previous night's shouting match seemed to have been forgotten or at least duct-taped over.

They mixed Bloody Marys and made a frittata and salad lunch while watching one of the Sunday talk shows with one eye each.

Chopping scallions, Pepper said, "What'd you make of all that Supreme Court hullabaloo?"

"They're all assholes," Buddy said thoughtfully.

"Whole process has become sort of a zoo, hasn't it?"

"Who'd want it?" Buddy said, cracking eggs.

"To sit on the Supreme Court? Are you serious?"

"Nine old farts in robes sending footnotes to each other."

"Rehnquist. Warren. Brandeis. Frankfurter. Harlan. Black. Holmes. Marshall. Old farts in robes? I'm beginning to see why you went into TV, darling. You have a genuine talent for the old reductio ad absurdum."

"Don't knock TV," Buddy grunted. "It bought you this room

with a view. By the way, I was thinking, what would you say to raising the show's metabolism a little?"

Pepper said cautiously, "What did you have in mind?"

"I was thinking, you know, instead of handing out these civil-type penalties, what if we could actually sentence people to jail?"

"Buddy," Pepper said, "we try civil-type cases. A, people don't get sent to jail for those, and B, I'm not a real judge anymore. So I'm not getting how we could send them to jail."

"I thought of that," Buddy said. "Instead of people signing these wimpy-ass agreements where they're contractually bound to abide by your decisions—if they lose, they have to serve actual time."

"What time? I can't send people to jail. I'm not a real judge. What am I supposed to do, call up the Metropolitan Detention Center and say, 'Judge Cartwright here, do me a favor, would you, and put some folks in jail for me?'"

"No—we build our *own* jail," Buddy said, smiling triumphantly.

"What are you talking about?"

"With cameras in every cell. Say you lose your case—you get sent to the slammer. Our own slammer. For, like, a week or whatever. We create a prison. Build our own. Somewhere grim. Down south. With guard towers and—a *moat*. A shark-filled moat. Throw in some alligators. Do alligators and sharks mix?"

"I'd have to get back to you on that," Pepper said.

"I hadn't even thought of that until now. The guards would have uniforms. Darth Vader–type. Scary. And the prisoners—they'd have uniforms. They'd get points for good behavior, et cetera, so you could get out a day early or whatever. And—Jesus!—a cash prize if they *escape*."

Pepper tried to concentrate on chopping radishes for the salad. "And if they get eaten by the sharks and alligators?"

"I'll talk to Legal about it. Figure something out. But don't you see it? *Oz* meets *Survivor*.* It could be incredible. What do you think?"

"Well, darling, you sure are innovative on the weekends. Let me think about it," Pepper said, continuing to chop.

Hᴀʏᴅᴇɴ Cᴏʀᴋ had been at his desk for only an hour on Monday morning and already he was having a bad day.

"Sir, all I'm asking is that we postpone further discussion until Mr. Clenndennynn returns. His plane gets into Andrews at—"

Dammit, Hayden caught himself. *Bad slip.*

"Andrews?" the President said, looking up from his paperwork. "Since when do private jets land at U.S. Air Force bases?"

"He's coming in on a military plane, sir. I sent one to bring him back."

Hayden Cork braced for a stern lecture on wasteful government spending. Instead the President said, "Good work, Hayden."

"Sir?"

"He's going to shepherd her nomination through the Senate. That is," the President chuckled, "if he can tear himself away long enough from helping overpaid CEOs negotiate debt relief with Chinese commies." The President was of the old school. He still called it Red China, in private.

"Sir," Hayden said plunging deeper into gloom, "I'm not sure how he's going to react to this . . . whole idea."

"I wouldn't worry about that. Graydon's an old pro. He'll get

---

* Popular TV shows, respectively about a brutal prison and a tropical island without Starbucks where city dwellers are forced to grow their own arugula.

it straightaway. And if it goes down in flames, he'll put the word out, *What else could I do? The President asked me to do it as a personal favor.* Crafty old badger."

"Sir, would you consider just *meeting* with Runningwater?" Hayden said. "I really think you'll be dazzled by him. His tribe was celebrated for—"

"Hayden," said the President, "get with the program."

"Yes, Mr. President."

IT IS A CLICHÉ in Washington that the most dangerous place to find yourself is between a politician and a TV camera or microphone, but in the case of Senator Dexter Mitchell the cliché had acquired a kind of Darwinian perfection. Dexter Mitchell loved—lived—to talk. He had uttered his first full sentence at the age of fourteen months and hadn't stopped since.

Once, famously, on his way into a state funeral at the National Cathedral, a reporter for one of the smaller cable TV new channels stepped forward to ask for a brief comment. One hour and fifteen minutes later, Senator Mitchell was still talking as the casket emerged, carried by the honor guard. One of his fellow senators was heard to remark, "Wouldn't it have been simpler to ask him to deliver the eulogy?" The tape of the interview is a cult classic and plays three or four times a year during the wee hours. Some consider it the best argument around for 24/7 cable TV.

Dexter was now in his midfifties, at the age when men begin to take cholesterol-lowering and penis-elevating medications. Now in his third decade of public service, he had a solid career behind him: prosecutor, congressman, three-term senator from the great state of Connecticut. For the last four years, he had been Chairman of the Senate Judiciary Committee, generally referred to as "the powerful Senate Judiciary Committee." And true enough: if you wanted to wield a federal gavel, you first had to get past his.

He was good-looking, in a shiny sort of way. He'd had his front teeth capped. They were now so blindingly white that when he bared them, you could almost hear a little *tingg!* and see a star of light reflect off the incisor, just like in the commercials. He cheerfully admitted to having Botox injections, and even had a nice line about it: "I need all the help I can get. My job involves a lot of frowning." He had an attractive wife named Terry, attractive children, and an attractive beagle named Amtrak. (Senator Mitchell sat on the Transportation Subcommittee and fought fiercely for subsidies for America's railroads, especially the one that ferried him from Stamford to Washington and back.)

If a computer were programmed to design a president of the United States, it might very well generate Dexter Mitchell. Everything about him seemed, indeed, calculated. And yet for all his qualifications, Dexter somehow added up to less than the sum of his considerable parts. His epic loquacity was not an asset. Successive campaign advisers had tried without success to get him to give briefer answers, but nothing had stemmed the logorrheic tide, the tsunami of subordinate clauses and parenthetical asides, the inexorable mudslide of anecdotage. His campaign "listening tours" were occasions of mirth among political reporters, since it was the people he met who did the listening. Dexter Mitchell would happily express himself on any issue, at any time, at any place.

He had run for president three times. The first time, he raised $12 million and came in third in the Iowa caucus.* The

* A device to attract reporters to a state that they would otherwise never visit; its secondary purpose is to give the media something to report when the candidates whose victory they have been forecasting for months come in second and third, or not at all.

second time, he raised $20 million and came in fourth. The third time, he raised $22 million and came in seventh. He was undeterred. Somewhere over the rainbow he heard the people chanting, *Mit-chell! Mit-chell!* But by now he had begun to acquire a slightly used feel; "certifiably pre-owned," as one pundit put it uncharitably.

When he declared his intention to run a fourth time, his wife, now working as a K Street lobbyist representing—as it happened—the U.S. rail industry, replied in no uncertain terms that she would not spend one more weekend, one more day, one more hour, one more minute at some coffee shop in Iowa, pretending to care about ethanol, or indeed any biofuel; or for that matter about the price of wheat, corn, soy, or anything that emerged from the loamy topsoil of the Hawkeye State. Dexter sulked off to the World Economic Forum in Davos, Switzerland, to drown his sorrow in feverish multilateral panel discussions on climate change and globalization.

Contemplating his thwarted presidential ambition, Dexter decided that a more sensible—and permanent—avenue to greatness would be to become a justice of the U.S. Supreme Court. And why shouldn't he? He was ideal for the job. In fact, he asked himself, why hadn't he thought of it sooner? He berated his friends for not having thought of it first.

It was this conviction, along with a refreshing absence of modesty, that had prompted him to call Hayden Cork some months before and request an Oval Office meeting with the President. He gave an equivocal reason, saying only that it was "important and confidential." The President groaned at the prospect, but agreed.

On arriving, Dexter plunked himself down and said to the President (we know all this from a tape recording in the archives at the Vanderdamp Library): "My information is that Brinnin's gone nuttier than a granola bar. You and I haven't always seen eye to eye, but I've always respected you." (Three weeks before, Dexter had called President Vanderdamp "the worst president since Warren G. Harding.") "But I say let's put aside whatever philosophical disagreements we have. I'd like you to consider putting my name forward as a successor to Brinnin."

There is a brief, perhaps eloquent, silence on the tape. Then Dexter continues: "Now, why do I propose myself? Frankly, because I think I'm the right person for the job. Why do I think that? I've narrowed it down to five reasons. Well, six. Don—if I may—when I first started practicing law over three decades ago . . ."

The tape continues on for twenty-six minutes. In the background, you can hear the President reaching for an imaginary—and much craved—EJECT button. At several points he tries to arrest the wall of sound with comments like, "I promise to give it the consideration it deserves." But Mitchell, having only gotten as far as reason number three (paragraph four), soldiers on.

Eventually, a door opens and an aide advises the President that his next meeting is now imminent (an almost certain lie). Vanderdamp's exhalation after the door has closed on his loquacious visitor is reminiscent of a man who has at long last reached a desperately sought urinal.

The President did not nominate Dexter Mitchell to succeed Justice Brinnin, for at least five reasons. When Cooney's nomination was released to the press, the President told Hayden Cork to leak it that Mitchell's name had not been on the short list—or even on the long list. (The ever-protective Hayden wisely ignored the instruction.) Mitchell was thus, to put it mildly, undisposed to treat the President's nominees kindly. Nor did he. After wiping Cooney's and Burrows's blood and brain matter from his gavel, he smiled and said—with uncharacteristic concision—"Next?"

CHAPTER 5

I t was just after four o'clock on Monday, which gave Pepper less than an hour to give the President her answer.

The day's taping had gone well. Buddy was in a good mood. She was summoning the courage to introduce the dreaded topic when he said, "You given any more thought to my idea?"

"What idea, sug?" she said.

"The prison," he said excitedly, as if suggesting they hop on the next flight to Paris.

"Baby, something's sort of . . . come up."

Pepper took a deep breath and explained the reason behind the visit to Camp David. Buddy listened in silence. He looked like a man being informed by his doctor that the MRI had found something.

"I guess he is a fan," Buddy said.

"It would appear."

"So," Buddy said, "what did you tell him?"

"Well, I wasn't about to tell him anything until you and I had a chance to talk it over."

Buddy let out what sounded like a sigh of relief.

"What was that?" Pepper said.

"Jesus, you had me going there. I thought you'd accepted."

"No. But I'd kinda come around to thinking that I might. I need to call him with an answer before five."

"Well, better call him."

"Oh, thanks, honey. I really—"

"And tell him you can't."

Pepper stared. "Why would I tell him that?"

Buddy gestured, as if the answer were self-evident. "Baby, we're going into Sweeps Week."

"Sweeps Week trumps . . . this?"

"Ah, look," Buddy said, "Vanderdamp's a total loser. They're about to impeach him. Look what happened to his last two nominees—and they were *serious* guys."

"If you're trying to talk me out of this," Pepper said somewhat coolly, "you're not going about it the right way."

"Hey, I think it's great he asked you. Fantastic publicity for the show. Hadn't thought of that."

"Buddy," Pepper said. "We are not having a satisfactory conversation here."

"What do you want me to say?"

"I don't know. You might try something like, 'Congratulations, honey. Right proud of you.'"

"Congratulations. Proud of you."

"You left out the 'honey.' And don't choke yourself getting too excited."

"Baby, this makes no sense."

"That's what I told him."

"Did you also tell him you have two years to go on your contract?"

"No, we didn't really get into that."

"You can't just walk away from everything we've created," Buddy said.

"Baby, it's the Supreme Court. My country's calling."

"Well, tell it to call back."

"Sweetheart—"

"You have obligations, Pepper. And not just to me. What about your millions of devoted viewers? Are you just going to tell them 'Fuck off'?"

"Actually," Pepper said, "I wasn't going to put it quite that way. And if they're really fans, I don't suppose they're going to shoot themselves on account of I'm moving on from a TV show to the Supreme Court."

"This 'TV show,' as you put it so condescendingly, is the only reason you've been asked to *sit* on the Court."

"I didn't say it wasn't," Pepper said, folding her arms across her chest.

"I get it. I'm the one you're telling to fuck off."

"No," Pepper said, "but keep this up and you might just hear those very words before this conversation is concluded."

"You can't do this to me."

"I'm not doing it *to* you. And by the way, who appointed you center of the universe?"

"You want to go to court? Fine, let's go to court. For breach of contract!"

"Well, aren't you the thorny rose." Pepper sighed. "Thank you for being such a honeybee for me and making the moment so special. I've got to call the President. You want to stick around and tell him yourself to go fuck himself?"

CHAPTER 6

Tuesday morning, Senator Dexter Mitchell was in his office on Capitol Hill when the phone rang. Graydon Clennden-nynn calling, mandarin in chief.

The two men knew—and loathed—each other. Graydon referred to Mitchell (in private) as "a jumped-up mediocrity." Dexter referred to Graydon (in public) as "an insufferable, overpaid egomaniac." Both points of view had some merit.

The phone call was like a meeting on the plain of battle when representatives of the about-to-clash armies came forward to offer terms and bribes by which carnage might be averted.

"So," Graydon Clenndennynn said, "*habemus papam.*" He enjoyed lording his knowledge of arcana over Mitchell.

Mitchell said, "I didn't go to boarding school, Graydon. Try it in English."

"It's what they say at the Vatican when they've elected a new pope," Graydon said, yawning from jet leg. "It appears we have a nominee. This is the obligatory courtesy call."

"All right." Dexter took a pencil and poised it above a legal pad, an old habit from his prosecuting days. "Shoot."

"I'm going to say something to you, without prejudice," Clenndennynn said. "Agreed?"

"All right," Mitchell said, suddenly curious.

"You will most likely deduce that this name did not originate with me."

You old fox, Dexter thought.

"That said," Clenndennynn continued, "I have given the President my word that I will do everything I can to move the nomination forward. And that is my intention."

"All right, Graydon. I get it. You're behind it one thousand percent. Is it Runningwater?"

"No. Cartwright."

Dexter Mitchell's mind raced. Wasn't there a Cartwright on the Sixth Circuit . . . ?

"Judge Pepper Cartwright," Graydon said.

"Did you say Pepper Cartwright?"

"Yes."

"Pepper Cartwright."

"Yes."

"The *TV judge?*"

"The same."

Dexter Mitchell leaned forward over his desk and massaged his forehead, still tender from that morning's injection of live botulinum cells. "What the hell, Graydon? Is this your idea of a joke?"

"Far from it. It is the President's view, and I must say I agree with him, that the last two nominations devolved into grotesque spectacles, thanks to you. So now he's trying another tack. You have to give him credit. It's out of the box, as they say. Are you familiar with the expression?"

"Those hearings were full and fair. It's not my fault if—"

"Let's dispense with the folderol, shall we? He sent you two men, two lions of the bar. Men of distinction, ability, probity. Reputations you could eat off. You turned it into a reprise of the Salem witch trials."

In moments of stress, Dexter Mitchell had a tendency to laugh unpleasantly. It came out as a high-pitched staccato burst, a sort of cackle. One observer likened it to the sound geese make when being force-fed. He had done it once or twice during the presidential debates, causing some in the audience to wonder if they really wanted to hear four years of it in the White House.

"That's just—*aack!*—absurd!"

"Please. It was unseemly." Unseemliness was the worst sort of crime to Graydon Clenndennynn, worthy of the death penalty.

"I'm sorry you and the President feel that way. I happen to disagree. Let me point out that—"

Clenndennynn was not about submit to a marathon Dexter Mitchell harangue. "Have you seen her television show?" he said.

"What? No," Dexter lied.

"Maybe you should. Everyone else in America seems to. She's very popular, I gather. A tall, cool drink of tequila. Yes. From Texas, too. Her grandfather was a sheriff."

"I don't care if she's descended from Sam Houston. This is unacceptable. It's an insult. A travesty. This is—"

"Unacceptable?" said Clenndennynn in his woodiest voice. "Unacceptable? To *whom*?"

"To the United States Senate!"

"Well, before you go speaking for the entire United States Senate, you might spend five minutes thinking about how the country is going to react. We happen to think it will go for her in rather a big way. Look up her ratings if you don't believe me. So, there we are. Courtesy call concluded. Good day, Senator. Always good talking with you."

"Wait a minute. Wait a minute. I get it. This is some kind of vendetta?"

"Oh, please, Senator. Let me point out a very basic fact to you about the man you and your distinguished colleagues like to call Don Veto. Donald Vanderdamp isn't Sicilian. He's from Ohio. He's a nice, really not terribly complicated man from—I can never pronounce it—Wapakoneta. Two boys grow up in Wapakoneta. One was good in math and became the first man to walk on the moon.* The other was president of the student council and became President of the United States. My idea of diversity. But if you prefer to think of it as a vendetta, why not? Adds a bit of garlic to the stew."

"Well," Dexter said, "you can tell Don Veto that he's going to wake up with a horse head in his bed."

"Threats, Senator? Well, if that's how you want to play it, what about that pathetic call you made on him in the Oval Office, begging to be appointed to the Court. He hasn't told anyone about that. Up to now."

"For the record, I did not 'beg.' I gave him six perfectly compelling reasons why I would be a reasonable, logical choice for the Court."

"He fell asleep after number three. Good-bye, Senator. See you on the field of honor."

---

* Neil Armstrong, though you'd probably already gathered.

CHAPTER 7

"How did it go with Mitchell?"

The President and Clenndennynn were watching television in the family quarters upstairs at the White House. Pepper's nomination was leading the news.

"He's going to chop off a horse's head and have it put in your bed."

"Good," the President said. He was absorbed in the TV, which was playing that morning's Oval Office announcement. "Gosh, she's attractive."

"Yes," Graydon said like an old water buffalo commenting on a butterfly that had just alit on its horn. "Quite attractive."

"She's going to do just fine. You watch."

"I'll be doing more than watching. I called Felten, Risko, and Bristz," Graydon said. (Other senators on the Judiciary Committee.) "I can't say they were pleased, though Bristz seemed amused. I think they're all a bit embarrassed over Cooney and Burrows."

"Darn well should be. This town has become more toxic than a waste dump. Eighteen more months to go. I count the days."

"You manage to make the presidency sound like a penitentiary. You'll be the first president since Johnson not to seek re-election. You know what they'll say."

"I don't care what they say."

"I know. But you might try. This midwestern imperturbability can be overdone."

On the TV screen, the President and Pepper were sitting side by side on the fauteuils in front of the fireplace, cameras snapping away, a boom mike hovering like a bat above them.

"Mr. President, do you watch *Courtroom Six?*"

"Never miss it," the President said. "My favorite show. After *Bowling with the Stars.*"

"Judge Cartwright, are you qualified to sit on the Supreme Court?"

"I doubt I'm qualified to be a clerk at the Supreme Court."

The reporters laughed.

"Then what are you doing here?"

"What I'm told."

"Judge Cartwright, is it true you're planning to continue with your show while the nomination process goes forward?"

"If you were in my position, would you quit your day job?"

More laughter.

Vanderdamp chuckled and slapped Graydon on the knee. "That's my girl. You tell 'em, Pepper. Oh, this is going to be rich. Rich, Graydon."

"Rich indeed."

They watched. The President said on TV, "Judge Cartwright may not be a traditional Supreme Court nominee, but I believe that, given the atmosphere in this city, and perhaps in the country as a whole, she is just what these times call for. She knows the country and the country knows her. She's a hands-on, commonsense, workaday judge. Calls them as she sees them. And I call on the Senate Judiciary Committee and the full Senate to approve her. Without delay."

"Nice touch, that, 'without delay,'" Graydon murmured. "A little final flick of the cape in the bull's face."

"Yes," President Vanderdamp smiled, "I thought you'd like that."

A WAR ROOM OF SORTS was arranged at the Retropolitan Club, a few blocks from the White House, where Graydon Clenndennynn and Hayden Cork could prepare Pepper for the hearings.

Tables had been arranged to approximate the Senate Judiciary Committee dais. A name card in front of Hayden Cork's place indicated he had the role of Senator Mitchell. Other senators were played by various White House and Justice Department people, as well as by a few seasoned proxies Graydon brought in. He himself sat aloof, serene, off to the side wearing his most eminently gray expression, in a leather armchair that looked like it had borne the weight of establishmentarians going back to the New Deal.

Pepper arrived, took in the surroundings, and said, "I was looking for the Cartwright event. This looks more like a Nuremberg trial."

Hayden nodded curtly and opened an enormous loose-leaf binder stamped CARTWRIGHT / CONFIDENTIAL.

"All that, about me?" Pepper said. "Didn't think I'd been alive long enough to leave a paper trail that thick."

"Judge Cartwright," Hayden began in a plummy voice, "what makes you think you're qualified to sit on the Supreme Court?"

"Never said I was. Senator."

"Then I'm asking you now. Are you?"

"I think I'll leave that to you distinguished-looking folks."

"It's a straightforward question. Just answer straightforwardly, if you wouldn't mind."

"Well, Senator, all I know is my phone rang one Saturday morning. It was the President of the United States. He asked me to do this. I didn't volunteer for the job. You ask me, I think the whole thing's nuts."

Hayden tapped his pencil on the table. "Is that really the tone you're planning on striking at the hearings?"

Pepper said, "I'm just a plain old girl from Plano. What you see is what you're going to get. You want to brighten me up, you might try silver polish."

"Why don't we move on," Hayden said heavily.

"You could just skip ahead to abortion. That's all anyone cares about anyway these days. Unless you're busting to hear my views on *Marbury v. Madison*."

"Judge—"

"Just trying to speed things along. I know how busy you folks are."

Hayden Cork pursed his lips and flipped to another section of his briefing book.

"Is there anything in your past that might prove embarrassing to this Committee?"

Pepper did a sweep of the faces staring at her. "Depends how easy you all embarrass."

"Judge Cartwright," Hayden said in a despairing voice, "this is a dress rehearsal."

"Look here, *Senator*. You got five thousand FBI agents out there going through my garbage and waterboarding everyone I ever talked to, starting with the ob-gyn who slapped my butt on my way out of the womb. Do you really think I'd put myself through all this if I had a whole catacomb of skeletons doing the cha-cha in my closet?"

Hayden Cork's lips had by now turned blue. He cast an exasperated glance at Graydon, who was looking on with leonine bemusement.

"But now that you mention it," Pepper said, "there was that Saturday night in college when I got up and danced on the table without panties. That the sort of thing you're looking for, Corky?"

Hayden blushed. A few other senators chortled.

Hayden turned to a different section of his phone book–sized dossier.

"Your husband, Buswald Bixby?"

Pepper said, in a different tone of voice, "Why don't you just call him Buddy. Everyone does."

"The television producer. Of your show. And others."

"That's right," Pepper said, edgily.

"His show *Jumpers*. Can you describe it for us?"

"You could just look it up in *TV Guide*. Maybe one of the seventy-two people you have on staff could do it for you."

"Seventy-six."

"I stand corrected. Thank you."

"My understanding is that it's about people who throw themselves off bridges. He produces another called . . . *G.O.* About grotesquely obese people?"

"That's right. He's got another one in development," Pepper said, "called *Assholes*. It's about White House staffers."

Graydon rose and said to Pepper, "Let's go have a cup of something." They left the faux senators and went and sat alone in a quiet lounge that reeked of long-ago cigar smoke and wood polish.

"You're quite good," Graydon said.

"Thank you," Pepper said tightly.

"That's why I was surprised to see you fall for that so easily."

"Whatever."

"Come now, Judge Cartwright. Let's not start feeling sorry for ourselves. You're playing in the big leagues now. This isn't *Courtroom Seven*."

"Six. Look, Mr. Clenndennynn—"

"Graydon."

"Mr. Clenndennynn, I don't see any point in acting like I'm some lion of the federal bench who's spent the last decade writing erudite footnotes, sitting on the U.S. Court of Appeals for the District of Columbia. I'm just a—"

"A plain old girl from Plano. Yes, yes. But you have a point. You might as well be yourself. That's presumably why the President asked you in the first place. Authenticity. The real America. Ah, the real America. That elusive thing . . ."

Pepper laughed.

"I amuse you?" Graydon asked.

"Not really. But I do get a kick out of the way you say *presooomably*. You're a real aristo, aren't you, Mr. Clenndennynn? Regular blue blood."

"Yes," Graydon smiled. "Very much so. So is Mr. Cork, though of a younger generation."

"Corky?" Pepper said. "No, he's not in your DNA league. He's just another Ivy League needle-dick." Pepper said, "Sorry. You went to . . ."

"Harvard."

"I don't think of you as a . . . that."

"Generous of you."

"Look, Mr. Cork made it clear as Evian water from the get-go what he thinks of me. I don't owe him a damn thing."

"Hayden Cork—Corky, as you call him in front of people who have been in public service longer than you've been alive— is the White House Chief of Staff. He has one goal in all of this. Serving the President. I wouldn't make an enemy of him, just for the sake of satisfying your own ego. This can be a mean town, Judge. Very mean. You have no idea. You might just find yourself needing a friend or two. On the other hand," the old man said airily, "you might just make it to the finish line. In which case, you won't need any friends for the rest of your life. You'll be home free."

"You don't sound exactly thrilled at the prospect."

"May I speak frankly, Judge?"

"Why not?"

"I know this is a big moment in your life. But to me, it's just another Thursday morning."

Pepper stared at the old man, who returned her stare implacably.

"Ouch," Pepper said. "But I appreciate the honesty."

"Whether you make it concerns me only to the extent it affects the President." Graydon crooked his head in the direction of the White House. "I happen to like him. I admire what's he's trying to do—against considerable odds. If you turn the hearings into some simulacrum of your television program, just to humiliate Mitchell and the others—which I don't doubt you can since you are a clever girl—they won't be able to retaliate directly if they sense that the country is with you. So they'll take it out on him. They're already trying to, with this idiotic Presidential Term Limit Amendment. The irony is he's . . . I gather he's let you in on the dirty little secret."

Pepper said, "What secret?"

"Very good. You know perfectly well what I'm talking about. That he's not planning to run for reelection."

"I wouldn't know anything about that."

Graydon smiled. "*Very* good, Judge. But you can relax, because he told me that he told you. He doesn't want to reveal it yet because the moment he does, he's a lame duck. For the time being he needs to have people assume he will, in order to exercise what power remains to him. But Mitchell and his band of assassins *can* make the rest of his months in office a torment. You, meanwhile, will be safe in your new marble bunker. Impervious. It's the ultimate job. No one can take it away from you," he said benignly, "until you start wrapping your ears in tin foil." His expression turned grave. "He's handing you the keys to the kingdom, Judge Cartwright. Be grateful. We understand each other?"

"Yes, sir."

"Sir?" Graydon smiled. "Well, well. I feel as though I've just been promoted."

THE MURDER BOARD* RESUMED. Pepper kept her lip buttoned, her answers businesslike and polite. She rose to no bait. Hayden kept the questions judicial—where did she stand on original intent, judicial temperament, the role of a judge versus a legislator, prayer in school, racial profiling, should the Pledge of Allegiance contain the words "under God," and naturally, abortion—the object, of course, being to say as little as possible in as many words as possible.

On a discreet signal from Graydon, Hayden turned to another page of his briefing tome and in a mild tone of voice said, "Judge Cartwright, your father was a Dallas police officer?"

Pepper stiffened slightly. "Yes, sir, that's correct."

Hayden let it hang there a moment, and then said, "Before continuing on to another profession?"

Pepper relaxed. "Correct again, Senator."

"He's a minister, down in Texas."

"First Sabbath Tabernacle of Plano. Giving witness to the Word, twenty-four seven, rain or shine, hell or high water, no sin too small, no crime too dire. Yeaaaah, Jesus!"

"Sorry?"

"It's how he begins his Sunday broadcast."

"Ah. Yes. Growing up in that environment must have affected your own religious views?"

---

* Committee of questioners convened to prepare someone for a tough grilling. Originally devised by Spanish clerics in the fifteenth century.

"Certainly, sir. But as to that, I don't really *have* any religious views."

"How do you mean?"

"Well, Senator, we all keep the Sabbath in our own way."

"May I ask how you keep it?"

"In bed with a crossword puzzle, coffee, and a croissant."

"I see."

"I could leave out the croissant part at the hearings, if you want, if you think it sounds too French. Want me to substitute bagel? Or is that too Jewish? What about crumb cake? Crumb cake sounds American enough."

Hayden and the other senators exchanged uneasy stares.

Hayden said, "Your lack of religious views, again, if I may, I don't mean to . . . what I'm trying to get at is . . ."

"Let me help you out here, Senator. When I was nine years old I watched my momma get hit by lightning. Now, my daddy interpreted that as the Almighty's punishment for playing golf on the Sabbath and built a whole church around it. I drew a different inference."

Hayden said, "The inference being . . . I don't mean to pry, but . . ."

"That God is a son of a bitch," she said.

SHE SAID *that*?" the President said.

It was later the same day. He had just handed a worn-out–looking Graydon Clenndennynn a double martini and had poured himself a frosty schooner of beer.

"Freely," Graydon said. "Gleefully. She's an atheist. Proud of it."

"Oh, my," said the President.

"From what I gather, it didn't help that that the gaga father baptized her by holding her head underwater in front of thousands of people at that absurd church of his. Hayden did a very lawyerly job of drawing it out of her. Not that she held back, mind you. We spoke to her privately about de-emphasizing it at the hearings. But it's an Achilles' heel. If it comes up, Mitchell will chomp down on it like a terrier."

"There have been Supreme Court justices who didn't believe in God. Haven't there?"

"Yes, but I don't think they presented their views quite so gleefully or vividly at the confirmation hearings. My reading of her is that she wants to disqualify herself. I'm not a psychologist, but that's my sense of it."

"Hm," the President said. "Well, maybe it will come off as refreshing. Santamaria practically wears his Knights of Malta feather cap to Court. She's honest. Transparent. A breath of fresh Texas air. The people will respond. I know it."

"Donald, according to polls, more people in this country believe in the Immaculate Conception than in evolution. I don't know why you're always carrying on about the so-called 'wisdom of the American people.' Half of the population seems to me to be demented. Belong in cages . . ."

"Maybe it won't come up," said the President.

"I wouldn't count on that. There are five thousand reporters out there, digging. Like worms."

The President sipped his beer. "Her father, the TV reverend. He'll balance out the religious aspect. It'll be fine."

"The Reverend Roscoe," Graydon said morosely. "Quite the trailer park we seem to have wandered into."

"I never realized you were such a snob, Graydon," the President said. "Actually, that's not true. I've always known you were a snob. But don't discount the Reverend Roscoe. He's a major player down there, you know. I've been to one of his barbecues."

"Really?" Graydon said. "Were the ribs to the desired consistency and flavor?"

"Darned tasty. Maybe we ought to get him up here for the hearings."

"God, please, no. He'll start speaking in tongues. And it would only remind everyone of the Ruby business. She seems fond of the grandfather. Former sheriff. His name is JJ, wouldn't you know? Droopy mustache, big shiny belt buckle, soulful eyes. He'll do. Your wise American people love that sort of thing."

CHAPTER 8

Declan Hardwether, at forty-nine years old the second youngest Chief Justice of the United States and the most powerful
man in the country—at least so it was often put—was stuck
in traffic.

The situation did not improve his mood, which had been
sour anyway since his wife had announced several months ago
that she was leaving him for a retired army colonel named Doreen, Doreen being the major's first name.

One week prior to that breakfast table bombshell, Chief Justice Hardwether had cast the deciding vote to legalize gay marriage in the United States. After telling him that she was leaving,
his wife, Tony (née Antoinette), told him that once their divorce
was final, she and Doreen would marry.

"And I want to say, from the bottom of my heart, thank you
for that, Dec," she said, without a trace of irony.

By noon she was gone, taking with her (so to speak) the large
house in McLean outside Washington, two of the three expensive German cars, the very expensive vacation home in Maine,
and the bank account, all of those being hers, anyway, benisons
of inherited wealth. Tony's maternal grandfather had poured
most of the concrete between Chicago and Milwaukee.

As he boxed up his personal effects, Chief Justice Hardwether pondered in his study over a depleting bottle of Scotch whether he should go after her for half her dough. He was entitled to it, according to his reading of the law. He entertained pleasant fantasies: freezing her assets, having secret police throw her in jail.

But the more he thought about it, the more he realized that a messy divorce would only keep the (goddamn) spotlight on him. He no longer dared turn on the TV late at night for fear of hearing himself made the butt of another monologue joke by some half-wit talk show host.

Declan Hardwether looked out the car window at the Potomac River. The turbid water was flowing faster than his car was moving. His head hurt. He chided himself. *Got to lay off the late-night snorts. For that matter, the midday snorts.*

It was, he knew, not a good sign that he had started to carry little bottles of mouthwash. Had he really fooled Justice Plympton, Court den mother, when he explained that his sudden minty freshness of breath was the result of "a gum thing" that required frequent rinsings? To judge from the look on her face, no, he had not fooled Paige. Would she have given him a warm hug and said, "You know we love you, Dec," because she was concerned about his gums?

The car continued its crawl across the Theodore Roosevelt Bridge. With any luck, he'd miss his flight.

He was on his way to give a speech at Lutheran Law in St. Paul. It had been arranged months before Tony's disastrous announcement. Canceling it was out of the question. Worse—he rubbed his forehead—he had agreed to do a Q&A after his speech. Meaning he had no choice but to face reporters. He had managed to limit his contacts with the press to smiling at the bastards and giving them a quick wave as he walked briskly from his front door to the car—*Hi, hello, good morning, wonderful to see you, wonderful . . .* —as they screeched at him, "Any second thoughts on gay marriage, Chief?" *Har, har, har.* The reporters weren't the only ones camped on his front lawn. It had turned into a shantytown of protesters who, to judge from the signs they shook at him, had way too much free time on their hands:

HARDWETHER—REAP AS YE SOW!
CHIEF **INJUSTICE** HARDWETHER!
HARDWETHER: ROT IN HOMO HELL!

His cell phone vibrated. Tony. A text message. *Can u be out of house by end of wk? Realtor wants to do Open House. Hope u r OK. Love T.*

Not yet ten a.m. on a Wednesday, and the most powerful man in the country wanted a drink. Needed a drink. Maybe if he just drank the entire bottle of Listerine. Mouthwash had alcohol in it, didn't it?

His cell vibrated again. A call. Mertz, his clerk, alerting him to a story in today's *Washington Times*, an interview with Justice Silvio Santamaria, in which he described the Chief Justice's vote in *Fantods v. Utley* (the gay marriage ruling) as "an abomination." Mertz hesitated before reading his boss Justice Santamaria's next comment, about how Justice Hardwether "should consider exchanging his black robe for a more appropriate color. Scarlet might be appropriate."

Thanks, Silvio. Damn collegial of you.

The fact was that the Hardwether Court was a divided court. One-third of the justices had been appointed by conservative presidents; one-third by liberal presidents; and another third by presidents of no consistent ideology. Half the justices had proved to be disappointments to the presidents who appointed them, the conservatives voting liberal and the liberals voting conservative and the middle-of-the-roaders swerving like drunk drivers from right to left. Nine times out of ten, the Court voted 5–4.

Consistent razor-thin majorities are not a sign of a happy

court—or a happy country. The Court had split 5–4 on affirmative action, right-to-life, right-to-death, gun control, capital punishment, school prayer, partial birth abortion, stem cell research, torture, free speech, border security, interstate commerce, copyright, immigration, pharmaceutical patents, even on a case involving graffiti. A Court that couldn't agree whether there had been a violation of the First Amendment rights of a seventeen-year-old arrested for spray painting obscene slogans on a pair of Mormon missionaries was not likely to reach consensus on larger issues.

"It is at this point unclear," the *Times* noted, "whether this Court could agree on the law of gravity."

Personal tensions, long simmering, had begun to bubble to the surface. Some justices had barely addressed a word to each other in years, which made for a frosty atmosphere in conference where they all had to sit at a table and discuss cases and vote. Paige Plympton, the only justice who was on speaking terms with every other justice, did what she could to warm things up, but it was tough going. When she arranged a picnic outing for the justices and their families, two showed up.*

The Court was in this regard perhaps reflective of the country as a whole. The last presidential election had been decided by four electoral votes and a popular plurality of 14,000. The majorities in the House and Senate were thinner than slices of

---

* The fact that the court was split was not Declan Hardwether's fault. The Chief Justice has only one vote, like the rest. A divided Court inevitably sends a disturbing signal. But when a Court is unanimous, or nearly so, the country is likelier to go along peacefully with its rulings, no matter how controversial they might seem. Chief Justice Earl Warren famously cajoled his fellow justices into unanimity so that he could say the word "unanimously" when announcing the 1954 *Brown v. Board of Education* ruling abolishing segregation in schools. Warren wanted the country to see that despite internal dissent, the Court had decided to stand together on this vital issue.

deli-cut salami. Even the Board of Governors of the Federal Reserve, normally not a hotbed of intramural dissent and backbiting, was now the scene of ad hominem remarks, leaks, and even shoving matches. The Yeats line about things falling apart and the center not holding was being quoted so often it had started to turn up on refrigerator magnets in airport gift shops. One pundit had suggested that the Treasury ought to stop printing the words *E pluribus unum* on the nation's coinage and substitute *Every man for himself.* Even the occasional terrorist attack didn't seem to bring the country together these days. Within a day or two, everyone was back to squabbling about whose fault it was and who should pay for it.

Scarlet, huh? You fat pompous Sicilian gasbag, Hardwether fumed.

Every court has its diva. Silvio Santamaria, 250 pounds, gel-slicked-back jet-black hair, former boxer, Jesuit seminarian, father of thirteen children, Knight of Malta, adviser to the Vatican on international law and even occasional guest *advocatus diaboli* in canonization cases.* What relish he brought to *that* task! A reproduction of Holbein's Sir Thomas More hung in his chambers. Indeed, his written opinions often quoted from the movie *A Man for All Seasons.* He was brilliant, with a wit as caustic as drain cleaner; good company if you were in his camp and look out if you weren't. Silvio Santamaria didn't take yes for an answer. He didn't disagree—he violently opposed. Didn't demur—he went for your throat. Didn't nitpick—disemboweled you and flossed his teeth with your intestines. First-timers appearing before the Court for oral argument had been known to wet their pants and even faint under his withering questions and commentary. His written dissents were of the type described by the press as

---

* The prosecutor who tries to convince the canonical court that the putative saint was not only not a saint, but someone you would never invite to dinner.

"blistering" or "stinging." He loved to write, and when he was not procreating more Santamarias or inveighing against the modern world, he wrote books. Scathing books. He'd published five while a justice. Their titles included *The Road to Sodom* and *Supreme Arrogance: How the Court Is Ruining America— And What You Can Do to Stop It.* He gave fiery—and rather good—speeches that had his audiences stomping on the floor and standing up on their chairs calling for—demanding!—a new Inquisition. On balance, Hardwether wasn't surprised by the scarlet robe quote; it was a miracle Silvio hadn't called for the Chief Justice to be impeached or—better—hanged, drawn, and quartered, his head impaled on a pike.

Hardwether's chauffeur, an ex–Secret Service agent adept at aggressive driving, suddenly drove up onto the median strip and got the CJ to Dulles in time for his flight. Alas.

Airport security whisked him through a separate entrance where he was not required to remove his shoes and surrender his gels or his bottle of Listerine—there were at least some advantages to being "the most powerful man in the country," even if you couldn't seize your wife's assets and have her submitted to *peine forte et dure.** But Declan noticed that the airport staff avoided eye contact. Everyone seemed faintly embarrassed around him these days.

Aᴛᴛᴇʀ sᴏᴍᴇ ᴘʀɪᴠᴀᴛᴇ ᴄᴜssɪɴɢ out loud and kicking of walls, Senator Dexter Mitchell had resolved to play it cool.

He would not denounce the President's nominee. On the contrary. He would appear to be entirely open to having a— God save us—TV judge sit on the Supreme Court of the United

---

* French term for being slowly pressed to death. Used today to describe waiting for the cable company to arrive.

States of America. He would appear to be even—what was the right word?—"intrigued" by the idea.

It's an interesting notion the President has proposed, and I and the committee look forward to hearing Judge Cartwright's views on the substantive issues. Yes. It's an intriguing idea. Intriguing. Yes.

He would be the soul of noblesse and politesse. He would not condescend. He would invite her to lunch with him in his private dining room. Yes.

Dexter Mitchell had decided on this bold course of action for the simple reason that his pollsters* had brought him the disturbing news that the voters back in Connecticut—and, indeed, most of the other forty-nine states—were thrilled with the idea of having Judge Pepper Cartwright of *Courtroom Six* on the Court.

That imbecile Vanderdamp had finally done something popular. It would have to be handled carefully. Very carefully. Yes.

He had given strict instructions to the Wraith Riders to find something. Anything. *If necessary, pin the JFK assassination on the demented preacher father.* But he would have to be a little careful about that: one of the senators on the Judiciary was from Texas, and he spent a lot of time flying around the country on the Reverend Roscoe's private jet. Yes.

THE DAY OF HIS COURTESY LUNCH with Pepper, Dexter came up with the superb idea of greeting her not in his office, as was usual, but on the front steps of the ceremonial entrance door of the Senate. *Oh, the magnanimity. Yes.*

His staff alerted the media to the impending grace note. It

---

* Overcompensated and usually self-regarding political functionaries who instruct leaders what to do, based on the biases of a largely uninformed electorate.

would lead off the coverage: the President's bitter enemy welcoming a completely unworthy nominee—at the front door. Dexter self-scripted the crawl at the bottom of the TV screen: GOOD-LOOKING, SUAVE, GRACIOUS, MAGNANIMOUS SENATOR MITCHELL OF CONNECTICUT DISPLAYS EXTRAORDINARY COURTESY AS HE GREETS IMBECILIC PRESIDENT VANDERDAMP'S TOTALLY INAPPROPRIATE SUPREME COURT NOMINEE . . .

Standing on the steps beneath the portico as he waited for Cartwright's car to arrive, Senator Dexter Mitchell pursed his lips (slightly sore from yesterday's collagen injection) and did a few labial calisthenics, practicing his thousand-dollar smile for the cameras.

"Arriving now, Senator," an aide whispered into his ear.

"Good," he said exuberantly. "I'm looking forward to this. Very much looking *for-ward* to it. Yes. Yes."

Moments later a vehicle hove up inside the archway. But it was not the expected dark Lincoln town car. Instead . . . *what's this?* . . . Dexter's brow strained against the Botox—a bright, cherry-red pickup truck?

He was digesting this incongruity when the driver's side door opened and out stepped—bounded—not a chauffeur but Supreme Court nominee Pepper Cartwright. Herself, in the flesh. And what flesh.

Claxons sounded in Dexter's ears as he realized that he had just been one-upped on his own front steps.

She was coming around the car—the *pickup. Smile!* She was wearing a figure-hugging pantsuit—*whoa, nice figure there, cookie*—a pearl necklace, turquoise stud earrings, and cowboy boots, expensive looking: ostrich, silver-toed. She was smiling for the cameras and the cameras were grinning back. She had her hand out. She was saying something.

"Senator Mitchell. Pepper Cartwright. Honor to meet you, sir."

Say something! Smile, dammit!

"No, no. The *honor* is mine. Your Honor. *Aack!*" Dexter grinned maniacally. "Great pleasure. Great pleasure. Yes. Yes."

He took her hand but as he tried to maneuver her to his left side for the cameras, she pivoted backward and, still gripping his hand, positioned herself to his right.

Dammit!

Dexter's smile tightened. In the photographs and TV shots, she'd be on the left—the dominant position. It would look like *her* meeting. Like *she* was welcoming *him*.

Keep smiling!

Dexter's mind raced: had she done this accidentally, or had she managed to one-up him twice, in less than thirty seconds?

Say something!

"That's a . . . dandy-looking truck you've got there, Judge," he said, looking straight ahead at the horde of photographers and cameramen.

Pepper paid him no attention. She smiled her lovely smile as the shutters snapped away like electric crickets.

"Shall we?" he said.

"You betcha," she said, heading right in—*ahead of him!*—like she owned the place.

They posed for the cameras in Dexter's office and made bland conversation for the microphones.

"I know I speak" *click click click click* "for all the members of the Committee" *click click click click click* "when I say that we're looking forward to getting to know you better." *Click click.*

"I sure appreciate that, Mr. Chairman." *clickclickclickclickclickclick* "And I'm sure looking forward to getting to know *you* all."

Aides shooed the national media out like cats, leaving the Chairman of the Senate Judiciary Committee and the Supreme

Court nominee alone in sudden, awkward silence. This was unusual for Dexter Mitchell. Normally he could fill a conversational vacuum from a hundred yards away.

"Should I call you Mr. Chairman?" Pepper said.

Dexter's mind raced. *Another power play?*

"Call me . . . whatever's comfortable."

"How about 'Senator'?" Pepper smiled. "You can call me Pepper, if you're comfortable with that."

"Fine. Fine. Yes. Pepper." Dexter grinned. "Wonderful name. So, now . . ."

"Do you feel kind of awkward, Senator?" Pepper said. "I sure do."

"Awkward? No. Not in the least. No, no."

"By the way, Mr. Clenndennynn sent his regards."

"Well, send them back. A character, Graydon. Yes."

"He said to watch out what I say to you," she smiled. "I don't think he likes you."

Dexter stared. "Really? What makes you say that?"

"Honestly? He told me as much."

"Aaack!"

"You okay, Senator?"

"Fine. Fine. You—*aack*—gave me a good laugh, that's all. Yes. A good laugh . . ."

"I was getting ready to Heimlich you."

"No, no, not necessary. What makes you think Graydon Clenndennynn . . . hates me?"

"Well, he said, 'Dexter Mitchell is the embodiment of everything that is rotten and vile in government today.' That was my first inkling."

"Really? Well. *Aack.* That's a compliment coming from *him*, I must say. But I thank you for your candor, Judge."

"Candor doesn't have anything to do with it. He told me to tell you that."

Dexter stared. This was not going the way it should. "Judge," he said, "this is highly unusual."

"Whole thing's unusual," Pepper said. She smiled. "Did you like the pickup bit?"

Dexter recrossed his legs. "Yes," he said, "nice touch."

"Figured I'd need all the help I could get. So, here I am. Could I ask you something?"

"Yes. Fine."

"You want this job for yourself, don't you?"

"What do you mean?"

"The Supreme Court job. The one I'm up for."

"Not at all. Well, everyone would like to be appointed to the Supreme Court. But I'm not sure I follow you."

"Yeah, but not everyone goes and, like, personally begs the President for it." She smiled. "Right?"

Dexter re-recrossed his legs.

"You got that restless leg syndrome thing?" Pepper said. "They got something for it. The company advertises on my TV show. I could probably get you a free sample if you'd like."

"There is nothing wrong with my legs, thank you. As for the other, I'm sure I don't know what you're talking about."

"Well," Pepper said, like a little girl repeating a story she'd been told, "Mr. Clenndennynn said that you asked the President to name you to the Court. And when he didn't, you got all blinky and took it out on Judges Cooney and Burrows."

"Blinky?"

"Sorry. Texas talk. Sour milk-like."

Dexter was about to cross his legs but didn't.

Pepper added in a lower voice, "Don't worry. I understand that it was a confidential visit and all. Only reason I brought it up is I wanted to make sure you didn't resent me for trespassing on what you consider to be your land. Texans are awful sensitive about that."

Dexter grinned and gestured. "There's some misunderstanding here. I have the best job in this town. I'm Chairman of the Senate Judiciary Committee."

"I noticed," Pepper said. "By the way, sir, fantastic office. That is one heck of a view there."

"Thank you. I don't know about this alleged incident Clenndennynn told you, but I will tell you that it's absurd."

"Okay."

"I certainly wouldn't take everything Graydon *Clenndennynn* says as gospel. Ha. No. No, no. The stories I could tell you about Graydon Clenndennynn. Ha."

"Well, I don't want to be the cause of some internecine thing between a couple of dominant gorillas," Pepper grinned. "Figure of speech."

"Yes. Well, why don't we get on with it. For starters, how do you see yourself fitting *in* on the Court. Your qualifications are—let's be honest—unusual."

"I'm not sure I'd fit in at all," Pepper said.

"I don't understand."

"Well," she said, "I can't imagine any of the justices are exactly thrilled at the idea of having some TV judge for a colleague. Can you?"

Dexter frowned. "Well, that was what I was driving at. So you think you would be a divisive influence on the Court?"

"Probably. On the other hand, they already look pretty divided, without adding some catty whompus to the mix."

"What?" Dexter said, exasperated.

"Sorry. More Texas talk. I revert when I'm nervous. A catty whompus is something that doesn't, you know, fit in."

"You don't seem nervous," Mitchell said, pulling his trouser leg down to cover bared calf.

"Well, I can fake it pretty good. So, let's get to it. You fixing to nail me to a cross like you did those other two?"

Dexter smiled suavely. "That's not the way we do things up here."

"Oh? Funny. I watched the tapes. Looked like a replay of Good Friday to me. A regular passion play, like they do over in Germany every year at that place I can't ever remember how to pronounce."

"I can't speak to that, but I will absolutely say that we gave them the hearing they deserved. Why do you smile?"

"That's exactly what Mr. Clenndennynn said you'd say. Well, okay, whatever, it's your show. But I might as well tell you, with all due respect, I'm not going to roll over and play dead for you."

"I wouldn't expect you to. You'll get the hearing *you* deserve."

Pepper laughed. "Yeah, I'll bet. Can I call you Dexter for just a second?"

"As you wish."

"Okay, Dex. How about we quit shoveling horseshit at each other and talk, lawyer to lawyer."

"Very well," Dexter said.

"Now, you don't like anything about me, starting with the fact that I'm sitting here in your office, not kissing your ass like you're used to. I understand. That's fine. But I wouldn't be here in the first place if you and your committee hadn't strung up Judge Cooney and Judge Burrows. Let me finish. Now I don't know what kind of witch trial you got planned for me, but this being a courtesy call, let me tell you how *I'm* going to play it. I've got the number one–rated TV show in the country. As of this morning—and I checked— Congress's approval ratings are at eighteen percent. So it's my numbers up against your numbers, Senator. And if you and your distinguished colleagues try to pull any shit, I am going to climb up on that nice wooden committee table of yours and beat you to death one by one with your micro-phones. We on the same page here, Dex?"

Senator Mitchell was not responding.

"Well," Pepper said, rising, "I've enjoyed this courtesy call. Thank you for your time."

THE NEWS REPORTS on Pepper's first day on Capitol Hill led off with the image of her bounding out of her cherry red pickup truck. Within hours, the manufacturer was reporting a spike in sales of that model.

CHAPTER 9

In an effort to appease Buddy, Pepper was taping back-to-back episodes of *Courtroom Six*. His gloom over the prospect of losing his star was only slightly mitigated by *Courtroom Six*'s having become—as Pepper had pointed out to Chairman Mitchell—the number one–rated show in the country. He acted as though Pepper's acceptance of a Supreme Court nomination was a betrayal and inconvenience. At this point Pepper wasn't clear which of the two Buddy considered the more heinous.

In her not-so-free time, she was cramming her head with the thick briefing book Hayden Cork's staff had prepared. It contained précis of significant Supreme Court rulings and transcripts of previous confirmation hearings, along with "suggested responses," which to Pepper seemed mainly to consist of smoke grenades of obfuscation.

Judge Cartwright, will you respect stare decisis* *with respect to* Roe v. Wade?

Answer: I'm delighted to have the opportunity to discuss this important aspect, Senator. Stare decisis *is, of course, itself an important concept dating all the way back to the days of the Roman Empire,*

---

* Latin phrase meaning "to stand by things decided," i.e., let the precedent continue in effect. The full phrase is *Stare decisis et non quieta movere.* Trans.: "For God's sake, just leave it."

when everyone was speaking Latin. We do things differently from the Romans, of course. We do not feed criminals to live animals, or crucify them, or make them row in galleys. We do not even use galleys, in fact, though it might be energy efficient if we put our two million prisoners to work powering our naval vessels. But to your question . . .

Pepper gathered that the object was to put the senators to sleep. She was having a hard enough time herself keeping awake.

One night after a tiring day as she was curled up on the couch doing her homework, Buddy came in from a late dinner and announced, "I'm not going to live in Washington. You can. I'm not."

Pepper looked up and said, "Okay."

Buddy said, "I've got way too much going on up here."

"I understand," Pepper said.

"There aren't any decent restaurants."

Pepper sighed quietly. "Whatever."

"That's all you have to say?"

Not looking up, Pepper said, "What am I supposed to say?"

"You might at least fake disappointment."

"Buddy, honey, if you're spoiling for a fight, could you just go punch the doorman? I gotta memorize all this mumbo jumbo."

"Don't you *want* us to live together?"

"Sure I do. But I don't want you to be miserable. It's not that far. I'll commute up on weekends."

"Swell," Buddy snorted. "Great."

Pepper took off her reading glasses. "Shall we do an instant replay? You came in the door and announced, like the Holy Roman Emperor, that you weren't going to live with me in Washington. I said okay. I don't recall lack of restaurants being the deal breaker in the marriage vows. I was actually under the general impression that Washington is halfway civilized and has decent, even fine restaurants that serve edible food. But recognizing that living there would be an inconvenience to you, I understand and agree. Whatever works for you."

"You're such a lawyer," Buddy said.

"What the hell is that supposed to mean?" She closed the briefing book. "But if you're spoiling for a fight, okay. What's the theme of this one? How I've ruined your life?"

"Don't let me take you away from your studying."

"Baby," Pepper said tenderly, "I got to ask you a serious question at this point."

"Go ahead."

"Are you aware that from the get-go you've been a total a-hole about all this?"

"Oh," Buddy laughed bitterly, "I get it. Thank you for pointing it out. I'm the asshole."

"Well, glad we got that settled," Pepper said, putting her glasses back on and reopening the book.

Buddy said, "How am I supposed to react? Am I supposed to be thrilled that you're willing to throw away everything that we've worked for so hard?"

"Baby. Your wife has been asked to sit on the Supreme Court. How does that amount to throwing it all away? Looky here. We've got more money than God. *You've* got more money than the Holy Trinity. I probably won't even make it past the confirmation hearings. But if I do, you'll find another judge for *Courtroom Six* in about twenty seconds. And you got six other shows running. Two of 'em in the top twenty."

"Right. People jumping off bridges and eating themselves to death."

"Well, honey, they were your ideas. And you're making a fortune off 'em."

"They're shit."

"Now, don't you be too hard on yourself. You've brought

awareness to the issue of people hurling themselves off bridges. And *G.O.* . . . that episode about that 750-pound food writer—what was her name, Mrs. Stern?—having to be surgically separated from her sofa, that was right . . . human. I'll bet you that touched a lot of chords with large folks who'll be inspired to get up off the sofa before they fuse with it."

"It's all shit. It's crap. *Courtroom Six* is a showcase. Without you, there's no *Courtroom Six*. Without you, I've got no class act. There. Okay? You see the problem?"

"Doesn't your wife being on the Supreme Court amount to some kind of 'class'?"

"Is this where I'm supposed to tell you—for the eighteenth time—that I'm proud of you? All right. Great. I am so fucking happy for you."

Pepper closed the briefing book and shoved it into her briefcase. She stood and disappeared into the bedroom, re-emerging a few short minutes later with an overnight bag.

"All right. What are you doing?" Buddy said, in a tone suggesting he knew exactly what she was doing.

"Going to a hotel," Pepper said. "That way, if I feel the overwhelming need to be congratulated in the middle of the night, I'll just ring down to the concierge and have him send someone up to pat me on the back."

"Go ahead," Buddy said. "You've become an expert at walking away from things. Be my guest."

"I'll be the hotel's guest," Pepper said, exiting, "but I will put it on your credit card."

NEW YORK BEING NEW YORK, there was a five-star hotel just a few blocks away, off Columbus Circle. Pepper checked into a suite on the fifty-eighth floor, tipped the bellman, and stood staring out the floor-to-ceiling window at the great black-and-white panorama before her: a million lights, ships tugging up and down the Hudson, the necklace strand of the George Washington Bridge in the distance. All it lacked was Gershwin's *Rhapsody in Blue.*

She was relieved to be here and not back at the apartment being nattered at by Buddy. Still she looked for her building amid all the others and found it at the edge of the park. She could make out the windows of their bedroom, and her study. What room was Buddy in now? What was he thinking? *I really am an asshole* or *What a bitch?* She didn't know the answer, and it troubled her, on reflection, that she didn't. They'd been together now seven years. He'd proposed to her the day the show was picked up by the network. And she'd said yes, automatically, a little joylessly, now that she looked back on it. It occurred to her, for the first time, that her feelings for Buddy might have been a little . . . self-referential, maybe? Or—she thought on it coldly and clearly—self-reverential. Being on TV does tend to bring out the inner Narcissus. Had they ever actually loved each other or was it the success they'd brought each other that they'd loved? Confronting this unpleasant, humiliating epiphany, Pepper decided she didn't want to dwell on it anymore just now. Which, she realized, was confirmation enough of its probable, essential truth. *Aw, hell,* she thought, *you—dummy. You deserve every bit of what you're getting. Every kick in the butt. It wasn't ever really a marriage. It was just a damn business arrangement.*

Her cell phone trilled. She rummaged urgently in her bag, then saw the call was from JJ.

"Hey," she said.

"What's wrong?" he said.

"Nuthin'. How you?" Her Texas accent tended to deepen when talking to JJ.

"Nuthin' name of Bixby?" JJ had never been a big fan

of Buddy. He was generally suspicious of anyone who had anything to do with television, the only exception being his granddaughter.

"He's being a pain in the butt. But I was the one who walked out. Never done that before."

"Where are you?"

"In a hotel."

"Hotel? Where?"

"Around the corner from my apartment. It was either that or whack him upside the head with one of my Emmys. Don't think I wasn't tempted."

"Hell, make *him* go check into a hotel." *Pwwttt.* JJ's sentences were punctuated by the sound of expectorated tobacco juice.

"Don't worry. I'm puttin' it on his plastic," Pepper said.

"Hope it's an expensive hotel."

"Oh, it is. I'm gonna eat all the macadamia nuts in the mini-bar. That oughta add a thousand bucks to the tab. So, what's up down there?"

"Everyone's having a fit and steppin' in it over this damn border-mining bill," JJ said. *Pwwttt.*

A Texas state senator had introduced a bill in the legislature calling for the state to mine its border with Mexico, on the grounds that the federal government had failed to stem the tide of illegal immigrants. It had started out as a symbolic protest, but America being America—and Texas definitely being Texas—the thing had acquired a life of its own. The bill now had so many supporters it looked like it might actually pass in the upcoming session. *Pwwttt.*

"I guess I feel as strongly about immigration as the next person," JJ said, "but I don't know if the solution is to start blowin' up Mexicans. Be a heck of a mess. But we got to do something. Juanita feels kinda strongly against it."

"I'll bet she does," Pepper said. Juanita was JJ's girlfriend.

She'd been the housekeeper and cook up until JJ's wife, Pearl, had passed. Juanita still did the cooking and housekeeping; a few other duties had been added.

"Hold on," Pepper said. "I think I'm supposed to have an opinion on that. I'm *supposed* to have an opinion on everything, including the moons of Jupiter. It's somewhere in here. . . ." She opened her briefing book, flipped through the pages. "Here it is. Get a load of this." She read aloud:

"Question: In the event the Texas Border Enforcement Initiative (TBEI) becomes state law and is challenged in the federal courts—as would almost certainly be the case—how would you vote on that?

"Answer: I am very glad you raised that, Senator. The issue of illegal immigration is indeed a complex and highly charged one, at the federal, state, and certainly local level. While it would not be appropriate for me to comment about this or for that matter any hypothetical case that might come before the Court, I would point out that in *Jimenez v. California*, the Ninth Circuit held, in a case involving a private aircraft chartered by an out-of-state corporation, that state legislation permitting the strafing of illegal aliens did not run afoul of the Dormant Commerce Clause. At the same time, in *Montez v. Arizona Minutemen*, the Fifth Circuit held, in another case involving a private aircraft chartered from an out-of-state corporation, that Title 14-266 of the Arizona Revised Statutes 19b, which permitted dropping incendiary devices on illegal immigrants, did, in fact, run afoul of the Dormant Commerce Clause. Now, as to reconciling these divergent opinions . . ."

"What in the hell is that?" JJ said. "I didn't understand one damn word."

"It's my homework," Pepper said. "I got to memorize that, along with a thousand other pages just like it."

"Julius Caesar. You sure you want this job?"

"Suppose."

"Suppose? That don't sound like 'whuppee' to me."

"I don't know, JJ," Pepper said, suddenly feeling like she was going to cry. "It's the Supreme Court, isn't it? Shouldn't I *ought* to want it?"

"Wouldn't make a damn bit of difference to me, either way. We're already proud of you just for being asked. Juanita's bought a new dress for the hearings. Oh, I'm supposed to ask you—she supposed to curtsy when we meet the President?"

"No, JJ. It's America. Nobody's got to curtsy to nobody. We fought a war over that."

"That's what I told her." *Pwwttt.* "But you know how she is. Hell, she's about the first person in her family ever to own a pair of *shoes*."

"Well, you tell her not to. Tell her I said. You talk to the bishop?"

"Bishop" was the word Pepper and JJ used privately for the Reverend Roscoe.

"I called him on Monday." *Pwwttt.* "He called me back on *Thursday.* I said, 'Been so long since I called I can't remember what I was callin' you about.' That boy's got the manners of a . . ."

"Now, JJ," Pepper said. "You go easy on him. You know Daddy ain't dealin' off a full deck."

Pwwtttt. "I know *that.* I think he's got a case of the guiltys. He offered me and Juanita a ride up there to Washington on that plane of his." JJ chuckled darkly. "Preachers with their own *planes.* I said to him, 'So what kind of private *plane* did the twelve *apostles* have?' He didn't laugh none."

JJ and his son, Roscoe, had a somewhat textured relationship. Though JJ had never admitted as much, Pepper suspected that he'd taken a major amount of ribbing from his fellow lawmen about his son being the one who told Jack Ruby where he could go shoot Lee Harvey Oswald. JJ was as down-to-earth as asphalt. His idea of a religious experience was a pretty sunset; of religious service, doffing his hat when a hearse went by. He tended toward skepticism in the matter of his son's ministry, with its rhinestone sermons and televised Sunday services, $20 million private jet and all-female choir that looked like the Dallas Cowgirls got up in angel costumes.

"Now, JJ," Pepper said, "you don't mind that plane none when he lets you use it to go trout fishing with your buddies up in Montana."

"That's different," JJ said.

Pepper laughed. "How is that different?"

"It's putting the plane to some decent use. I don't mind if he's flying some kid with cancer to a hospital or whatnot, but most of the time, he's lendin' it to politicians so they'll give his church another tax break. What's he need another tax break for, I want to know. Hell, he's already got enough money to burn a wet dog."

Pepper said, "President's folks asked me to try to keep him from coming up to the hearings."

"Can't say's I blame 'em."

"They're just worried it'll give the media the excuse to drag up the whole damn Ruby business. I told them under no circumstances. And I told them they ought to be ashamed for asking me. Maybe he's a little unusual, okay, but he's my daddy and he's going to be there."

JJ snorted. "'Unusual.' You got that right."

"Now, JJ Cartwright, you look here," Pepper said. "It would be nice if while the senators are peeling the bark off me, the two of you weren't sitting behind me pecking at each other like a pair of snake-bit roosters."

"Don't you worry none about that. We'll be quiet as the Tetons. As for those senators," JJ pronounced the word with disdain, "if there's one thing they can do, it's read polls. You're about the one thing this country agrees on right now."

"Well," Pepper yawned, "we'll see about that. All right. I'm gonna eat a thousand dollars' worth of nuts and memorize another forty pages of this horseshit. I love you."

"Love you, too, Pep."

THE NEXT MORNING at six-fifteen on the set of *Courtroom Six,* Pepper was sitting in front of the mirror, eyes closed, as the makeup lady was doing her thing when Bob the director entered and, looking embarrassed, said that he had a "couple of notes" for her.

"They're from Buddy," he added. "Not me. So you know."

Pepper opened one eye warily. She was tired from staying up late with Corky's Gutenberg Bible–sized briefing book. Macadamia residue sat uneasily in her tummy.

"He wants a guilty verdict in the Robinson case. And in the Bofferding case. And in *Nguyen v. Rite-Aid*, not guilty."

Pepper cocked her head to one side. Both eyes were open now. She liked Bob. He was an affable old pro in his midsixties, with nothing left to prove professionally, nicely devoid of ego. In six years she and he had had maybe three arguments, all of them forgotten within an hour.

"Bob," Pepper said, "what in hell are you talking about?"

"Like I said, they're from Buddy." Bob shrugged. "I told him you'd probably want to hear it from him directly, but he said for me to tell you. So I have. You look terrific, by the way."

"Who does he think he is . . . Hammurabi? Since when does he dictate verdicts?"

"I know. It's . . ."

"Well, you tell our producer for me he can kiss my Texas . . ."

Bob smiled and gestured with open palms—universal sign language for *I really,* really *do not want to get involved in this.*

Throughout the taping of the Robinson case, which involved a leaf blower that had (allegedly) been used for indecent purposes, Buddy sat in his usual chair behind Bob. Instead of following the proceedings, he ostentatiously thumbed his BlackBerry. Pepper concentrated on the case. When it came time to pronounce the verdict, she said, a little more loudly than usual, "Not guilty," adding, "and I ought to fine the plaintiff for costs for wasting this court's time. Shame on you, sir. And you will apologize—right now—to Mr. Gomez here."

Buddy looked up from his BlackBerry, tapped Jerry on the back, and drew his hand across his throat.

"Cut," Bob said.

Buddy whispered something to him. Bob rose, walked over to Pepper, crouched down beside her behind the bench.

"Sorry about this, kiddo. Boss says you need to find the guy guilty."

Pepper, blood pressure rising, said calmly, "He isn't guilty. He was blowing leaves. He wasn't aiming under Mrs. Robinson's skirt on purpose. Look at him. Mr. Gomez hasn't probably had a sexual thought since he left El Salvador thirty-five years ago."

Bob nodded and winced. "That was my—right. Right. But he's the producer. I'm just the schmuck director."

"And I'm the judge in this courtroom."

"Nolo contendere. But I'm still just the salaried schmuck."

"In that case," Pepper said, "just tell our producer what I said back in makeup. You can finish the sentence, too."

Bob smiled. "I'm between the rock and the hard place here."

"You tell the rock what I said he could do."

"You want me to tell the rock to kiss the hard place's ass."

Pepper rose. "Okay," she said, "stand aside." She walked over toward Buddy, all eyes on the set and the audience on her. He'd gone back to his BlackBerry.

Pepper said to him in a lowered voice, "Am I interrupting?"

"Problem?" Buddy said, not looking up.

"Not if you let Bob and me get on with it, there isn't."

"You have my notes."

"Since when do you dictate verdicts? Where do you think this is, North Korea?"

"No, I was under the impression it was New York City. Where *actors* abide by their *contracts*."

"I see. So that's what this is about. Well, stupid old me. Here I thought it was about whether Mr. Gomez was on a beaver hunt up Mrs. Robinson's skirt."

"We'll discuss this later," Buddy said in a bored tone of voice. "Bob, let's take it from 'Mr. Gomez, it is the opinion of this court that you are guilty et cetera et cetera of using a leaf blower with indecent et cetera and sentences you to et cetera.'" Buddy turned to Pepper. "And can you put some oomph into it? You've been a little flat this morning."

Bob looked at Pepper. Pepper stared at Buddy, said nothing, took her seat.

"Quiet on the set, please. Five seconds, Three, two, one, and . . . *action*."

"Mr. Gomez," Judge Cartwright said, "it is the opinion of this court that the producer of this TV show here is full of a substance I cannot name, on account of this being a family show; further, that he is hereby sentenced to have that leaf blower of yours inserted in a portion of his anatomy I also cannot name. Case dismissed. Sorry for your trouble."

On her way off the set, she said to Buddy, "Enough oomph for you?"

That concluded the day's taping of *Courtroom Six*.

Pepper rechecked into the hotel, having checked out of it that morning. The front desk clerk asked how long she would be staying this time.

"Damn good question," Pepper said.

Well, she thought on her way back up to the fifty-eighth floor, *least I'll get plenty of studying done.*

The incident was all over the blogosphere and Internet within minutes and was well covered in the papers the next day. Page Six ran an item:

SEPARATE CHAMBERS

Supreme-to-be Judge Pepper Cartwright has moved into a suite at the Mandarin Oriental Hotel, a few blocks from the $14 million penthouse duplex co-op she shares with husband-producer Buddy Bixby. Producer and star nearly came to blows yesterday while taping a segment involving a leaf blower. A spokesman for *Courtroom Six* denied rumors of marital troubles and said the move was simply to provide Cartwright with "a little peace and quiet" so she can prep for next week's grilling by Senator Dexter "Hang 'Em High" Mitchell's Judiciary Committee. But a source tells Page Six that Supreme Hubby Buddy, whose other TV fare consists of reality shows about bridge suicides and human hippos, is in a reality lather over the prospect of losing the jewel in his crown. Yesterday, Her Honor stunned the studio audience by telling a puzzled Honduran gardener-defendant to insert the evidence—the leaf blower—in a unmentionable portion of her husband's anatomy. Speaking of anatomical metaphors, our source says that the atmosphere between

the two of them lately has been "chillier than a penguin's ass."

Pepper was boning up on *Griswold v. Connecticut* when her
cell phone rang.

"What?" she said after glancing at the caller ID.

"'Chillier than a penguin's ass'?" Buddy shouted. "Are you
trying to drive away our sponsors?"

"That's not my quote," Pepper said coolly.

"Bullshit. And I can't believe you told that fucking illegal
alien *gardener* to put a leaf blower up my ass. In front of everyone! Jesus Christ . . . But okay, okay. Will you just please come
back to work? We've missed a whole day's taping. I'm paying
union wages—caterers—for nothing. I'm running a million-
dollar soup kitchen here."

"Baby," Pepper said, "you got a genuine gift for prioritizing."

"Okay," Buddy said. "I'm a second-rate hustler. At least I
know who I am."

Pepper said, "What in the hell's that supposed to mean?"

"It means what it means. And it's from the heart."

"You are dis-missed," Pepper said, reaching for the END
button.

"Whoa. You can wield absolute power when—and *if*—you
get to the Supreme Court. Until then, I'll remind Your *Honor*
that you have a legally binding contract. And don't tell me to
shove that up my anatomy."

Pepper said, "I was going to suggest that you first fold it up
like a nice origami giraffe. Well, darling, before I terminate this
conversation, which I am on the brink of doing, I want to thank
you for all your loving support at this critical point in my career.
It's meant so much to have you behind me." With that, Pepper
pressed END.

The phone rang again.

"What?" she said.

Buddy said calmly, "If you're not on the set tomorrow, I will sue you for breach of contract."

"Okay then, guess I'll see you in court." She said, "Funny . . ."

"What?"

"Always wanted to say that."

CHAPTER 10

There's been a development—I suppose you could call it—in the Cartwright matter," Graydon Clenndennynn said to the President over the phone.

"Go ahead," the President said warily. He had been president long enough to know that the word "development" was synonymous with *something truly dreadful has just happened.*

"Her husband—the producer of the television program—has informed her that he intends to sue her for breach of contract in the event she leaves the show."

President Vanderdamp absorbed this bizarre piece of information. He stared at the polished surface of his wooden desk, made from planks of an eighteenth-century U.S. warship. He'd served on an aircraft carrier in the navy. At times, he imagined that his desk was a flight deck onto which a never-ending succession of wounded, flaming aircraft crash-landed. *Boom, boom, boom.* The trick was repairing and relaunching them.

"Well," he said at length, "for heaven's sake."

"Yes," Graydon said.

"He should be strewing rose petals in her path. Giving her neck massages. Telling her sweet nothings and *I'm so proud of you, sweetie pie.* What's his beef, anyway?"

"Who can say? Remember what Tolstoy said about unhappy families."

"Graydon," the President said, "cut it out."

"I believe Tolstoy's basic point was that they're all unique. I don't know the gentleman—if that's the right word in Mr. Bixby's case—but it would seem he's reluctant to part with his star. I gather she lends his operation a touch of class. His other programs feature somewhat less high-minded fare. Fatsos and suicides. But who's to say what's art and what isn't."

"Is Hayden aware of this development?" the President said, simultaneously pressing a buzzer to summon his chief of staff.

"I wanted to give you the news first directly. To be honest, I was concerned that it might cause him to insert his head in the nearest oven. As you know, Hayden has not been overly enthusiastic about this appointment."

The door to the Oval Office opened. Hayden Cork entered. "Sir?"

The President pressed the speaker button on his phone and said, "Graydon, why don't you tell Hayden what you just told me?"

When Graydon was finished, Hayden Cork emitted a long, exquisitely soulful sigh, like the last gasp of a dying, landed salmon.

"So," the President said to his men, "where does this leave us?"

"She's offered to withdraw," Graydon said.

"Oh? Well, fine. Fine," Hayden said, suddenly as full of life as a salmon returned to the water. "In that case, I'll give her a call and tell her we're deeply appreciative of her—"

"Hold on," the President said. "Steady. Let's stay on course here. What did you tell her, Graydon?"

"It's not my decision. I said I'd relay her offer."

"Mr. President," Hayden said, "I really think it would be

best for everyone if we just accepted her wonderfully gracious offer—before this—"

"Sit down, Hayden."

"Sir—"

"Sit. Down. How did she sound to you, Graydon?"

"I sensed that she was putting up a brave front. I think she's a bit busted up inside. Can't say as I blame her. But the offer sounded sincere."

"I like that. Shows character. Judgment. Not enough people these days offer to resign. Not nearly. Lost art, modesty."

"Mr. President," Hayden said. "I'm sure all this isn't pleasant for her. But these hearings are going to be brutal enough as it is. I mean, she threatened Senator Mitchell—during her courtesy call."

"Good for her. Wish *I'd* stuffed a microphone down Dexter Mitchell's yap long ago. Graydon?"

"Well, sir, it is a bit of a mess. Hayden's perfectly right. The media will feast. But all that said, I've grown rather fond of the lady. She is a pistol."

Graydon heard a soft moan from Hayden in the background.

"I don't see," the President said, "why we should punish her because her husband is a complete j-e-r-k. No. Call her. Call her right now. Tell her I'm behind her all the way. Tell her," the President said, with a meaningful look at his chief of staff, "that the entire White House is behind her. You tell her that. You tell her that for me."

"Very good, sir," Graydon said, and hung up.

"Now," the President said, "Hayden."

"Yes, sir," the chief of staff said glumly.

"I think I'd like to know a little more about this . . . husband."

"Oh, sir," Hayden said, "we're not going to . . . no, sir. Please."

"The FBI is already conducting a full and vigorous background check, aren't they?"

"Yes, sir, but—"

"Hayden," the President smiled. "This is no time to go wobbly."*

GRAYDON AND HAYDEN met late that afternoon at the Retropolitan Club for a last murder board with Pepper, who was flying in from New York. Hayden greeted Graydon with a sarcastic, "Thank you. You were a big help this morning with the Chief."

"What can I say?" Graydon shrugged. "I've grown accustomed to her face."

"This is going to end in tears," Hayden said. "Or blood. Mitchell's hotter than lava."

"Dexter Mitchell is a horse's ass," Graydon said, "but he's not stupid. He's seen her numbers. The people want her on the Court."

"I didn't realize," Hayden said, "you were such a populist."

"I'm not. But it doesn't hurt to give the mob what it wants every now and then. Keeps it quiet."

"I take it back. You know what the Chief is asking for, don't you?"

"I'd rather be able to look the grand jury in the eye with a trace of sincerity and say, 'I really don't know what the special prosecutor is going on about.'"

"Thanks. And what do *I* tell the special prosecutor?"

"Oh," Graydon said with a Cheshire cat grin, "you'll think

---

* The President is quoting British Prime Minister Margaret Thatcher, who famously said this to President George H. W. Bush after Saddam Hussein invaded Kuwait in 1990. Bush promptly counterinvaded Kuwait, expelling Saddam. Mrs. Thatcher had that effect on men.

of something. And if you don't, I'll come visit you on Sundays. Bring you croissants and a file."

The stand-in senators filtered in and took their places behind the committee table. Pepper arrived shortly, only fifteen minutes late, looking as though she'd had a tough day. Graydon greeted her warmly; Hayden with a perfunctory handshake and nod.

"Nice to see you, too," Pepper muttered under her breath.

"I'm sorry about this brouhaha with your husband," Graydon said. "But as I told you this morning over the phone, the President is behind you all the way." He added pointedly, "As is Mr. Cork."

Hayden pursed his lips.

"You look a bit tired," Graydon said to her. "Are you up for this?"

"Yeah," Pepper said without enthusiasm.

Hayden and the others fired questions at her for several hours—on privacy, interstate commerce, immigration, on whether the Eighth Amendment had been properly applied in *Miskimin v. Incontinental Airlines.** He cleared his throat and said, "Now, Judge Cartwright, would you stipulate that a person's private life is relevant when determining his—or her—suitability to serve in a high public office?"

Pepper stared at him a moment and said, "Well, Senator, I guess that would depend on the office, wouldn't it?"

"How do you mean?"

"Let's say this hypothetical person turned out to be a member of al Qaeda or an arms dealer or hooker. I suppose that would be relevant if they were up for the Supreme Court or Secretary

---

* Miskimin was a passenger aboard a plane that was held on the runway at Chicago's O'Hare airport for three days over Christmas. She finally took the controls herself while the pilots were playing backgammon with the first-class passengers and flew the plane to Omaha.

of State or some big job like that. But if they were just running for, say, the Senate, I'd say a reprobate background would be a qualification."

The senators burst out laughing.

Hayden shook his head. "Is that really how you're going to play it at the hearings?"

"I don't know, Corky," Pepper said, yawning. "Just trying to get through the day, you know?"

"Would you kindly not call me that?" Hayden said, flushing.

"I didn't mean any disrespect. My shrink says it's a way I have of processing feelings of insecurity."

Hayden stared. "Your . . . did you say 'shrink'?"

"Psychiatrist. You know, someone who helps you sort things out upstairs, like."

"Are you saying that you are under the care of a psychiatrist?"

"Well, sure. Everyone in New York is. Aren't they down here, what with all the stress and such?"

Hayden was flipping anxiously through his briefing book. "I don't . . . recall that on the questionnaire. Did you include it on your . . ."

Pepper smiled demurely. "Well, no, sir. It's kinda personal."

"God Almighty," Hayden said. "This is . . ."

"I didn't mean to cause you any trouble. As far as the shrink goes, I didn't really have a whole lot of choice in the matter."

"What do you mean?" Hayden said, his voice a squeak.

"Well," Pepper shrugged, "they more or less told me I had to see one."

Hayden stared. "'They'?"

"The folks at the rehab place. It was a condition for letting me out after just a month. Instead of the full six."

"Full six?" Hayden spluttered.

"You can't hardly see the scars," Pepper said, holding up her wrists. "Least not when I'm wearing these bracelets. Say, any of you folks got any Valium? I left in such a rush I forgot to bring mine."

Graydon rose. He said, "Shall we break there? Judge, if I may?"

He and Pepper left the others staring at each other in horrified stupefaction. Graydon led the way to a book-lined corner of a parlor where they sat in facing leather armchairs.

"Young lady," he said, "you ought to spanked."

"I was," Pepper said. "Many times. Just trying to lighten things up. Corky's wound so tight his bow tie's gonna start spinning any minute now."

A waiter appeared.

"A double martini, Hector, thank you," Graydon said. "For the lady?"

"Tequila, straight up. Beer back. Bottle, lime."

Hector seemed amused by the order.

"That's probably the first time anyone has ordered that here since the Johnson administration," Graydon said. "So, Pepper. Think you'll make the whistle?"*

Pepper smiled at the question. "Been to a rodeo, have we?"

"Yes. About a century before you were born."

"You do surprise me, Graydon. You don't seem the type."

"We used to summer in Wyoming when I was a boy. Why do you laugh?"

"Wasn't until I got East to school I realized 'summer' was a verb. So you been out west."

"My grandfather built the railroad to it," Graydon said, stirring his martini idly with his forefinger.

"Oh," Pepper said. "Well, beats flying coach."

---

* Staying on the bull for the full eight seconds.

"As to rodeos," he said, "I have made the whistle. You, you're only just mounting up."

"I'm wearing different colored socks."*

The old man smiled. "All right, then. But hold on. This bull's an arm-jerker."

---

* Rodeo cowgirl superstition.

CHAPTER 11

Senator Dexter Mitchell looked radiantly senatorial on the first morning of the Cartwright hearings: dapper, smiling, with the air of a man upon whom the great issues of the day heavily weigh. He looked . . . historic. How often had it been said of Dexter Mitchell that he was every inch the part?

The TV cameras followed him as he mounted the dais and moved from colleague to colleague, shaking hands, sharing a greeting or quip, nodding thoughtfully, here and there offering a furrowed brow or blinding grin. Whatever your feelings, you had to admit—the man had poise. The cameras did love him.

This was not lost on Buddy Bixby, who was watching the proceedings on television.

Normally, the spouse of the nominee sits directly behind the nominee at the hearings. Normally, too, the spouse is warmly introduced to the nineteen senators, who couldn't really care less, but who generally offer pleasant brief smiles of acknowledgment. Not today.

Buddy's New York office had quietly put out the word that Mr. Bixby would not be joining his wife in Washington "owing to an inner ear infection." Buddy's ears—inner, outer and middle—were in fact fine. The truth was that Buddy had been keeping a low profile since the weird, unsettling visit late Friday afternoon. Buddy Bixby was freaked.

He'd been in the apartment, innocently preparing to drive out to the house in Connecticut for the weekend—alone, since Pepper was still at her goddamn hotel with her panties all in a twist, probably racking up a monster bill on his Amex card— when the doorman called and said there were "two gentlemen from the FBI."

Gentlemen? Jesus, they looked like something out of *The Sopranos*. Polite—very polite—too polite. There's something inherently nervous-making about overly considerate armed men.

Was this an inconvenient time? They didn't want to intrude. From your bag there, Mr. Bixby, it would appear that you're leaving on a trip. Are you leaving town? Leaving the country? Now Mr. Bixby, in the course of conducting the background investigation into your wife, Judge Cartwright—by the way, everyone at the Bureau is a major, major fan of the show. *Uh, thank you.* One or two items have turned up that we're hoping you might be able to shed some light on. By the way, sir, this is not an investigation of you per se. But should you at any point in this conversation feel the need to have an attorney present, you are certainly within your rights to have one. *Attorney? No, that's fine, but could you just tell me what this is—about?* Sir, during a routine search of your Internet records— *Internet records? Whoa. Internet records? Hold on. Who the fuck—I mean, sorry, who gave you the right to go poking around my Internet records?* Sir, are you sure you wouldn't be more comfortable having an attorney be part of this conversation, sir? *Yes. I mean no. I mean . . . just . . . tell me what this is about, would you?* Well, sir, it appears that you have been ordering Cuban cigars on line. *Jesus fucking Christ, guys, you almost gave me a fucking heart attack.* Well, sir, these records appear to go back over a period of eight years. *Cigars! I thought you were going to tell me I'd been sending money to al Qaeda, for Chrissake! Hah! I'm joking.* But "the guys" were not laughing. They were staring, doing that G-man thing. Mr. Bixby, ordering contraband items online and receiving them is not a humorous matter. Technically, it's a felony. *Felony? Guys, fellas, what are we talking about here? Cigars—* That's correct, sir. Cuban cigars. Prohibited under The Trading with the Enemy Act, USC Title 50-106. And by virtue of being a repeated and consistent violation of federal law, you may have exposed yourself to charges of participating in an ongoing criminal conspiracy. *Conspiracy? Guys . . .* But that's for the U.S. Attorney to decide, not us. *But—cigars . . .* Additionally, by virtue of your paying for the cigars over the Internet with your . . . I see you used your personal American Express card for most of these transactions . . . you could be susceptible to charges of wire fraud. *But—* Nothing needs to be done at this point in time. This is just to advise you, semiofficially, as it were, that—depending on how the U.S. Attorney decides to proceed—we are opening a file. *Opening a what? A file? What does "opening a file" mean?* Well, sir, that's just standard procedure when the Justice Department initiates a criminal investigation. *Criminal? This is nuts, guys. Completely—* Thank you for your time, sir. By the way, do you have a number where we can reach you? Would this number be good night and day?

By the time they left, Buddy was covered in sweat, his heart was going like a jackhammer, and his hands were shaking. He dialed Pepper's cell phone. She didn't pick up, since she wasn't speaking to him. He left a one-word message.*

When Pepper retrieved the call some hours later, she was somewhat startled but put it down to Buddy's general hysteria—a bit too much bourbon, perhaps?—and went back to prepping for the hearings. She was pleasantly surprised

---

* Four letters, beginning with *c*.

when, over the course of the following days, no process server knocked on her hotel door to notify her that her husband was suing her for breach of contract. Maybe he'd just gotten it off his chest with that little phone outburst and come to his senses. Meanwhile . . .

. . . Buddy, watching from New York, found himself fascinated by Senator Dexter Mitchell. He knew of course from Pepper that he was Public Enemy Numer One, the main obstacle standing between her and a seat on the Court. He'd seen photos and clips of Mitchell over the years. But up to now he'd never realized just how . . . *perfect*-looking the guy was.

Senator Mitchell finished shaking hands and patting shoulders as he made his way to the far end of the dais, where the most junior senator sat. Having come to the end, instead of turning back to his seat at the center, he walked the few steps down onto the committee room floor and made a beeline toward Pepper, who was just then taking her seat at the green baize table facing her inquisitors.

Behind her sat Graydon Clenndennynn, leonine, pin-striped, exuding calm, confidence, serenity; JJ in bolo tie and the white forehead of a man who has lived his life under a burning sun and hat; beside him Juanita, handsomely multicultural; next to her, the Reverend Roscoe, in his trademark white patent leather boots with crucifixes, trying to look relaxed but fidgeting, a purple morocco-bound Bible on his lap.

"Don't you worry none, Daddy," Pepper had gently reassured Roscoe going in, "they ain't gonna get into the Ruby thing. I won't let them."

Senator Dexter Mitchell strode toward Pepper, his eyes beaming like halogen headlamps.

"Judge Cartwright," he said, full of bonhomie, "on behalf of the Committee, let me say, welcome. Welcome. This must be your lovely family here."

"I'm the godfather," Graydon said drily.

"Dexter Mitchell. You all must be so proud. Yes. Proud. Reverend Roscoe, sir. Welcome to Washington, welcome."

When it came JJ's turn to shake, he extended his hand as though it were strictly on temporary loan.

The cameras followed it all.

"That's very unusual," a TV commentator said. "Very. Mitchell never came down to shake hands before. At least I've never seen him do it. What does that tell us, Bob?"

"Jim, I think it tells us that Senator Mitchell knows that he has to handle this carefully. Very carefully, in fact. Some feel that Mitchell and his committee members may have overplayed their hands with the previous two Court nominees. And as you know, polls are showing that a striking majority of people favor Judge Cartwright's nomination. They like this lady. Of course, she's on TV regularly, so they feel they know her already and that's a major plus right there."

"Those polls, Bob—what do they tell us about where we are, that is, as a nation?"

"I guess if nothing else, they tell us that we've reached the point—for better or worse—where being a TV personality is a qualification for the Supreme Court."

"Good news for us, I guess, right?"

Senator Mitchell liked to tap with the handle of his gavel rather than the hammer, signaling that he wielded his authority lightly. He invited Judge Cartwright to read an opening statement.

"Thank you, Senator Mitchell," she said. "I do not have an opening statement."

"You don't?"

"Other than to thank the President for the great—if perplexing—honor of nominating me to this considerable position. And to thank the Committee for considering it."

The Botox in Dexter Mitchell's face felt like it was gelling. "You don't have a statement? It *is* customary, Judge."

"I realize that, sir. But I guess at this point everyone pretty much knows who I am and what I'm doing here. Don't see much point burning up your time yapping on and on about how wonderful I am."

[Laughter.]

"But I would like to introduce my family. That's them behind me. This is my daddy, Roscoe Cartwright. You may have seen him on TV. He's real popular down there. This my granddaddy JJ Cartwright, who used to be a lawman down there. And this is my might-as-well-be grandmomma, Juanita Vazquez. They all three raised me, so if you don't like what you see, it's *their* fault. [Laughter.] I could honestly give a whole opening statement just about how wonderful *they* are, but why don't we just get to the grilling. I see you're all wearing your best barbecue mitts."

[Laughter.]

Fifteen seconds in and she's already taken over. Goddammit. Keep smiling.

"Well, Judge, it *is* unusual—"

"Senator," Pepper smiled, "with all due respect, this whole blessed *thing* is unusual."

[Explosion of laughter.]

"Now, with the Committee's indulgence," Pepper continued, reaching under the table, "I brought with me my whole judicial record." She placed boxed sets of *Courtroom Six* DVDs on the green baize.

[Wave upon wave of laughter.]

Say something, dammit.

"I think I can safely speak for the Committee," Senator Mitchell gleamingly grinned, "that this Committee has never looked forward so much to reviewing a nominee's judicial records."

[Laughter.]

Thank God. Okay, Mitchell thought. *Good. Keep it up.* . . .

Pepper said, "I'm happy to have made the Committee's job more pleasant. Might I respectfully suggest that when referring to any of my distinguished legal cases, the Committee instead of citing by case number simply refer to 'season two, episode four,' and so forth?"

[Laughter.]

"The Committee gratefully accepts your recommendation," Mitchell said, flexing his maxillofacial muscles to a point approaching pain. "Shall we . . . ?"

"Commence firing?" Pepper grinned. "Absolutely. Fire at will, sir."

For reasons of self-preservation, Mitchell had decided to invite Senator Harriett Shimmerman of the great state of New Jersey to try to draw first blood. Better, he thought, to let two women have at each other.

Senator Shimmerman was no fool. She was not in the least thrilled by the assignment. Her office had already received an unusual volume of e-mails, letters, calls, and even personal visits from constituents insisting that she vote to approve Judge Cartwright.

"Good morning, Judge Cartwright," she began, trying her best to sound more like a kindergarten teacher than the fabled "Iron Maiden of Newark" who had sent scores of mafiosi to spend the rest of their lives staring at the ceiling of their cells for twenty-three hours a day in super-max prisons. "You've made a number of public statements to the effect that you do not consider yourself qualified to sit on the Supreme Court." She smiled and made a help-me-out-here hand gesture. "I'm just wondering . . . should we be disagreeing with you about this?"

"No, ma'am. I stand by my previous statements. Realizing, as I do, that that doesn't happen a whole lot in Washington."

[Raucous laughter.]

Senator Shimmerman kept smiling. "Yes, well, welcome to our little town, Judge," she said. "I wonder if perhaps you might tell the Committee a little about your judicial philosophy."

"Basically, do your best to keep an orderly courtroom. Make sure everyone abides by the rules. Punish the wicked and acquit the innocent. That's about it. Want to fast-forward to *Roe v. Wade*?"

"I . . . well . . ." Senator Shimmerman said, glancing at Dexter, who was looking on with a frozen smile.

Pepper said, "I've reviewed transcripts of the last dozen or so Supreme Court nomination hearings and they all seem to pretty much boil down to that."

Senator Shimmerman straightened in her chair. "No. Not at all. I think this committee would like to hear your views on a great variety of topics."

Pepper gave an unconvinced shrug. "Okay, if you say so. Just trying to save time. We can talk till the cows come home about original intent and strict constructionism, the living Constitution, judicial temperament, the role of the court versus the role of the legislature, what-have-you, and all the rest. I'm happy to do that. I've spent the last couple weeks cramming my locomotive with suggested answers Mr. Hayden Cork and his folks supplied me with."

Hayden, watching on TV with the President, closed his eyes and silently groaned. The President beamed.

"The White House told you what to say?" Senator Shimmerman said.

"Heck, yes. They gave me these briefing books," Pepper continued. "Great big *pile* of 'em. Looked like a back-to-school sale at Wal-Mart. You'd need a forklift to carry 'em all. Anyway, I memorized all the answers. I warn you, though, Senator. They're pretty darn dull. Seems to me, they were designed to have everyone at home reaching for the channel changer, going, 'Wake me up if they find pubic hair on any Coke cans.'* But however you want to play it, Senator. This is your rodeo."

Graydon Clenndennynn smiled.

Senator Shimmerman's mouth opened. Nothing came out. She looked like she'd been smacked across the face with a haddock.

In the Oval Office, President Vanderdamp purred. "That's our girl, Hayden," he said, slapping his desk. Hayden Cork said nothing.

Nineteen senators stared mutely at the nominee.

"Well," Pepper smiled, "doesn't *anyone* have a question?"

---

* Reference to an unfortunate moment in a prior Supreme Court nomination hearing, best not dwelt upon.

CHAPTER 12

W hy should *I* be the one to bring that up?" Senator Pebblemacher of the great state of Nevada said with some truc-
ulence to Chairman Mitchell during a fraught caucus of
half a dozen Committee senators prior to day three of the Cartwright hearings.

For two days, Dexter had been sending his party's senators
out onto the field of battle. They had all returned whimpering.
Hanratty of Massachusetts had tried to nail Pepper for her athe-
ism, to which Pepper had calmly replied, "Well, Senator, perhaps if you'd seen your momma get zapped by the Good Lord
when you were nine years old, you might feel the same way."
Hanratty had received so many death threats he was now under
Secret Service protection, spending nights at several undisclosed
locations.

Bouscaran of Delaware, a former judge himself, had tried to
trip her up on technicalities, only to have Pepper correct him on
the actual wording of *Leegin Creative Leather Products v. PSKS*.
(Hayden's people had astutely included it in the briefing book.)

Harmookian of Wisconsin wanted to know if she would
have granted certiorari in *Gretchen's Frozen Pike v. Milwaukee
Block Ice*. Pepper cited three precedents, going back to 1956,
where the Court had refused to intervene in similar cases, on

the grounds that decomposing fish was simply too revolting to contemplate.

"I only thought," Dexter said to Senator Pebblemacher, trying to sound magnanimous, "you might like to take a shot at her. It's a low-hanging fruit."

"Then why don't you reach for it?" Pebblemacher said suspiciously.

"I'm holding myself in reserve," Dexter said.

"What do you think this is? Battle of the Bulge?"

"Yeah," said Murmelly of the great state of Idaho. "When *are* you going join the fight, Dexter?"

"All in good time," Dexter said. "All in good time. People, people. Come on. Let's keep it together." He appealed to Pebblemacher. "Jimbo, look, you can't miss with this one. Her father practically *invited* Jack Ruby to shoot Oswald."

"For God's sake, Dexter, she wasn't even *born* in 1963. What the hell's this got to do with her?"

"I'm not saying she was involved personally," Dexter said. "But the whole thing stinks. And the mother. Killed by lightning? Don't you think that's a little bit too pat? My Riders found someone who says he was in the ER when they brought her in and he'll swear she was still alive."

"Proving what?" Pebblemacher said, arms crossing defiantly over his chest.

Dexter lowered his voice. "Well, our information is that they, uh, finished her off there."

Pebblemacher snorted. "You want to make that case? Be. My. Guest."

Dexter shrugged. "Suit yourself, Jimbo. Just thought you were a team player. Anyone?"

A half-dozen senators stared back silently at their chairman.

"All right then. But I think we're missing an opportunity here."

Dexter turned to Senator Ramos y Gualtapo of the great state of Florida. "Silvia," he said. "Hit her on the commerce clause. That answer she gave Fritz yesterday on *Feinhard v. Moon*—she was on thin ice. I could hear it cracking."

Senator Ramos y Gualtapo gave Chairman Mitchell a dubious look. "I didn't hear any ice cracking."

"Well, I think," Dexter said, tapping the table impatiently with his pen, "that she's vulnerable on interstate commerce."

"When are you going to question her, Dexter?" Silvia said.

"Yeah."

"Yeah."

"Don't you worry," he said calmly. "I've got questions for Judge Cartwright. Oh, yes. Oh, yes. Yes."

"Like what?"

"All in good time."

"You haven't said boo so far," said Senator Bloggwell of the great state of Mississippi. "All you do is make goo-goo eyes at her."

The senators murmured. Murmuring is one of the higher senatorial arts.

"You let her run over Harriett," said Senator Manxzen of the great but not spacious state of Rhode Island. "Wearing cleats."

"Harriett Shimmerman is as tough as aluminum siding," Dexter said. "She didn't need any help from me."

"Oh, yeah?" said Senator Ezratty of the occasionally great state of North Carolina. "Is that why I found her sobbing in the cloakroom?"

"No, no, no, no," Dexter said. "That was on account of her dog. It got cancer. Leukemia. Some fatal dog something."

"That was last week."

"Well, maybe the dog had a relapse. Look, people. I am

going to hold Judge Cartwright's little piggies to the fire, don't you doubt it. In the meantime, I don't think any useful purpose would be served by . . ."

"Telling us what you're going to ask her?" Senator Ramos y Gualtapo said.

"No, Silvia. By broadcasting our strategy," Dexter said. "Let's get it together, people. She's got us all running around in nineteen different directions."

"Well, unless you come up with a smoking gun, Mr. Chairman," said Senator Murfledorken of the great but somewhat pointless state of North Dakota, "I might as well tell you I'm going to vote for her."

The senators murmured superbly.

Dexter shook his head. "Ralph, that is so . . . not helpful."

"Would you like to see my mail?" Murfledorken replied. "I can't get in the door of my office it's piled up so high in the hall. My Web browser crashed last night from all my e-mail. I'm not going to commit hara-kiri over her. She seems all right to me. If you want to know the truth, I *like* her."

"Yeah."

"Yeah."

"Ralph," Mitchell said, "voting for that"—he was about to say *woman* when he caught Silvia glowering at him—"TV personality. I mean, it would go against every sacredly held principle we're sworn to uphold. My God. Do you realize this Committee is the only thing standing between the Supreme Court of the United States and . . ."

"What?" Silvia said.

"Mediocrity."

"I don't find her so mediocre."

"Me, neither."

"People. *People.* Let's all just take a deep breath. . . ."

But by day three of the Cartwright hearings, it was clear that the air was going out of—not into—the members of the Senate Judiciary Committee. Senators who had dared to ask even mildly snarky questions of Judge Cartwright were receiving death threats—the kind that specify what caliber bullet will be used. It was abundantly, pellucidly clear that the people wanted Judge Pepper. Even President Vanderdamp's approval ratings had shot up—by almost ten points.

"President Vanderdamp," the *Financial Times* commented wryly, "finally appears to have done something politically astute—almost certainly by accident."

After the unhappy caucus had huffed and stomped its way out of Senator Mitchell's office, Dexter summoned his chief of staff, a man named Pickerill.

"What was that stuff the Russians used on the ex-KGB guy? The radioactive poison. Do we have any? A few drops in her water pitcher . . . What a catastrophe. Anything from the Riders?"

"There is something, but it's—not much."

Dexter had been praying for some eleventh-hour smoking gun, but the Wraith Riders had come back from their investigation, shrieking and neighing and wailing, with empty hands. Pepper Cartwright had not had an abortion; had not dated anyone named bin Laden; had not distributed pamphlets calling for the overthrow of the U.S. government; snorted cocaine; called anyone by a racial epithet. She'd sniffled through the final scenes of *To Kill a Mockingbird*. There had been a brief, giddy moment of hope when it was learned that Cartwright and Bixby's housekeeper was Nicaraguan, but it had been cruelly dashed when it turned out they were legally sponsoring her for a green card and citizenship.

"Let's have it," Dexter said.

"Senior year at her boarding school, she and another girl put shaving cream on the headmistress's toilet seat."

Dexter stared at his chief of staff. "Well, that'll drive a stake through her heart."

"Sorry, Senator. We'll keep trying."

And so, on the brink of the final day of the Cartwright hearings, Senator Dexter Mitchell found himself standing on a diving board above a large pool full of—nothing.

"Good morning," he said, giving the gavel handle the lightest little tippy-tap. "Senator Ramos y Gualtapo, your witness."

Silvia dutifully asked Judge Cartwright a technical question about the applicability of the commerce clause.

"Well, Senator," Pepper said, "as you know, in the nineteen eighties the Court was divided and reversed itself on *Garcia v. San Antonio Transit Authority.* . . ." Silvia nodded, as though thoroughly versed in the case, shooting a venomous glance in Dexter's direction. Dexter for his part was thinking, *I've seen episodes of* Mister Rogers' Neighborhood *that were more contentious. Why don't you just ask her for her recipe for upside-down pineapple cake?*

Silvia finished. "Thank you, Judge Cartwright. I have no further questions."

And so, finally, it was Senator Dexter Mitchell's turn. There had been much speculation about this moment. All eyes were on him. Normally he reveled in the sensation. Not today.

Even Terry, his wife, high school sweetheart, life's companion, sharer of his heart's secrets, lover, best friend, mother of their attractive children, had said to him that morning over the shredded mini-wheat, "I hope you're not planning to embarrass yourself with Judge Cartwright."

Planning? *Planning?* To be rendered splutteringly speechless, with a mouthful of shredded mini-wheat, on this day of days, by his own . . . wife? *Yes, honey,* he felt like saying, *funny you should mention it. I was up all night "planning" how to make myself look like a complete fool on national television. Do you have any tips for me? How about if I blew my nose on Senator Tronkmeyer's neck-tie? Do you think that would bring about the desired level of embar-rassment? Or should I simultaneously summon a thermonuclear fart right as I'm boring in on her interpretation of the equal protection clause?*

"*I* think she's terrific," Terry continued, not looking up from her newspaper.

"Thank you, honey," Dexter said, "for the input."

"Anytime," Terry said, still not looking up.

"Judge Cartwright," Dexter Mitchell began, leaning forward as he faced Pepper. There behind her was Graydon Clennden-nynn, looking like a public library stone lion. There was the grandfather, Sheriff JJ, droopy mustache and all. His arms had been folded tightly across his chest for three days now as he scowled at the Judiciary Committee. *Mess with my little girl, and I'll cut out your livers.* Next to him the Mexican woman. And there's the Reverend Roscoe. *Nice going with Ruby, there, Reverend. . . . No,* Dexter warned himself, *don't go there.*

Dexter cleared his throat. "Judge Cartwright, were you . . . You must have been pretty surprised when President Vander-damp nominated you for this job."

"Is that a question, Senator, or a statement of the scream-ingly obvious?"

[Laughter.]

"Ha-ha," Dexter nodded, "quite right. Yes, yes, I suppose you must have been. Because someone in your . . . position, that is, in your line of work, wouldn't normally . . . I guess what I'm trying to get at—"

"Let me throw you a lifeline, Senator," Pepper said. "The President's telephone call knocked me flatter than butterfly roadkill. I stipulate that, Senator. But didn't we kind of establish that about five minutes into these hearings?"

[Laughter.]

"Yes. Yes. . . . Right you are, Judge."

"It would take someone with bigger cojones than I have," Pepper continued, giving Dexter a foxy look that only the two of them—along with the President, Graydon Clenndennynn, and Hayden Cork—could fully appreciate, "to *ask* for this. It's not the sort of job anyone would solicit outright. Is it?"

This moment in the Cartwright hearings has been much discussed. Many have wondered why Senator Mitchell never paused to ask for a clarification of the meaning of "cojones." Instead, he seemed to recoil slightly and stammer, "Judge, you've done, in my view, a-a-a very thorough, indeed, excellent job of answering this Committee's questions."

Pepper, staring evenly, said, "Very generous of you, sir."

"There were those on the Committee," Dexter said tsk-tskily, "who wanted to ask—to raise certain issues, going back . . . well, a long way."

Pepper's eyes narrowed.

"But it was decided that the Committee would not, so to speak, go there."

Dexter Mitchell's face suddenly and weirdly turned exuberantly magnanimous, like that of someone who has just decided to give away his entire fortune at the stroke of a pen.

"Yes," he beamed. "And if I may say so myself, that was the right decision."

His fellow Committee members stared at their chairman, jaws agape.

"As chair of this distinguished Committee, I feel strongly that no *decent* purpose would be accomplished by going there. No, no. And so, Judge, I am pleased—indeed, very pleased—to say, to declare right here and now, without further delay, that it is the collective sense of this Committee that your nomination is . . ."

Dexter let it hang there a moment, a little bright origami kite wafting on lung-warmed thermals.

". . . likely, indeed almost certain to be approved by this Committee."

A shiver of pleasure went through the room, and, through the airwaves, beyond into the land. For a moment, the entire country exhaled together, as a vast, happy *ahhh* spread from sea to shining sea, rippling the amber waves of grain as it went.

"Now," Dexter said, looking abruptly serious, "this is not to say that I did not entertain certain . . ."

The *ahhh* paused, hovered tremulously over the Great Plains.

". . . call them . . . if you might . . . well, misgivings. . . ."

Amber waves of grain trembled.

Dexter spoke gravely, as if trying to look like a Daniel Chester French statue of himself. "I have, of course, certain responsibilities, transient and historical . . . but there are times—and this, surely, is one of them—when a leader, in order *to* lead, must follow. And so, let me be the first to say, as leader, that I will vote to approve your nomination."

The room erupted into applause. The Committee members, most of whom were by now casting withering looks at their sure-to-be transient "leader," began one by one to join in the applause.

CHAPTER 13

Pepper's nomination was approved by the Senate Judiciary Committee 18-0 (one abstention) and 91-7 (two abstentions) by the full Senate.

Graydon Clenndennynn warmly accepted congratulations for his stewarding of the nomination, and dropped hints that it had been his idea all along. President Vanderdamp's approval ratings shot up another few points. Complimented on his role, Hayden Cork mustered a tight smile and changed the subject.

Dexter Mitchell went on *Greet the Press* to assert manfully that there are times when "the courageous thing to do is to accept the will of the people and move on." He quoted a leader of the 1848 Revolution in France, someone named Alexandre Ledru-Rollin, who had declared, completely sans irony, "There go the people. I must follow them. I am their leader."

Though he put on a brave front, Dexter Mitchell felt inwardly humiliated. His fellow committee members now viewed him with outright loathing. There was murmuring (of high senatorial quality) in the cloakroom about the need for "fresh leadership." Nights he lay awake grinding his molars after failing to satisfy his wife maritally. How, he wondered, had it come to this? Three decades of dutiful, steady, occasionally brilliant public service—to be outgunned and outshone by some chick TV judge from Texas. Where—Dexter Mitchell asked the ceiling gods—was the justice in that?

A few days later he took some satisfaction (however guilty) in reading in the *Washington Post* that Judge Cartwright's marriage was apparently unraveling.

"Associate justice–designate Pepper Cartwright's office today issued a statement announcing that she and her husband, producer Buddy Bixby, are 'amicably separating' after seven years of marriage."

Fortunately, certain details did not make the paper.

Pepper had returned, triumphant, from Washington, eager to make up and move on with Buddy, only to find that her key no longer opened the door to their apartment. When she called him on her cell phone to ask what was going on, he informed her in a businesslike voice that she was no longer welcome.

"Buddy," Pepper said, tapping the toe of her cowboy boot on the marble of the entryway, "what are you talking about? This is our *home*. You can't just go changing the locks. What's gotten into you?"

"If you will recall," Buddy said coolly, "the apartment is in my name. But then you're pretty casual about remembering the wording of certain documents. Like employment contracts."

Pepper groaned. "You still going on about that? I thought you were going to sue me for breach of contract."

"I was. Until you sicced the FBI on me."

"What are you talking about?"

"Oh, ha-ha-*ha*. Like you know nothing about it."

"I haven't got the slightest idea what you're talking about. But I would like to get into my apartment. Among other things, I got to pee."

"Try the coffee shop around the corner. They have a restroom." He hung up.

On her way to the coffee shop, cussing and fuming, Pepper called Hayden Cork.

"Do you know anything about the FBI visiting my husband and making some kind of threat? He's having a conniption the size of Guatemala about it."

There was a lengthy pause. "I have no direct knowledge of such an event," Hayden said.

Pepper said, "Is that 'no' in Washingtonese?"

"That's all I'll say," Hayden said. "Congratulations on the Senate vote. The President is very pleased. He looks forward to the swearing-in." He hung up.

Fighting hot flashes, Pepper called Graydon Clenndennynn, reaching him aboard someone's jet en route to Tokyo.

"My dear," he said mellifluously, "you don't make the whistle in this town by knowing things you don't need to know. My warmest congratulations to you." He hung up.

She called Buddy, who didn't answer. She left a message.

"I made a few calls. No one'll tell me anything, but I guess something happened. Whatever it was, I didn't have anything to do with it. You're going to have to believe that. Either way, I hope it isn't going to end like this for us, leaving messages on each other's phones."

The next day after an uneasy sleep in the fetal position, she heard a knock on her hotel room door. Expecting maid service, Pepper opened it to find a man she instantly recognized as a process server, who with some embarrassment handed her two sets of documents, one a suit for divorce, another for breach of contract.

Pepper accepted the papers. She told the man, "Hold on." She returned and handed him a twenty-dollar bill.

"What's this?" he said.

"It's a tip," Pepper said.

"Why?"

"You'll see."

Two days later, the *New York Post* reported that Judge Cartwright had tipped the process server. The item appeared under the headline CLASS ACTION.

Figuring that Buddy would leak it that he'd served her with papers, Pepper decided she might as well get in the last lick.

DEXTER MITCHELL was at his desk morosely contemplating his future, which, as Judiciary Committee Chairman, did not promise to be long-term. His secretary entered with the news that a Mr. Buddy Bixby was on the phone. His mind raced. What would he be calling about? If it was information that could torpedo his wife's nomination, he was a day late and a dollar short. Cautiously but curiously, he took the call.

"Senator Mitchell, I'd like to discuss a proposition with you."

"Proposition," Dexter said. "Could you be a little more precise?"

"Not over the phone. Is there some way we could meet privately? It probably wouldn't make sense for us both to be public, given the situation."

Alarm bells rang in Dexter's brain, but he was intrigued. He told Bixby that he would be on the Acela train from Washington to Stamford, Connecticut, the next day, seated in the last seat on the last car.

The next afternoon as the train stopped at Penn Station, Buddy Bixby slid into the empty seat next to Senator Mitchell.

"Feels like a spy movie, huh?" Buddy said.

"What can I do for you?" Dexter said.

"In addition to *Courtroom Six*," Buddy said, "I produce a number of other TV shows."

"Yes," Dexter said. "People jumping off bridges and eating themselves to death."

Buddy laughed, "Yeah, well, those are the ones that pay for the quality shows."

"Mr. Bixby, I'll be getting off in Stamford in about thirty-five minutes from now. Shall we get to the point?"

"You bet. Ever considered going on TV, Senator?"

Dexter stared. "I 'go on TV' all the time. Recently, in fact. You may have seen me. I was on with your wife."

"Nah. Your *own* show."

"What kind of show?" Dexter said, trying not to sound too interested. "I'm not leaping off any bridges. Or gaining five hundred pounds."

"Nothing like that. Senator, how'd you like to be President of the United States?"

"I tried," Dexter said drily. "Several times."

"This time, you win. And you don't have to enter the Iowa caucuses or the New Hampshire primary. You don't have to kiss babies or anyone's ass. You don't have to pretend you give a shit about the Middle East—"

"Mr. Bixby. I *do* give a shit about the Middle East."

"That's great. Someone has to, right? Look, I've been watching you. You were born to play this part. You've got this incredible . . . *authority*. You really look like the real deal."

"Thank you. I like to think that I am the real deal. You want me to play a president, is that the idea?"

"Exactly."

"Like *The West Wing*?"*

"Yeah. But without all the hand-wringing. With balls. Gritty. And *sexy*. Hot. I'm casting Ramona Alvilar as the First Lady."

"Really?" Dexter said. "I saw her in what-was-it-called. She's quite . . ."

---

* Popular TV series about a hand-wringing liberal U.S. president and his hand-wringing liberal staff; based on the novel *Let Freedom Wring*.

"Hot? Oh," Buddy chuckled, "let me tell you. I came three times during the meeting."

Senator Mitchell's expression suggested to Buddy that this might not have been appropriate. Buddy shrugged. "Figure of speech. You know what sold her on the deal?"

"No," Dexter said, "I don't."

"When I told her I was going to approach *you* to play the President."

"Oh. Really."

"She's a *huge* fan."

"Well. Please tell her that I'm a fan of *hers*. Look, Mr. Bixby—"

"Buddy. Please."

"I already have a job. A good one."

"I recognize that and appreciate that," Buddy said. "And I respect that. I would say this: if at this moment in your life you're completely fulfilled, if you feel that you have nothing left to prove, no heights left to scale, then . . . I'll shake your hand, thank you for your time, and be out of here. I guess someone in your position, when they retire, they can make a few dollars working for some lobbying firm on K Street, right? On the other hand, if you're up for taking on something that could be extremely exciting, very high profile, to say nothing of insanely lucrative, then . . . sleep on it."

Dexter looked out the window, seeing his own face staring back at him. It was a handsome reflection, he reflected. He tilted his head just so. Yes. It did look presidential. Yes. Yes.

"Are you doing this to spite your wife?" Dexter said.

"Well," Buddy shrugged, "sure. But there's also the money."

IN A VAST MARBLE BATHROOM of a vastly expensive hotel suite with a splendid view of the Washington Monument, Pepper

Cartwright, associate justice–designate of the U.S. Supreme Court, was throwing up.

JJ and Juanita hovered on the other side of the door.

"*Amor,*" Juanita said, "*por favor, abre la puerta.*"

From Pepper's side of the door came a hollow, bellowy sound of the kind heard in the sea mammal section of the zoo as feeding time approaches.

"You all right, honey?" JJ said somewhat pointlessly.

"Of course she's not all right," Juanita said.

JJ took out his gold pocket watch and said, "Maybe I oughta call the White House."

"*Sí.* Call them."

"What am I supposed to tell 'em?"

"That she's sick."

"I can't tell the President of the United States she's got her head in the toilet. It ain't dignified."

"Tell them that she ate something."

Pepper, listening to it all from behind the door, said, "I'm all right. Just give me a . . ." This was followed by another aquatic sound.

She had, to be sure, been through rather a lot at this point and had run through a lifetime's supply of adrenaline. A few hours earlier, as she lay awake, sweating into her 800-count hotel sheets, staring at the time display on the clock, it had dawned on her that there was now no going back. Her new office was in a marble building that looked like it belonged on the Acropolis. She'd had recurring dreams in which its great bronze doors clanged shut behind her. When she turned around, she saw hooded figures welding the doors shut, to the accompaniment of demonic cackling. She stared into the blue water in the toilet bowl. *Even the toilet water looks expensive.* The President of the United States and the world media were cooling their heels waiting for her in the Oval Office.

Oh, girl, she thought, struggling to her feet and looking at the ghastly reflection in the mirror. *What in hell have you got yourself into?*

"What about a nip of bourbon?" JJ suggested through the door.

"*No seas tonto, JJ.* She can't have *bourbon* on her breath for the President," Juanita said crossly.

"Wasn't suggestin' she drink the whole bottle."

Pepper opened the door, pale, but upright. "All right," she gasped. "Let's do this thing."

Juanita marched her back into the bathroom to attend to hair and lipstick and other necessaries. JJ shrugged and drank the bourbon himself. The swearing-in went without incident, with Chief Justice Hardwether doing the honors. Pepper had gargled beforehand with about a quart of mouthwash and smelled like a spearmint forest. The Chief Justice smelled kind of minty himself. There was a nice small lunch, and President Vanderdamp autographed his place card for Juanita.

CHAPTER 14

On Capitol Hill, Senator Dexter Mitchell was having an officially unofficial meeting with his old friend Senator Clement Cranch of the great state of Mississippi. Cranch was Chairman of the Senate Ethics Committee, almost never referred to as "the powerful Senate Ethics Committee."

The meeting was not going to Dexter's satisfaction. Cranch kept shifting in his chair and doing things with his mouth as if he were a recent recipient of oral surgery.

"I just honestly don't see the problem, Clem," Dexter said. "It's not like I'm trying to hide income."

"Dexter, you'd need a mine shaft to hide that kinda income."

Dexter made a dismissive gesture. "Now that's only a best-case scenario, like if the series goes into syndication. For starters I'd only be pulling down, you know, fifty grand," he lowered his voice, "per episode. Tops."

Cranch snorted. "That's one-third of a Senate salary, Dex. How's that gonna look on the front page of the *Washington Post*? How's it gonna look back in Hartford? You think of that?"

"Yes, Clem, I have, and I think the people of Connecticut would be proud to see their senator on TV."

"You're already on TV."

"I'm not talking about C-SPAN, for God's sake. We're talking network, prime time. Look, Clem, there's all sorts of dimensions to this thing."

"Whenever people tell me 'There's all sorts of dimensions to' something, it always boils down to one—money."

"Listen, Clem—and this is strictly between us. Can I trust you on this?"

"Dex, I'm the Senate Ethics chair. I guess you can trust me."

"Okay. I don't give a rat's ass about the money. You think I'm getting into this so I can move to McLean and build myself some forty-thousand-square-foot McMansion? This money—all of it—is going into my war chest."

"What war chest?"

"For when I run again, Clem. For the big job."

Cranch shook his head. "Dex, I don't care if it goes for a McMuffin in McLean, for Vegas hookers, or for cleft palate surgery for kids in the damn Congo. The rules are the rules."

"Fuck the rules."

"That's a fine thing to say to the Ethics chair."

"That's right, Clem. It's a chair. Not a throne."

"Well, whatever it is, it ain't a toilet, and you ain't about to take a crap in it."

"Write new rules," Dexter said. "For God's sake. No one expects ethics in the Congress, anyway. Try Googling 'ethics' and 'Congress,' see how many matches you get."

"Be that as it may. It's my *job,* Dexter."

"With all the dire things going on in the world right now . . . the economic situation, Texas about to mine its border with Mexico, these Russian submarines snooping off our shores like great white sharks, *TV judges* on the Supreme Court . . . and you're all bent out of shape because a U.S. senator wants to lift the image of the entire government and maybe make a little walking-around money on the side. . . ."

"I'm tired of this conversation, Dex. The rules say no outside regular salary. And that's that. Over and out."

"It's not a salary."

Cranch slammed his fist on his desk. "Then what in tar hell is it? And don't you tell me it's an *honorarium*. We get into more pissin' matches over that goddamned word *honorarium*."

Dexter stood before a window, looking at his presidential—yes—reflection. He sighed philosophically.

"It's sad," he said. "You devote your entire life to public service . . . your whole life . . . and an opportunity comes along to do something good for your family, a little money—"

"I thought the money was going to your war chest."

"I consider my family part of my war chest, Clem. And the next thing you know you're being trampled into the ground by the Four Horseman of the Ethicalypse. No wonder young people don't want to go into politics these days."

"That was a fine oration. Up there with Cicero. You done?"

"Will you walk with me, Clem? Will you take a few steps with me?"

Senator Cranch sighed. "Dammit, Dex, it ain't *up* to just me."

"This could be good for all of us. A sitting senator on a popular prime-time TV show, dynamically playing President of the United States."

"Hold on. Hold on. How did you wantin' to play Mr. Hollywood President become a mission of mercy on behalf of the U.S. Senate?"

"Have you seen the latest polls? Do you know what percent of the American people have quote-unquote high confidence in the Senate?"

Cranch groaned.

"Twelve percent," Dexter said. "Twelve percent. Donald Vanderdamp—who has brought incompetence and dishonor to the office of the President—*he* has better numbers than us."

"If it comes to that," Clem said, "I don't have a whole lot of quote-unquote confidence in the American people. But we're stuck with each other. As for Don Veto, I wouldn't worry none about his popularity ratings. Maybe he got a little temporary uptick from the Cartwright thing, but he's a long way from winning any beauty contests. Hell, the Presidential Term Limit Amendment just got voted out of committee. Bussy Filbrick says it's gonna sail through the House faster than shit through a goose. According to my whip count, it's got over sixty-eight votes in the Senate.* Personally, I wish I could vote for it twice. That self-righteous cocksucker just vetoed my shrimp boat building initiative in Pascagoula."

Dexter said, "What good is denying him a second term? From what I hear, he doesn't even *want* a second term."

"How'd you like to go down in history as the president who caused a constititutional amendment keeping presidents from having more than one term? I'd call that a serious humiliation, far as a legacy goes."

"Wouldn't it be simpler just to impeach him?" Dexter said.

"Be *simpler*," Cranch said, "to shoot the sumbitch. But they got laws, so they tell me." The two men stared at each other.

"I didn't say that," Cranch said. "Looky here, Dex, I'd like to help. I sure would. I love you like my brother."

"You don't have a brother, Clem."

"Well, if I did, I'd try to love him like I do you. But I can't just go creating a loophole the size of the Grand Canyon for you. They'd run me outta here faster than a nukular particle accelerator. Sorry, old buddy, but you're gonna have to choose between the U.S. Senate and this TV show."

*　*　*

---

* To be ratified, an amendment to the U.S. Constitution must be approved by two-thirds votes in the House and Senate and then by three-fourths of the state legislatures.

Just a few blocks away at the marble palace, everyone was being very nice. Pepper had been bracing for wrinkled brows and sneers of cold command from her fellow justices. They practically greeted her with sugar donuts and hot chocolate. Paige Plympton, apparently a fan of *Courtroom Six*, gave her a little hug. Paige was an unflinty Maine Yankee; former Chief Judge of the State Supreme Court. Her ancestors had come over on the second boat to land after the *Mayflower*. "We sent the servants on ahead."

Only two handshakes from her new peers were on the cool side: Justices Santamaria's and Richter's.

Pepper suspected that Silvio might feel a little awkward inasmuch as he'd given an interview after her nomination was announced calling it "another installment in the Great Dumbing-Down." She'd been tempted to bring along a thirty-six-ounce bottle of Mountain Dew and a bag of pork rinds. Paige had advised against it.

Ruth "Ruthless" Richter wasn't outright hostile, but her vibes were of the what-are-you-doing-here kind. But then she, like CJ Hardwether, was going through a rough patch as a result of a vote. Ruth had written for the majority in *al-Muktar v. United States*, the ruling that freed "suspected terrorist"—as he was then called by the media—Sheik Mohammed al-Muktar from the U.S. military prison in Guantánamo. Two months later, Sheik al-Muktar graduated to "confirmed terrorist" after blowing himself up on a parking lot shuttle bus at Disney World along with twenty-three visitors to the Magic Kingdom.

Justice Richter stood by her opinion on constitutional grounds, but her approval ratings were now such that she had to be moved about town in an armored personnel carrier with helicopter gunships patrolling overhead. So she was understandably a bit on edge these days. One morning while the justices were in conference, a law clerk passing outside dropped a volume of *U.S.*

Reports onto the floor of the marble corridor, causing a bang. Ruth dove under the table.

Ishiguro "Mike" Haro was the first Japanese-American Supreme Court justice, and persuasive evidence that Asians really are intellectually superior to the other races. His hobby was doing the *Times* of London crossword while blindfolded. He'd graduated from Stanford Law School at age twenty. By twenty-four he was a Silicon Valley billionaire start-up lawyer; at twenty-eight, the youngest judge on the federal bench (Ninth Circuit). He was, like many of advanced intelligence, impatient with those of more modest brilliance. He was not shy of expressing deeply held opinions, such as that President Truman was—as he put it, perhaps unwisely within view of someone's cell-phone video camera—"a runty genocidal haberdasher" for having dropped the A-bomb on some of his relatives. He was not overly popular with the law clerks—even his own—who made puns on his surname's similarity to an Asian mispronunciation of "hello."

Justice Morris "Mo" Gotbaum had been, until joining the Court, senior senator from New York. He was a famously soft touch when it came to staying executions, having granted seventy-eight stays so far. This caused tensions between him and Silvio, an ardent champion of the ultimate sanction. Silvio kept a little guillotine cigar-cutter on his desk—for the amusement of visiting children (he claimed). Mo never missed an opportunity to tweak him. Once during oral argument in a case involving a public school teacher who had been fired for expressing a favorable opinion about Intelligent Design, Mo had asked the teacher's attorney, "If Intelligent Design exists, how would you explain the U.S. Tax Code?"

In other ways, Mo was atypical for a New York Jewish liberal. His great passion in life was putting on black leather and touring the country on a Suzuki Rocket motorcycle—he privately called it his Crotch Rocket—with his wife, Bella, hanging on behind for dear life. He faithfully attended the annual biker rally in Sturgis, South Dakota, every year and gave passionate, well-footnoted speeches to the bikers, calling for a motorcycle exception from the national speed limit. When bored during oral arguments, which he frequently was, he would hum "Born to Be Wild."

Crispus Galavanter was second in juniority to Pepper. He occupied the "black seat" on the court, though it is seldom openly referred to as such. He had first come to prominence in an unusual way: by taking on the Ku Klux Klan—Web site slogan: "Bringing a Message of Hope and Deliverance to White Christian America! A Message of Love NOT Hate!"—as a client.

The Klan had wanted to open a store in a mall in suburban Boise, Idaho, where it could sell Klan notions and memorabilia, his and hers ceremonial robes and caps, dinner-table flaming crucifix candelabra, hangman noose light switches, Third Reich memorabilia, reissues of *The Protocols of the Elders of Zion*, manuals on breeding pit bulls and Alsatians, and other heartwarming gewgaws. The mall owners, however, perhaps seeking a more elevated tone, refused to rent them space.

Crispus, then a young local attorney, volunteered to handle the Klan's case "for costs." The Klan was initially somewhat taken aback, but after some head-scratching and palavering decided what the heck, they might look kind of good in court if they had themselves a smart "colored" lawyer, so they said, okay, just so long as we don't have to eat with you or share bathroom facilities, and forget about dating any of our daughters. No problem at all, Crispus said. Put it out of your minds. You concentrate on spreading that message of love to White Christian America and let me deal with these small-minded mall owners.

He was brutally pilloried in the press for his efforts on behalf of the Idaho Klan, accused of all manner of outrageous grandstanding, called all sorts of names, about the mildest of which was Black Judas. Through it all Crispus smiled and kept his head down and diligently argued his client's case. He framed it as a civil rights case and fought it all the way up to the Idaho Supreme Court.

In his argument before the state's highest court, Crispus eloquently championed his client's views on the superiority of the white race; Jewish control of the media, the international banking system, and bottled drinking water; the Vatican's secret deal with NASA to put a Catholic on Mars; and Occupational Safety and Health Administration regulations that required filling out endless, unnecessary paperwork before burning a cross on public land. By the time Crispus was finished, he had all the judges doubled over with laughter. They ruled in favor of the mall, made the Klan liable for the mall owners' legal costs. Crispus thereupon smiled and presented the Klan with a bill that, coincidentally, amounted to one dollar more than it had in the bank. It filed for bankruptcy.

When questioned about whether his representation of the Klan was consistent with a lawyer's duty to represent his client vigorously, Crispus would say that he had made precisely the arguments the Klan had wanted made, and that the fee he had charged was reasonable. As for the Klan, it was entitled to full consideration of its legal claims, and that legal consideration had destroyed it.

Crispus was appointed to the federal bench and a few years later moved on up to the high court. He golfed with Tiger Woods.

CHAPTER 15

Three years earlier, a man named Jimmy James Swayle had walked into the Rough River Savings and Trust Bank in Hotbridge, South Dakota, and presented the teller with a note written in incongruously polite language. *Pleace hand over $TEN THOUSDAND or I will be compelt to shoot the poor customers. Sorry for the inconvenients. Hurry up OK.*

The teller duly activated the silent alarm and, reciprocating Mr. Swayle's politeness, insisted on counting out his request in one- and five-dollar denominations, apologizing for not having larger bills. Presently, Sheriff's Deputy Edward Fogarty entered the bank with drawn shotgun and commanded Mr. Swayle to drop his weapon and lie facedown on the floor. Mr. Swayle pointed his pistol at Deputy Fogarty and pulled the trigger. The gun, a Rimski 9mm semi-automatic, failed to fire. Deputy Fogarty walked over to Mr. Swayle, gave him an understandably robust butt in the face with the shotgun, and hauled him unconscious off to the pokey.

After a not very long trial, Jimmy James Swayle was found guilty of attempted armed robbery and murder and sentenced to twenty-five years. And there, but for the genius of the American legal system, the books might have quietly closed on a not distinguished criminal career. However . . .

. . . a second-year law student doing a project at the state penitentiary advised Mr. Swayle to file suit against the Rimski Firearms Corporation on the grounds that their product, which he had legally purchased, had failed to function properly "during a business transaction," causing him not only loss of income but also significant psychic and physical distress, entitling Mr. Swayle to damages under South Dakota law. Since Mr. Swayle was a citizen of South Dakota and Rimski was a Connecticut corporation, Mr. Swayle was able to bring suit in federal court. The case had worked its way up the judicial ladder from the district court, the Court of Appeals, and had finally fetched up on the steps of the U.S. Supreme Court.

Mr. Swayle's petition for certiorari was just one of about 7,000 the Court receives each year asking to be considered for review. The justices accept only seventy or so of these for oral argument. Four justices have to agree to grant cert in order for a case to be accepted. Generally, the Court accepts only cases that it finds interesting; but sometimes a "what the hell" element seems to come into play. Justices look solemn in their formal black robes, but every so often they like to have a little fun by taking on a strange case, or overturning a presidential election, that sort of thing.

One of Haro's clerks, knowing of his justice's zest for embarrassing firearms manufacturers, yanked the Swayle petition from the cert pool pile and brought it to his attention. Haro immediately signed on. Justice Galavanter, who liked a little mischief himself, added his signature. Though it went against her Yankee instincts, *Swayle v. Rimski Firearms* somehow appealed to Justice Plympton. She had written for the majority in *Lestrepo v. Tompkins Compressed Air Injector*. In that closely watched case, the Court ruled that Tompkins, based in upstate New York, was not responsible when one of its air compressors, used at a facility in Alabama, overinflated 10,000 beach balls manufactured in Oregon. Tompkins wasn't liable, the Court found, because

Mr. Lestrepo, a worker inflating the beach balls at the Alabama facility, was an illegally employed alien who couldn't read the English instructions on the air injectors. It was a controversial ruling, to be sure, and emotionally fraught, since beach balls had been exploding all over the country, ruining picnics, making children cry, and inducing fourteen heart attacks. Plympton approved Swayle's cert petition. Barry Jacoby, an ardent foe of gun manufacturers, added the fourth signature, and in due course Jimmy James Swayle got word that his case would be heard by the U.S. Supreme Court. This is a big moment in your day if your days—all 9,125 of them—tend to be quite similar: up bright and early, avoid being stabbed for your packet of breakfast jelly, work in the prison laundry, avoid being anally penetrated in the showers.

"Do I get to go to Washington, Warden?"

"No, Swayle. You aren't going anywhere."

"But what if I win?"

"Then I'm gonna beat the shit out of you. Now get out of my office."

News that the Court had granted cert in *Swayle v. Rimski* caused an immediate stir. The Coalition Against a Runaway Judiciary, a Washington-based watchdog group, stridently denounced it.

"By agreeing to consider this case," declared Fortinbras P. Fescue, executive director, "the Court sends a chilling signal up and down the spine of law enforcement officers throughout the country." The Fraternal Order of Police also denounced it. On the other side, the American Foundation to Bankrupt Gun Manufacturers made approving noises.

IT HAD BEEN THE PRACTICE, in the previous court, for the justices to shake one another's hand before hearing oral argument, but given the dissensions and strains in the Hardwether Court, this agreeable protocol had fallen into desuetude. Paige Plympton had made efforts to resuscitate it, without success.

Silvio Santamaria refused to speak to Mo Gotbaum, much less shake his hand. In conferences, he wouldn't even look in his direction. Mike Haro couldn't care less for pleasantries. To judge from his thousand-yard stare and attendant spearminty aroma, Chief Justice Hardwether was focused on other things. Pepper felt sorry for him. Watching him across the room as the justices prepared to file out in threes and take their places behind the long mahogany bench in the Great Hall, Pepper thought, *He looks like he could use a hug.* But she was nervous enough on this, her first day of oral argument. Somehow she didn't feel it would be appropriate to go slap him on the back and say, *Hang in there, pard.*

She caught Ruthless staring at her. Pepper instructed herself mentally that she had to stop thinking of her that way, lest it pop out in conversation. *Oh, hey, Ruthless, how's it going?* Ruthless—that is, Justice Richter—gave Pepper a sort of wincy smile. Justice Crispus Galavanter stood in front of Pepper, who, per her most junior status, was at the back of the judicial choo-choo train. Crispus gave her a companionable wink and smile as if to say, *What* have *you got yourself into?*

Precisely at ten o'clock the Marshal of the Court nodded to the justices, held back the red velvet curtain, and pronounced the thousand-year-old French words, "Oyez! Oyez! Oyez! All persons having business before the Honorable, the Supreme Court of the United States, are admonished to draw near and give their attention, for the Court is now sitting. God save the United States and this Honorable Court!"

Pepper felt her stomach go tight. *Don't screw up,* she said to herself.

Her chair was on the end. Your seat gets closer to the

middle as you accrue seniority. The night before, she'd come into the Great Hall and rehearsed the simple act of sitting down in it so she wouldn't roll off the edge or tip over backward on her first day.

She took a deep breath and looked out at the people gathered before the Court. On her right, she recognized various reporters. On her left was where the guests and various—

—*Aw, hell.* JJ and Juanita. They must have flown in to surprise her. JJ was beaming at her as if to say, *You didn't think I was gonna miss my little darlin's first day on the Court, did you?*

She wondered: did he know that this case was about whether a criminal who'd tried to shoot a sheriff's deputy had grounds for grievance because his gun had misfired?

Justice Santamaria looked at Jimmy James Swayle's attorneys. There were three of them, including one with a ponytail, a famous New York lawyer who took on cases just to annoy the law enforcement establishment. Santamaria regarded them as he might a three-course meal that he intended to devour whole.

"You cite *Norbert v. Stigling Auto Parts*," Santamaria said. Oral arguments plunge right in without preamble. "Where's the relevance. I don't see it."

The ponytailed lawyer said, "The South Dakota Supreme Court ruled that the carburetor made by Stigling—"

"Hold on. You're comparing a carburetor to a firearm?"

"They are both—"

"Made of metal? I grant."

"With respect, Justice Santamaria, I was only going to point out, *sub specie aeternitatis* . . ."

"*Sub specie infernalitatis*, I should think," Santamaria shot back.

Pepper thought, *What in the hell are these people talking about?* Had she been teleported back to the rostrum in the Roman forum?

The lawyer pushed on. ". . . that a carburetor and a firearm, however distinct from a mechanical point of view, are both devices that come with implicit guarantees of functionality."

"Like an electric chair, say?"

A susurrus of laughter rippled through the Court. Justice Santamaria was frisky today.

The lawyer smiled wanly. "If you will. The relevant aspect here is that Mr. Norbert forfeited victory in his NASCAR race because his carburetor malfunctioned on the next-to-last lap. Not only did he forfeit the prize money but considerable income from product endorsements. It was this aspect that the State Supreme Court found—"

"What if Norbert's kidneys had failed on the next-to-last lap? Could he have sued his urologist for damages?"

Another ripple of laughter.

"Actually, I'm glad you brought that up," the lawyer said. "Absent invasivity, of course, there would be no grounds there. However, as I'm sure you're aware, in *Bosco v. Worcester Stent*, the Court held that Worcester Stent was in fact liable when one of its vascular stents implanted in Ms. Bosco's left thigh become dislodged while she was singing 'O mio babbino caro' at the Pierre Opera—"

"Yes, yes, yes," Justice Santamaria said peevishly. "But that was purely on *sub tecto* grounds."

A tiny ripple of approval went through the spectators, the sound of a dozen bees coming upon a satisfactory rose.

"Yes," said the lawyer unblinkingly, "but as you'll recall, in *Norbert* the Court concluded that the contract between Norbert's racing organization and Stigling provided that the governing law was Delaware's. Paragraph 7.23, I believe. It was in fact *that* clause that—"

"Are you saying," said Santamaria, in tones that suggested his intelligence had been insulted, "that money earned from product endorsements is *qua pecunia* no different from money demanded at the point of a gun during a bank robbery?"

"Oblatively, no, Justice. However, from a *pro tanto* standpoint, I would say that—"

"Uh-uh. No way. Not in Delaware," Justice Santamaria grunted. "And in case you were thinking of citing *Minnesota*, my advice to you, sir, would be, don't go there. The Eighth Circuit practically hired a skywriting plane to spell it out."

Santamaria sat back heavily in his chair, which emitted an authoritative squeak.

"I wasn't going to adduce *Minnesota*," said the ponytailed lawyer, beginning to show signs of hyperventilation, "but you might agree that in *Arkwright v. Gadmunster*—"

Justice Plympton, who by now had had enough of Silvio's theatrics, ventured into the turbid water. "I'm a little confused," she said, "perhaps even a mite troubled by your invocation of *Greenox v. Pesterson Hydraulics....*"

Pepper's cheeks flushed. She felt like a chickadee that had alighted on a branch with eight owls. Eight horned owls. While she could pretty much make out the references—her clerks had prepared a detailed bench memo for her—it was just all so darn . . . boring, really.

She thought, *Here we got an idiot bank robber suing the maker of his gun. What I could do with this on* Courtroom Six.

She looked over at JJ. It was clear he didn't have the foggiest idea what they were all talking about. How could he? Should she say something? On her first day? Some justices waited weeks, months, *years*, before saying a word.

Justice Haro had jumped in.

"I don't have any problem with *Greenox*," he was saying to the lawyer. Justices rarely if ever address one another in oral argument. "From my review, I'm not satisfied Mr. Swayle was even aiming the gun at Deputy Fogarty. So absent *mens rea*, you'd have concommittant diminuendo of *ballistico ad hominem*. Unless," Justice Haro shrugged with transparent insincerity, "I'm being obtuse."

Justice Santamaria shot his fellow justice a sidelong glance of withering contempt.

Satisfied that his rhetorical question had carried the day, Justice Haro continued. "Not that that's relevant *in quem particularem* insofar as the functionality of the firing pin is concerned. Which, really, is neither here nor there. But let me ask, *was* the firing pin manufactured by Rimski? Or was that outsourced to some . . . sweatshop?"

"No, Justice Haro," the lawyer said, delighted, "the firing pin was manufactured *at* the New Haven facility. By nonunion labor. You'll recall, per *Sikorski v. United Strutfitters Local 12*, that Rimksi was *in judicare*."

"Um," said Justice Haro, as though he had been reminded of a fact translucently well known to himself. "So clearly there's no *in remoto* aspect here?"

"None whatsoever," the lawyer said triumphantly.

Chief Justice Hardwether leaned forward into his microphone and said softly, "You seemed to go out of your way not to adduce *Persimmon v. Aberdeen Wheelchair*."

There was a slight but perceptible intake of air in the hall.

The lawyer smiled demurely. "I had a feeling you were going to bring that up, Mr. Chief Justice. I reread *Persimmon*. But try as I might, I could find no iteration of *quem protesto*."

Hardwether curled the side of his mouth, not unpleasantly, in a sort of *Oh-come-on-now-do-I-really-look-like-I-just-fell-off-the-turnip-truck?* look. "Did you read as far as page 653 before declaring moral victory?"

The lawyer froze. "I . . . *believe* . . . yes. . . ."

"Then you're well aware that *quo warranto* has no provenance here, absent guided direction."

A sound went through the court like a hundred snakes slithering across the marble floor. Hardwether had just scored a palpable hit! You could hear the muttering: *Declan may be hitting the sauce, but he hasn't lost his edge.*

"You have me there, Mr. Chief Justice," the lawyer conceded, his face reddening, "but might I tempt you with *Ordpurvis v. Sioux Falls Hydro-Electric.*"

By now Mo Gotbaum was on the third verse of "Born to Be Wild." Herself, Pepper felt like the Norwegian painting of the guy silently screaming.

Chief Justice Hardwether continued, "You could try. But I would stipulate, if I were you, that the South Dakota Circuit Court went out of its way in *Ordpurvis* to point out that in its view it was a clear-cut case of *interrebus quod aspecto* and that it had absolutely zero bearing *per res sciatica*. Now," he said, the picture of a reasonable man, "if you want to go *that* way, I'd say take a look at *Shrump v. Hartsdale Motorworks*—"

"Could I just say something here?" Pepper blurted.

Everything froze in the Great Hall of the United States Supreme Court. Time stopped. At which point Pepper, with dawning horror, realized that all eyes were on her.

Oh. My. God, she thought. First time out—first time out—and she had just interrupted a fellow justice. And not any justice. The Chief Justice. *Way to go, girl.* In the hierarchy of no-nos, that was right up there with vomiting on the Pope during High Mass at St. Peter's. She wanted to shrink inside her robe like a turtle.

Justice Hardwether, somewhat taken aback, nodded faintly and said, "Yes, Justice Cartwright. Of course."

Whereupon Pepper's mind suddenly went as blank as a crashed computer screen. She pressed every button, but all she could see on the screen was a blinking icon that said, YOUR HARD DRIVE IS EMPTY.

"I . . ." she tried, "with respect to"—she couldn't even remember what case they were discussing—"... there is ... it seems to me to boil down to *quem* ... I mean, *quasi* ... *modo*. ..."

A deep and terrible silence came over the Great Hall during which the sound of subatomic particles coming together would have been louder than clashing cymbals.

Justice Santamaria leaned forward into his microphone and said to the lawyer, "It's an interesting point and one, to be honest, I hadn't considered. So, Counselor, do you think *Quasimodo v. Notre Dame Bellringers Guild* has application here?"

The Great Hall erupted with laughter. It filled the marmoreal space like helium. Never in the memory of the eldest present Court watcher had there been such a spontaneous explosion of levity. Justice Hardwether, struggling himself not to join in, finally tapped his gavel to restore decorum.

PAIGE PLYMPTON came to Pepper's chambers, where the newest justice had been having a good sob.

"*My* first oral argument," Paige said, "I became so befuddled that I kept referring to *Gideon v. Wheelwright.*"

Pepper dabbed at her eyes and stared blearily.

Paige added, "And of course it's *Gideon v.* Wain*wright*. Well, my dear, let me tell you, 'mortified' is no mere expression."

"Thanks, Paige," Pepper said, honking into her tissue, "that makes me feel a whole lot better."

The next day's *Washington Post* brought a predictable harvest of shame: a story in the Style section about the TV Justice's first day of oral argument. It was illustrated with a still photograph from the movie *The Hunchback of Notre Dame*, with Pepper's face superimposed over Maureen O'Hara's offering a sip of water to Quasimodo.

There was a second serving of crow, this one in the form of a headline:

DEXTER MITCHELL (FINALLY)
BECOMES PRESIDENT
CONNECTICUT SENATOR TO STAR
IN NEW TV SERIES

Pepper's eyed widened as she caught a familiar name in the second paragraph.

Buddy Bixby, producer of TV's "Courtroom Six" and other reality shows, today confirmed that he has offered Senator Dexter Mitchell (D-Conn) the lead role in a projected prime-time dramatic series tentatively named "POTUS." The term is the White House abbreviation for "President of the United States."

Bixby said that he became interested in casting Senator Mitchell during the Pepper Cartwright hearings.

"I've been in this business long enough to know talent when I see it," Bixby said in a telephone interview from his Manhattan office. "He's got it— intelligence, looks, and credibility. He's been there and done that. He'll make a completely believable president. Who knows where it could lead," the producer said with a laugh, "look what happened to the last person I discovered."

His wife, Pepper Cartwright, was recently confirmed to the Supreme Court. The couple are reportedly divorcing. Bixby is also suing Justice Cartwright for breach of contract for leaving "Courtroom Six."

CHAPTER 16

Dexter was pleased by the turnout of reporters for his farewell press conference. Buddy had wanted him to hold it outdoors, on the West Front of the Capitol Building, where incoming U.S. presidents were now inaugurated. Dexter briefly mulled the notion before (wisely) vetoing it. He'd have his moment on the West Front someday. For now, the Strom Thurmond Memorial Room would do nicely enough. His press secretary made sure that the podium was within camera range of the bust of JFK, to remind the viewers subliminally of another New England senator who had gone on to bigger things.

"This is a bittersweet day for me," Dexter began, casting his eyes downward while biting his lower lip, a gesture he had learned from a master politician. He gave Terry—"my life's partner," as he put it—a brave glance. Camera shutters clicked away like demonic crickets. Dexter's face was momentarily bathed in so much flashlight that he feared he might never see again. Terry did her best to look wistful while inwardly doing cartwheels and jetés of unbridled joy. *We're in the mo-ney, we're in the mo-ney!* Dexter gave his life's partner a little nod of encouragement as if to say, *I know it's hard, honey, but together, we'll get through this.* Terry looked back at him as if to say,

Yes, dear, it is *hard. It's all I can do to keep from shouting "Free at last, free at last! Thank God Almighty, I'm free at last!"* Terry tried not to think of the bigger house. Of the beach house. Of a house in the south of France. Of not having to spend another day on K Street wheedling railroad subsidies out of her husband's colleagues.

She stirred from the delicious reverie and crashed back into reality and the sound of her husband's voice. What was he talking about now? She heard the phrase "decades of public service." *Oh, no. God, no. Please, someone—interrupt him with a question or we'll all be here until the polar ice caps melt.*

"When I first arrived in Washington twenty-three years ago," he was saying, "this was a very different place from the one it is now. . . ."

Unlike, say, any other place on the planet? Jesus, Dex. Please. Someone—for the love of God—ask a question. . . .

"But whatever Washington has become, I feel—at least, I'd like to be able to feel—that I've made some small difference. Some contribution. I believe it was Christopher Wren, the architect of St. Paul's Cathedral over there in London. . . ."

"Over there in London"? Put a sock in it, Dex.

". . . whose epitaph reads . . ."

No, no. Do not compare yourself to the architect of St. Paul's Cathedral. . . .

"'If it's monuments you want, just look around.' Well," Dexter continued with transparently insincere self-deprecation, "I certainly don't merit a marble bust. But I am darn proud to leave behind some solid pieces of legislation. In particular—"

"Senator—?"

Oh, thank you. Thank you, from the bottom of my heart. . . .

Dexter, halted in mid-self-adulation, said with a trace of irritation, "Yes, Judy?"

"What about these reports that you wanted to stay on in the Senate while doing the TV show?"

Fucking Clem.

"Oh . . . no. No, no. No. I mean, there were—we had—there was . . . there may have been some very theoretical . . . discussion. But no. Well, there were those who *wanted* me to stay on, but—"

"Such as who?"

Dexter laughed. "Well, now, we don't need to get into all that. Myself, I never thought that was realistic. Being in the Senate is a full-time job. A more than full-time job. Just ask my life's partner, here. *Aack.*"

Terry stalwartly grinned. *You're* such *a dick, Dexter.*

"And it's a full-time honor, let me add. So I . . . That never really made much sense as an option. Yes, Candy?"

"Is it true you're getting fifty thousand dollars per episode?"

Fucking Buddy.

"Well now—*aack*—I don't—there's no point in . . . Someone else is handling all that. But I can tell you this much—on an hourly basis, it pays a *little* better than the Senate. But let me talk for just a moment here about some of the things I'm proudest of having accomplished during my years in the—"

Someone—please—ask him another question.

"Is it true Ramona Alvilar has been cast to play the First Lady?"

"My understanding," Dexter said, "is that those negotiations are ongoing. You'd have to ask Buddy Bixby. Of course, from my perspective, it would be wonderful if she were to be my wife." Dexter stopped and looked over at Terry. "I think I just said the wrong thing."

Laughter. Terry smiled. "Yes, honey. You did." *You ass.*

More laughter.

"But if I might get back to some of the judiciary reform

initiatives that I'm proudest of . . . let me point to the Uniform Appellate Modification Act of—"

"Senator, this presidential one-term limit amendment that just cleared the House and looks to be approved overwhelmingly by the Senate."

"What about it?"

"How do you feel about it?"

That cocksucker Vanderdamp deserves everything he gets.

"Well, I guess it's no secret that President Vanderdamp and I have had our differences. Is it fair to punish future presidents because of one disastrous . . . Well," Dexter grinned, "I didn't come here today to criticize the President. I'll let the historians do that."

"Will you be voting in favor of the amendment?"

"It has some merit to it, I believe. On the other hand, who knows, I might find myself in a position one day where I'd like to be able to have a second term. *Aack.*"

Terry looked stricken.

"Are you saying that you plan to run for president again?"

"I . . ." Dexter looked over at Terry, whose eyes had gone cold as liquid nitrogen. "The only presidency I'm interested in at the moment is Mitchell Lovestorm's."

"Who came up with that name, anyway?"

"The name?" Dexter said. "Well . . . the writers. That's what they . . . but it suits me. Yes. It conveys a lot about this President. He's a strong man, a passionate man, with . . ."

Terry wondered, *He's already talking about himself in the third person.*

". . . a man who's been through the fire, but who has heart. Yes. Lovestorm. A perfect Lovestorm. Ha-ha. Like that movie. . . ."

Dexter looked over at his life's partner, who was sending him a message that decoded: *Wrap it up right now or I will Super-Glue your lips shut tonight while you sleep.*

"Thanks for coming," Dexter said, giving his audience a valedictory salute. "Thank you. This has been a tremendous experience. I like to think that I'm not really leaving you. Just moving to another channel. Don't forget to tune in Monday nights."

CHAPTER 17

Pepper was nervous, going into her first conference. Her stomach felt like a butterfly farm.

Justices vote in order of seniority, so she'd go last. As the justices began voting on *Swayle*, she prayed that there would be a clear majority before it got to her. Not today. The Hardwether Court was as divided as the Korean peninsula. When Crispus cast his vote against, it became 4–4. All eyes were on Pepper.

"Justice Cartwright?" the Chief Justice said gently. He didn't seem comfortable calling her "Pepper."

"I . . ."

She felt sixteen eyeballs boring into her like drills. Paige Plympton had warned Pepper beforehand that Hardwether didn't go in for lengthy debate in conference. "He runs a pretty swift ship," she said. This was not a debating society.

Every atom in every fiber of Pepper Cartwright screamed at her to vote against Jimmy James Swayle. Rule in favor of a bank robber who felt aggrieved because his gun didn't fire? If it had been *Courtroom Six*, Buddy would have had workmen in building a gallows to hang the sumbitch from before the first commercial break. But it wasn't *Courtroom Six*, and she found herself, oddly, thinking that the sumbitch actually had a case on the technicalities of the thing. Awkward, but there it was.

"I . . . uh . . ." she stammered, "for the motion."

"You're finding in favor?" Hardwether said.

"Uh-huh. Yes."

Justice Santamaria let out an exhalation that would have billowed the sails of a four-masted schooner. He tossed his pencil onto the conference table with disgust. Paige gave Pepper a look of bemused curiosity.

"It's just that I thought the South Dakota Supreme Court's decision in *Mortimer v. Great Lakes Suction* seemed to . . . uh, speak to the validity of Swayle's argument," Pepper said.

Silence.

"Well," she added, "it *is* a bitch, but that's kind of where I came down."

Justice Santamaria muttered something that sounded to Pepper like "Jesus wept." He let out another majestic sigh, leaned back, looked at the ceiling, and rolled his eyes.

Pepper said, "Justice Santamaria, do you have something to say to me? Or are you waiting for one of your clerks to come put drops in your eyes?"

There was a general intake of breath around the table. Santamaria's head turned toward Pepper like a tank turret swiveling to fire. Before he could get off a round, Chief Justice Hardwether, suppressing a smile, said, "In that case, Justice Cartwright, will you write for the majority?"

Pepper froze. "You want me to write the opinion?"

"If you would."

"Uh, okay. I mean, yes."

"Silvio," Hardwether said, "I assume you'll handle the dissent."

Silvio snorted assent.

After the conference, Paige stopped by Pepper's chambers. "Well," she said, "you certainly don't hold back."

"I shouldn't have popped off like that. But I couldn't take any more of that high dudgeon crap from him. His eyeballs were going like tumblers in a Vegas slot machine. And I'm a little tired of him yammering off to the nearest passing reporter about what a featherweight I am."

"Oh, he's a big boy. It's not him I'm worried about," Paige said.

"All right," Pepper said. "Let's have it. You think I voted wrong?"

Paige had voted against Swayle. "It's not that. But I had the feeling back there that you were voting against your instincts."

"It's not about instincts, is it?" Pepper said. "It's about the law. Right?"

"Are you trying to convince me, or yourself?"

Paige stood to go. "Sandy O'Connor kept a needlepoint cushion in her chambers. It said, 'Maybe in error. Never in doubt.'" She smiled. "I look forward to reading your opinion. Good luck with it."

Mr. President. We've just intercepted a coded signal from Chinese Naval Command Shanghai."

"Go ahead, Admiral."

"The *Wung Fu*, their fast frigate—it's armed with specials. Nuclear-tipped missiles."

The President's face darkened. "Goddammit. They lied. Their premier looked me straight in the face. And lied." He slammed his fist on the Situation Room table.

The Secretary of State said, "Sir, we don't know that for an absolute fact. All we know for sure is that when you met with him, Li Pu Fang was making moves to consolidate his power base with Xiang Zhu."

"Goddammit, Brad—he lied. What the hell kind of proof do you need? A mushroom cloud over San Francisco?"

The room fell silent. All eyes turned to the President.

"All right," said the President. "No more Mr. Nice Guy. Send in the *Nimitz*. Maybe a carrier battle group will get their attention."

The Chairman of the Joint Chiefs and the Secretary of Defense exchanged fraught glances.

"Sir," said the Admiral, "they'll take that as a provocation."

"You having a hard time with the English language today, sailor? I gave you an order."

"Aye, sir," the Chairman replied. He nodded to his chief of operations and said gravely, "You heard the President. Send in the *Nimitz*."

The Secretary of State said, "Sir, I beg you. This could lead to—global annihilation."

"You had your chance, Brad. I'm sorry. Better pull your people out of Beijing."

"But—there's no time!"

"Then they'll have themselves a ringside seat at the barbecue. Sorry, Brad, but this is my call."

"One more day, Mr. President. Give us just one more *day*."

The President shook his head. "I told those little yellow bastards not to—"

"Cut."

President Mitchell Lovestorm turned to the director. "What's the matter? I thought we were doing fine."

The director, a man named Jerry, said, "It's going great, Senator. Terrific. The line is 'I told those bastards,' not 'I told those little yellow bastards.' Okay? Let's take it from—"

Dexter said, "I think it's better my way. Tougher . . ."

"You could be right," Jerry said. "But let's trust the material."

"That's how they talk in Washington. Behind closed doors, anyway. Trust me. I've been in the room."

Jerry nodded. "I don't doubt it. But—"

"We want this to be realistic, right?"

"Absolutely. But let's trust the script. Okay? All set . . ."

"I mean," Dexter persisted, "they're threatening the United States with nuclear weapons. You think in the Situation Room at the White House everyone's going to stop and go, 'Oh, gosh, oh, dear me,' because the President, in a moment of—justifiable—stress, calls them a name? I don't think so."

Jerry glanced over at Buddy, who was perched in his producer's chair, looking as though he were conducting a silent one-man Socratic dialogue on the ethics of racist epithets.

"Samsung is a sponsor," Buddy said softy. "Toyota is a sponsor. Will they be comfortable with 'little yellow bastards'? I'm guessing not. I could be wrong."

"Those are Korean and Japanese," Dexter said. "They *hate* the Chinese. Are you kidding? They'll lap it up."

"It's tempting, but let's save it for season two."

The makeup lady dabbed at Dexter's forehead. He said poutingly, "I thought the whole idea was to be edgy."

"Edgy? You've just ordered in the *Nimitz*. Three pages from now, you're going to send a B-2 bomber over Shanghai, giving one point three billion little yellow bastards a case of the shits. I call that edgy. So, we good to go? I'd love to wrap the scene where you tell the Speaker of the House to fuck off before we break for lunch."

"All right. Where do we—what's the line?"

The script assistant said mechanically, "'I told those bastards not to screw around. Now they are going to get a taste of their own cooking, and it will make hot and sour soup taste like Cream of Wheat.'"

"Okay, everyone. Places. Scene six, take four. Action. . . ."

Dexter managed to get to the end of the scene without further denigrating one-seventh of the human race. He was doing better than credible work as President Mitchell Lovestorm, especially for a nonprofessional actor. Buddy's casting instincts had not failed him: a senator who yearns to be president brings verisimilitude to the role.

Buddy had been screening the first three episodes of *POTUS* for the media, and indications were favorable. They were amused by its camp aspect. In the opening episode, Mitchell Lovestorm—at the time, vice president—is reluctantly thrust into history's spotlight when the President is accidentally killed by a foul ball during opening day. His wife, Consuela "Connie" Lovestorm, played by the steamy Ramona Alvilar, is a panther in pantsuit who will stop at nothing to advance her husband's fortunes, but who is unable to deny—much less control—her ardor for National Security adviser Milton Swan. Icy blue–eyed Gore Peckermann of the TV show *St. Paul Trauma* brought a cool ambivalence to his role as the former Navy SEAL turned National Security adviser, who must balance his loyalty to President Lovestorm and the country with his burning desire to throw the First Lady over his desk and brief her until dawn.

CHAPTER 18

Pepper was in a sweat. She had an opinion to write, and since it proclaimed the right of criminals to sue gun manufacturers when their holdup weapons misfire in the middle of a crime, it needed to be good. Really, really good.

Her clerk, Sandoval, had offered to do "a draft" of it for her. Some justices let their clerks do pretty much all the "drafting" of their written opinions. But Pepper was determined to do her own even if it meant pulling all-nighters. She'd had enough problems in the media already without reading a snippy item in the *Washington Post* about how Judge Lightweight was relying on her clerks to do her heavy lifting. She didn't doubt Sandoval's discretion or loyalty, but clerks were a gossipy bunch who these days talked to reporters and authors and sometimes even wrote their own clerk-and-tell books.

After ten p.m. on what was shaping up to be her second sleepless night, Pepper was at her desk trying to figure out how to make the *Swayle* opinion sound like something Moses left behind on Mount Sinai along with the commandments. There was a knock on the door and in walked Justice Ishiguro "Mike" Haro.

"Busy?" he said.

It was a curious statement to make to someone who was in

her office after ten p.m., looking like hell while staring desperately at a computer screen.

"Kind of. I'm working on the *Swayle* opinion," Pepper said. "It's been a while since I . . ."

"That's why I came by."

"Oh? How's that?"

"Thought you could use some help."

This struck Pepper as falling somewhere between a breach of etiquette and an outright insult. Though new here, she was pretty certain justices didn't go around offering to help each other write opinions.

"I think I've got it under control. But thanks for the offer."

Justice Haro stood awkwardly. He was in his early forties but looked ten years younger and had about him a mild air of contemptuousness, as though the world did not measure up to his standards.

"I liked the way you gave it to Santamaria at the conference," he said. "Pompous prick."

Eager as Pepper was for peer approval, collegiality predicated on a shared dislike of a third colleague was off to a false start.

"I shouldn't have run my mouth like that," she said. "I wrote him an apology." She made a mental note to do that after Haro left.

"You don't owe him an apology," Haro said. "Not after the things he's said about you. And not just in print."

Was this an invitation to say, *What things?*

"I better get back to this."

"Do you like wine?"

"Generally. Not right now." Something made her add, "I'm more of a beer girl."

"I have eight thousand bottles in my cellar."

"Sounds like quite some cellar."

"Yes, it is. Maybe I'll show it to you sometime."

Haro turned to leave. As he did, he said, "By the way, *Mortimer* isn't the key to this case. But I'll take care of it when your draft circulates."

Pepper wondered if the woman who'd poured out her ex-husband's wine and replaced it with grape juice was available, and went back to her Augean stable.

She finished the opinion late the next day and sent it out for comments by the four other justices in the majority. She felt as though she were back in school, hoping to find an "A" in red ink at the top of the returned term paper.

One morning a few days later she logged on to SupremeNet, the Court's secure Intranet, and found the opinion in her inbox. There was no grade on it, but it was full of comments by the justices. Next to one section she found a "Good—DH." Chief Justice Hardwether was not known to be liberal with his compliments, so she purred to find this. The pleasure was short-lived. On the next page, he had struck out a line in which she had used the Texas phrase "more confused than a cow on Astroturf"—a sentiment she had felt condign enough in a case like *Swayle*—and written, "Let's try to keep it dignified." Ouch.

When she came to the centerpiece of her argument citing *Mortimer v. Great Lakes Suction*, she found that every line— indeed, the entire page—had been ~~struck out~~. In the margin was a note: "*Mortimer* is a rotting branch—see attachment. IH."* The attachment consisted of twelve pages in which Justice Haro essentially took over and rewrote her opinion from top to bottom. It hinged on a case called *Kozinko v. Mixmaster*, in which, as Justice Haro eloquently explained, "the South Dakota Supreme Court rightly held that liability was not *in quem pro*

---

* Somewhat florid legal term for a prior ruling or law considered likely to be overturned.

tanto automatically waived simply because the blender was being used to manufacture methamphetamine, a federally prohibited controlled substance. Indeed, the very absence of legality in that case, pari passu, argues convincingly on behalf of Swayle's assertion of denial of equal protection."

Pepper read it several times, each time getting madder, but in the end conceded that it was, alas, a better argument than hers. Nonetheless, she typed KISS MY ASS on the top of the attachment, closed the file, and went to the gym to cool down. When she got back from the gym, she reopened the file, deleted KISS MY ASS, and typed, YES, RIGHT—THANK YOU, and closed the file and e-mailed it back to the Clerk of the Court and went home to have a good cry, only to find a court summons in her mailbox relating to Buddy's breach of contract suit. It sure was great, being on the Supreme Court. But there was better yet to come.

The Court was due to render its Swayle decision from the bench on Friday. On Tuesday morning, Washington awoke to a riveting story in the *Washington Times*:

> The Supreme Court is expected to rule Friday in favor of a bank robber who is suing the manufacturer of the gun he used in the commission of the crime because it failed to fire when he tried to shoot the arresting officer.
>
> According to a source within the Court, the justices have voted 5–4 in favor of the plaintiff, one Jimmy James Swayle, a career criminal currently serving 25 years in federal prison. The deciding vote was cast by the newest justice on the high bench, former TV personality Pepper Cartwright. Justice Cartwright, the source noted, has made "an already polarized court even more antipodal."
>
> The word means "diametrically opposite."

It was a breathtaking leak, even by the standards of Washington, DC, where everything short of actual nuclear launch code sequences routinely turns up on the front page of the paper. Pepper's clerk, Sandoval, reached her at home just before seven a.m. to alert her to it. An hour later, two Court marshals knocked on her door to announce that they had instructions "to provide for your security, ma'am. Orders of the Chief Justice."

By the time she had arrived at the marble palace, Chief Justice Hardwether had already sent a SupremeNet e-mail to all the justices deploring the leak, apologizing to Justice Cartwright "on behalf of the *entire* Court," announcing that he would initiate an internal investigation, and hinting that he might even bring in the FBI. This last part did not sit well with various justices, unleashing a torrent of furious postings on J-Blog, the justices' Intranet chat room.

Emphatically resent implication my chambers might have had anything to do with this tawdry affair and shall in no way cooperate. Strong letter follows. SS [Silvio Santamaria]

Dismaying as the episode may be, I find even more outrageous the imputation that suspicion should be so casually and widely applied here. What happened to Equal Protection? RR [Ruth Richter]

Why don't you just install a polygraph machine in the Great Hall? IH [Ishiguro Haro]

Quis custodiet . . . sigh.* MG [Mo Gotbaum]

Come on, everyone—let's all take a deep breath and calm down. PP [Paige Plympton]

Reading them, Pepper was struck by the fact that most of them seemed most outraged about being subjected to an investigation, not the leak.

---

* Juvenal: the full quote is *"Quis custodiet ipsos custodes,"* meaning "Who shall guard the guardians themselves?" Generally invoked when figures in authority make a hash of things.

Outside, the world at large was howling not for the head of the leaker but for—hers. The article had managed to focus all the rage over the decision on Pepper, not on the other four justices who had joined her. The blogosphere and airwaves were in meltdown. By noon, the first calls to IMPEACH CARTWRIGHT had been posted and a crowd had gathered in front of the Court. A candlelight vigil was duly announced.

In the midst of the storm of outrage, Pepper's secretary announced that her grandfather was on the phone. This was the moment she had been dreading above all. She had even sent him and Juanita round-trip business-class tickets to Cancún, Mexico, and paid for a suite at a fancy hotel (with casino—JJ loved to gamble) for the express purpose of getting him out of the country when *Swayle* hit the news. With any luck he'd be in the casino when CNN reported the decision. Now this.

"Hello, JJ," she said.

"Is this true?" he said.

She sighed. "Yep."

There was a long silence, not even a *pwwttt*.

"Did you call just to not say anything?" Pepper said. "Why don't you just cuss me out and get it over with?"

"I just don't see how you coulda . . ." JJ said. "That coulda been me that son of a bitch was aiming at."

"I know. But there was this case called *Kozinko v. Mixmaster* where . . ." Her heart wasn't quite in it.

"Is that why you sent us those tickets?"

She drew in a breath to lie, but couldn't. The air came back out, unpolluted by mendacity. "Yep," she said.

Another long silence. "I know most everyone who goes to Washington loses their way sooner or later. But I didn't think it happened this fast."

"It's a complicated case, JJ. The Second Circuit found that—"

Pwwttt. "No, Pepper. It ain't complicated." Silence. Pepper couldn't think what to say. JJ said, "Guess I'm gonna hang up now," and he did.

A GRIM-LOOKING HAYDEN CORK had brought in the news yesterday morning, having just gotten a whip count from the White House Congressional Liaison. The Senate was about to pass the Presidential Term Limit Amendment, 77–23.

"Apparently the *Swayle* vote was the final nail," he reported.

Graydon Clenndennynn had been yanked back from another remunerative negotiation, persuading Russia to equip its domestic security forces with U.S.-made Taser guns, there being increasing need in Moscow these days to deal with a restive citizenry.

Hayden said to the President, "We're going to kill him if we keep putting him through this kind of jet lag." But Clenndennynn showed up in the Oval Office looking crisp and ready to lend wisdom and eminence to yet another presidential emergency.

"I'm not sure I see what the crisis is," Graydon said, setting down his china coffee cup. "I was under the impression you didn't *want* to run again."

"I don't," the President said gloomily.

"Then what's the problem?"

"Because now I'll have to run. To show them what I think of their ridiculous amendment."

"Why don't you just denounce them and be done with it?"

"I denounce the Congress all the time. Now, if I don't run, everyone will think it's because I was intimidated or scared off. I won't have that. Because it's not the truth."

"All right. Then in that case, run."

"Graydon," the President said, "stop pretending to be obtuse. I don't *want* to run. Everything I've tried to do has been predi-

cated on being in office for only one term. There's a principle at
stake here."

How many times had Graydon heard that hoary asservera-
tion. "Then *don't* run," he said with a fleck of petulance.

"Hayden," the President said, "would you please call Andrews and have a jet fueled to take Mr. Clenndennynn *back* to
Moscow?"

"Donald," Graydon said, "there are times when a leader has
to choose—"

"If this is one of your what-would-Winston-do lectures," the
President said, "I don't want to hear it. I'm not in the mood for
Churchillian wisdom today, thank you."

"—between the between the unpalatable and the poison-
ous. All right. The amendment is an insult, a slap across the
face administered by a bunch of self-dealing scoundrels. So
what else is new? You've been warring with the Congress since
day one. All I'm saying is, you're perfectly right. If you don't
run now, it'll look like . . . cowardice. That you're throwing in
the towel."

"So I'm damned either way. Is that it?"

"Sorry. Look," Graydon said, "if it's the prospect of serving
another term that's got you tied up in knots, I wouldn't worry
too much on that score. You certainly have my vote. But I didn't
pass huge crowds here on my way in from Andrews chanting,
'Four more years.' Where are we in the polls, Hayden?"

"Low thirties," Hayden said. "We had some bounce from
Cartwright, but *Swayle* eliminated that."

"How could the Court have ruled for that . . . Oh, well."
Graydon sighed. "Supreme Court justices almost always disappoint. Remember what Truman said when they asked him if
he had any disappointments. 'Yes, and they're both sitting on
the Supreme Court.' Well. There we are. Point is, sir, I think
you can safely run for reelection and expect to be back on your

front porch in Wapa—however it's pronounced—by the following January 21."*

"It's too cold in Wapakoneta in January to sit on the porch," the President said, "but I appreciate the sentiment. Well, this is going to be one heck of a queer campaign."

THE SENATE VOTED the next day, 78–22, in favor of the Presidential Term Limit Amendment. Having cleared both the House and the Senate, the measure would now go to the states to be ratified. Getting three-quarters of state legislatures to agree on something can take a long time. It took four years (1947 to 1951) to ratify the amendment limiting presidents to two terms; but lowering the voting age to eighteen took a mere one hundred days to pass (during the Vietnam War). The punditariat† predicted that given President Vanderdamp's unpopularity, the amendment stood a good chance of being briskly ratified. They confidently predicted that Vanderdamp would not seek reelection. He might be politically inept, they said, but he was not a fool, nor one to seek further humiliation. He would finish out his term and slink back to Wapawhatever with his tail between his legs.

A solemn-faced Hayden Cork, making a rare personal appearance in the White House pressroom, announced that the President would shortly address the nation from the Oval Office.

---

* The day after the new president is inaugurated on January 20. Until the 1930s, presidents were sworn in on March 4. The new date was chosen by the Congress for the probability of its being frigid and miserable.
† Collective term for the one-seventh of the population of Washington, DC, who opine on political matters on television.

CHAPTER 19

The President looked as though all the cares of the world rested upon his shoulders alone.

"It's not going to happen," he said to the somber faces around the table. "They will not become a nuclear power on my watch." No one spoke. "Is that clear?" he said, his voice grave. "Are we all on the same page here?"

Heads nodded reluctantly. The Secretary of State had gone ashen, slumped in his chair.

"All right then," the President said. "Let's quit dicking around. Send in the *Nimitz*."

"Cut."

"What was wrong with that?" Dexter said.

"The line is, 'Let's quit messing around,'" the director said. "We can't say 'dicking.' We'll get fined by the FCC."

"Don't worry about it. I know the chairman of the FCC. He's been to dinner at my house. We're pals."

"That's great. Always nice to have friends in important places. But for now, let's stay with the script. By the way, Senator, the energy in that scene—great. Amazing. I was blown away. Weren't you blown away?"

The assistant director nodded. "Totally."

President Mitchell Lovestorm grumbled assent. They reshot the scene. Lunch was called.

He remained at the table while the other actors dispersed in the direction of the craft services table, adrift in reverie. He was finding it harder and harder to turn his character on and off. One day, discussing it with the makeup lady, she'd told him about something called Method Acting, where you stayed in the character you were playing. He'd decided to try it. It worked. His wife, Terry, didn't quite get it and seemed to resent it when he told her not to "tie up the hotline," but generally it worked.

Dexter looked up at the screens about the Situation Room table. They depicted the paths of incoming missiles. But also outgoing missiles. Oh, yes. Yes. After lunch, they would shoot the scene where the Chief of Naval Operations informs him that cruise missiles launched from the *Nimitz* carrier group were on their way to destroy the presidential palace of Mumduk bin Shamirz—"Mad Ali" as he was known—the America-despising ruler of Badganistan. *Our friend Mad Ali has a nice warm surprise headed his way. Oh, yes. Yes. Yes.* Dexter visualized the two cruise missiles, hurtling in tandem toward their target, contour-hugging Badganistan's wild and rugged terrain, zooming past a minaret, their rocket engines torching the *muzzein* in the tower as he called the people to prayer. The *muzzein* falling to the ground, a human torch, screaming. *Nice touch. Clever, those writers. Overpaid, but clever.* Well, it had to be done, didn't it? Mad Ali had given him no choice. He'd tried to reason with him—again and again and again. He'd gone to the UN. He'd offered concessions. Trade agreements. Medicine for oil. An exchange of ambassadors. All rebuffed. *Okay, then, Ali, my friend. Have it your way. But for this President, no more dicking— messing . . . whatever—around.* Mitchell Lovestorm was not going to sit around and cool his jets while this towelhead went nuclear. Hell's bells, even the *French* are with us this time. *Allons, enfants de la Patrie . . .*

And yet . . . how lonely it felt. At such a moment, only a president, on whose shoulders these matters ultimately rest, could truly know the terrible loneliness of command, the terrible isol—

"Dex."

"Um? Oh. Yes, Buddy. What is it?"

"You looked like you were heading past Pluto there. You okay?"

"Yes. Yes. Just . . . reviewing the situation. Going over my lines."

"The loneliness of command, huh? It's a bitch, isn't it?"

Dexter stared at Buddy. *You have no idea. But then, how could you?*

"You going to eat something?"

"Not hungry," Dexter said.

"We got a lot of scenes this afternoon. Don't let your blood sugar drop. We need you *in the zone*, baby."

Baby? This was no way to talk to the President.

"I'll get something," he said. "Buddy—a word?"

"Sure."

"It's about the First Lady."

"What's up?" Buddy said cautiously. Ramona Alvilar was on fire as the ironically named Constance Lovestorm. Her steamy flirting scenes with National Security Director Milton Swan had even the crew breaking out in sweats and adjusting their trousers. "She's doing a hell of a job, don't you think?"

"Yes," Dexter said. "She's a fine actress. It's not that."

Buddy nodded. "So?"

"I just feel . . . she's my *wife*, Buddy. She's the First Lady of the United States of America. Why is she rubbing the thigh of my National Security adviser?"

Buddy stared. "That's the story line, Dex."

"Well, I'm not sure I'm comfortable with it."

"Ramona is helping to make this show hotter than one of

those cruise missiles you just launched. Nothing's broken. Let's not fix it."

"But where's the dignity? Mitchell Lovestorm is a good and decent man. President of the United States. He's fighting off the Islamic hordes and the Russians and the—"

"Little yellow bastards. Don't forget them. They're still shitting themselves in Shanghai over the *Nimitz*'s little visit there. Ha-ha."

"Yes, meanwhile, my wife is reaching for the zipper of my right-hand aide. And he a former Navy SEAL commander. A decorated war hero . . ." Dexter shook his head distastefully. "To me it just feels . . . demeaning. To everyone."

"Look," Buddy said, "Milton hasn't boinked her. We haven't even decided if he's going to boink her."

"I for one would greatly prefer that he *not* boink her."

"We're having a script meeting on that very point this afternoon. I'll definitely—we'll take a good hard look at it."

"I just don't think that the President of the United States ought to be made out to be a—cuckold."

"I respectfully disagree. To me, it enhances your humanity."

"How?"

"Didn't Abraham Lincoln have some problems along those lines? And look at how well *he's* regarded."

"No, no. No. His wife was a nutcase, but she wasn't diddling the help. Look, according to all these amazing reviews we're getting, the viewers like President Mitchell Lovestorm. They admire him. Shouldn't we respect *their* feelings?"

Buddy resisted the impulse to swat Dexter with the rolled-up script in his hand.

"Dex," he said, "to me, to them, all this personal stuff makes you an even greater president. Look at the situation. The whole world is on fire, the economy's crashing—through no fault of your own, remember, it was your predecessor's reckless fiscal

policies that screwed everything up. Meanwhile, your wife is trying to give the National Security adviser a hand job under the
cabinet table. This is *precisely* where your dignity comes in. Do
you let it get to you? No. No, sir. Mitchell Lovestorm rises above
it. I see tremendous dignity in that. I see *greatness* in that."

"From where I'm sitting," Dexter said, "it's the NSC Director who's doing the rising."

"Your wife is a beautiful, highly sexualized being—from the
barrios of Puerto Rico. So, okay, she's a bit frisky."

"Frisky?" Dexter snorted. "She's a complete slut."

"Hey, that's the First Lady you're talking about. No. I think
that's a tad harsh. *Passionate. Latina. En fuego!* And any guy
whose crotch she was stroking would rise. *Lazarus* would rise
from the dead again if Ramona were reaching for his wiener.
But you're forgetting about episode fourteen."

"What about it?"

"The reconciliation scene? On *Air Force One?* Talk about hot.
I got blisters on my fingers just from holding the script when I
read it the first time. You've won the war. Mad Ali's on his way
to a month of serious CIA waterboarding. Connie's come to her
senses and realizes that it's you she loves, not Milton Swan. You
tumble into the bed on the plane. Through the window while
you're ripping each other's clothes off, we see F-16 fighter escorts
framed in the setting sun. Jesus, I get a hard-on just thinking
about it. I want to put a warning after the opening credits, like
the ones they have for the pills? *In the event this episode causes
an erection that lasts more than four hours, seek immediate medical help.* Then, in episode fifteen, what happens to NSC Director Swan? Hel-lo? The Russians put that radioactive shit in his
borscht at the state banquet at the Kremlin and the next thing
you know, he's glowing like a lava lamp. And you and the First
Lady—going at it like *rabbits.* I need a cold shower just from
thinking about it."

Dexter considered. "What about if it turned out that Swan was working secretly *for* the Russians? Yes. And they didn't want that to get out, so that's why they killed him."

Buddy sighed. *Actors.* He yearned for the day when they were computer generated. "Why," he said patiently, "would your National Security Director have been working for the Russians?"

"I don't know," Dexter said with annoyance. "Can't the *writers* figure that out? Isn't that why you pay them so much?"

"It's an intriguing idea. Let me discuss it with them. Meantime, let's stay with the program, okay? Speaking of which, did you see that write-up in *People*?"

"No," Dexter lied. "I didn't. Was it good?"

"Good? *'Monday nights this season, vote Dexter Mitchell for President. He'll give you goose bumps every time he says, "Send in the* Nimitz*!"'*"

"Nice," Dexter said aloofly. "Yes."

"Nice? By the end of season two, they'll be screaming to have you in the real White House. Now, go get some lunch, would you please, Mr. President? You don't want to send in the *Nimitz* on an empty stomach."

CHAPTER 20

President Vanderdamp sat at his desk in the Oval Office, warming up his instrument. He had been in the glee club in high school and found that it helped before a speech.

"Do do do doooo do do doooooooo. Da da da daaaaa da da daaaaaaaa . . . Dee dee dee deeeeeee dee dee deeeeeeeeeeeeeeeeee . . ."

He knew that he must look somewhat ridiculous to the dozen people in the room: the ever-fretful Hayden Cork, the TV techs, his press secretary, the gloomy-looking Secret Service agents. He glanced at the TV camera suspiciously. His predecessor had been caught on tape picking his nose before a speech. It got twelve million hits on YouTube.

"Is that thing on?" he asked.

"Yes, Mr. President, but no signal is going out."

"Hope not. Wouldn't want to see myself doing this on the Internet. Would I?"

"No, sir," the technician said.

"Two minutes, Mr. President."

"Thank you."

"Dum dum dum dum dum dum dummmmmmmmmmm . . ."

A makeup woman leapt forward like a gazelle to powder puff the presidential forehead.

"Am I sweating?"

"Oh, no, sir. Just a teensy . . . sheen. These lights, they're so gol-darned hot."

"They certainly are. And what's your name?"

"Maureen, sir."

"Well, thank you for taking such good care of me, Maureen."

"No sweat, sir."

"That's very funny."

"I beg your pardon, sir?"

"You said, 'No sweat.' And we were talking about sweat."

"Oh. Yes, sir. I guess it was funny."

Donald Vanderdamp considered. He probably should be sweating. Odd—darned odd—to find himself in this position. All he'd wanted to do was get the job done and go home. The address he had planned to give, from this very desk, was a paraphrase of what his hero, Calvin Coolidge—that least appreciated of American presidents—had said: "I do not choose to run for President in 1928." And now here he was. Doing . . . this.

"One minute, Mr. President."

"I've. Got. A. Lovely. Bunch. Of. Co-co-nutsssss."

"Sorry, sir?" the technician said.

"Vocal exercise."

"Yes, sir. Stand by."

"Good evening," the President began. "This is the—let's see—third time that I have spoken to you from the Oval Office? I've tried not to do this too often. I used to hate it when I was growing up and the President would come on and preempt *The Jack Benny Show* or *Bonanza* or some other favorite television program. Of course these days we have a jillion channels, so you can always just switch. And anyway most of the networks won't preempt for a presidential announcement unless it's nuclear war. Well, it's all about ratings, these days. Ratings and polls and endless numbers.

"Speaking of that, my approval ratings—if you could call them that—are pretty darn dismal. Most of you think I'm doing an awful job. Well, I'm sorry about that. But I've always said, and you've heard me say it—you can look it up—that the presidency ought not to be a popularity contest. Certainly doesn't seem to have been one in my case. But let's get down to it.

"Every president's hope is to bring the country and the people together. I seem to have accomplished that. I've managed to unite most of you in disapproval of me. And now both houses of the U.S. Congress have set aside their partisan differences and passed an amendment that, if ratified by the states, would limit presidents to one single four-year term. I have a few things to say about that.

"First, I congratulate Congress on—finally—passing a bill that wouldn't require billions of dollars, plunging the nation into even worse debt.

"But now let's be honest. This amendment isn't about future presidents. This is about me.

"Let me remind the Congress that we already have mechanisms for denying presidents a second term. They're called elections. And—what do you know—we have one coming up just sixteen months from now. If the Congress can't wait that long, they could just impeach me, but since my crime consists of trying to force the Congress to be fiscally responsible, I'm not sure that dog would hunt. So they've gone about it this other way. And here we are.

"Now, the plain truth of the matter is I wasn't planning to run for reelection. It's been an honor and a privilege to serve as your president, but I wasn't going to ask for seconds.

"But this amendment, this absurd, ridiculous, petty amendment, changes that.

"This is politics at its worst, if that isn't redundant. So now I *am* going to run, if only to make a point. I will not be dictated to—nor will I allow future presidents to be dictated to—by what I consider to be, quite possibly, the worst Congress in United States history.

"Let me go further. I don't think there's been such concentration of rascality and unscrupulousness under one dome since the worst days of the Roman Empire.

"Frankly, it feels darn good to get that off my chest.

"Now, since we're speaking candidly, I'll tell you something else. I hope I *don't* win in November. I'm not the sort to hang around where I'm not wanted. But there's a point to be made and, by gosh, I'm going to make it.

"I've got a swell family back home in Ohio. And some really swell grandkids I haven't seen nearly enough of. I've got a dandy front porch with a swing chair on it. To be honest, my fellow Americans, I wouldn't trade all that for four more years of the White House if you made me emperor for life and threw in the Hope diamond and a Las Vegas chorus line.

"I'm sorry it's come to this, but here we are and here we go.

"And I'm sorry if I butted into your favorite TV show. Good night, my fellow Americans. God bless us, and God save the United States of America."

There was a hush in the Oval Office after the President finished speaking. No one moved. Then one of the TV technicians began to clap and suddenly the whole room was applauding, even the Secret Service agents, who never, ever register emotion, much less applaud.

President Vanderdamp, frowning at this unexpected display, thought, *Oh, shit.*

CHAPTER 21

"*mor*, I have been a fool. But now I am yours. Totally yours—if you will have me. Take me, Meetchell. Take me. Send in the *Neemitz. Now!*"

"All right, Connie, but no more Mr. Nice Guy."

"Cut."

"Problem?" Dexter said grouchily, dropping the panting Ramona Alvilar onto the satiny sheets of the presidential bed on Air Force One.

"Five minutes, everyone," Jerry the director called out. He and Buddy approached. "Everything okay, Dex?" Jerry said.

"Yes. Yes," Dexter said a touch petulantly. "Everything's fine. Why? Is it not fine for you?"

"No, no," Buddy said heartily. "It's fine. Great. I think it's going totally great."

"Really great," Jerry echoed. "But I'm—maybe it's just me—I'm not sensing a lot of heat. Buddy, does that sound fair?"

"Yeah," Buddy said. "I think it sounds fair."

"This is a hot, hot, hot scene here," Jerry went on. "Ramona's—Jesus—she's on fire. We're going to have to pack her in ice between takes. But when you hit the 'No more Mr. Nice Guy' line, it's coming through like a—I don't know—BlackBerry text message or something." Jerry turned to Buddy. "Does that sound valid to you?"

"I think so," Buddy said as if considering an amendment to Newtonian physics. "She was giving *me* an erection, and I'm ten yards away."

Dexter sighed. "Fair enough. I'm sorry, guys. I've . . . I guess I've got a lot on my mind right now."

"Is everything all right?" Buddy said solicitously. "Anything I can do?"

"No. No. It's fine."

It wasn't, actually. The day before, Dexter had had another argument with Terry over the Park Avenue co-op she wanted to buy—or as he now referred to it in conversations with her, "the fucking co-op." She'd found one she liked, on Park Avenue and Seventy-fourth Street, the most expensive latitude and longitude on the planet. It was the bottom floor of a vintage apartment building, something called a maisonette. Dexter assumed the word was French for "hideously expensive."

"Four million? Four million *dollars*? Terry. Hail Mary, full of grace."

"It's New York, Dexter."

"Thank you for clarifying that. I'd assumed you were talking about a diamond mine in South Africa."

O<small>KAY</small>," Dexter said to Buddy and Jerry. "Let's do it again. I'll rip her clothes off with my teeth."

"Whoa, Tiger," Buddy said, giving Dexter a manly shoulder punch. "That's an original Carolina Herrera. But I love the energy. Throw her onto that bed, send in the ol' *Nimitz*, and we're out of here. Good to go, Mr. Prez?"

"Yes, yes," Dexter said, sounding profoundly bored at the

prospect of ravishing a woman voted by *People* magazine the third sexiest woman on planet Earth.

There was something in addition to the four-million-dollar maisonette that was taking up a lot of gigs on Dexter Mitchell's hard drive: a poll that morning in *USA Today*. *If the election were held today, who would you vote for?* Answer: *President Mitchell Lovestorm*—by thirty points over the next most popular choice.

Dexter had shown the poll to his wife, palms moist with excitement. Terry had glanced at it in a bemused way, as if it were a postcard from Aunt Hattie in Bora-Bora. "That's wonderful, darling. And isn't it wonderful you aren't running?"

"But Terry. Look at these numbers. *Thirty points!*"

"Dexter," she said, "Mitchell Lovestorm is a television character."

"So?" Dexter said. "We're all television characters these days."

"I'm not. Look, sweetheart, it's a lovely compliment to what you've been able to do. And for a nonprofessional actor, too. We're all so proud of you. But the poll is"—she laughed—"meaningless. Anyway," she said brightly, like a mother trying to convince a recalcitrant six-year-old that he didn't really want to go to the zoo today after all, "you're already president."

Dexter sighed. "It's hardly the same thing, Terry. Have you ever heard of the term 'synchronicity'?"

"Yes," Terry said. "It's when you suddenly have a lot of money and just the right apartment comes on the market."

As soon as Dexter had wrapped the steamy reconciliation scene on *Air Force One* he went off to his dressing room and placed a call to Buster "Bussie" Scrump, the Washington pollster and political operative. It had been unkindly but accurately said of Bussie Scrump that his ethics were of a piece with Groucho Marx's manifesto, "I've got principles. And if you don't like them, I've got other principles."

"Mis-ter President!" Bussie said jovially. They'd known each other for years. "How's the *Nimitz*? I swear I get goose bumps every time I hear you say that."

"Fuck the *Nimitz*," Dexter said. "Now listen, Buss, this is between you, me, and the Holy Ghost."

CHAPTER 22

The investigation into the *Swayle* leak, now in its fourth week, had so far failed to produce any result other than a deepening of the already sour mood within the marble palace.

A defiant and continuingly minty-breathed Chief Justice Hardwether had, true to his threat, called in the FBI, causing almost unanimous ill will. (For once the justices agreed on something.) Clerks asked to submit to polygraph examinations appealed to their various justices, who in turn registered Olympian proxy umbrage and fired off furious, copiously footnoted letters to the Attorney General, with ostentatious cc's to their own Chief Justice. One such letter had been reprinted in full on the front page of the *Washington Post*.

The skies over Capitol Hill darkened with writs and subpoenas, but the Supreme Court being supreme, there wasn't a whole hell of a lot the Justice Department could do other than to stamp its feet and put out grumbly leaks on the theme of "supreme arrogance." Juvenal's *quis custodiet* was quoted so often on TV that three-year-olds became conversant in Latin. Court observers shook their heads in dismay. Not since *Bush v. Gore** had the

---

* Untidy, still controversial case involving somewhat confused, largely Jewish, Democratic retirees in Palm Beach who in 2000 voted by mistake for Patrick Buchanan, an anti-Israel Republican, instead of pro-Israel Democrat Al Gore, eventually resulting in the presidency of George (not H.) W. Bush, 9/11, the Iraq War, a 40 percent decline of the U.S. dollar, the subprime mortgage crisis of 2007–2008, a fatal tiger attack at the San Francisco Zoo, and a Nobel Prize for Gore.

Supreme Court been held in such contempt by the country. Had Chief Justice Hardwether lost his grip? *This never would have happened under Rehnquist.* And these rumors that he was drinking. It was all so very sad.

At the epicenter of this fury and unpleasantness stood Justice Pepper Cartwright, the aggrieved party insofar as the leak went, yet increasingly perceived in the public eye to be the epicentric cause of all the problems. Editorials had begun to appear calling for her impeachment. Every now and then, as the saying goes, Washington needs to burn a witch.

Meanwhile, the President who had elevated her to the high court was mounting the most quixotic reelection campaign in history. He had announced his firm intention not to spend one dime on television advertising, nor a single day campaigning in Iowa or New Hampshire or any of the early primary states. His campaign slogan was almost defiantly prosaic: "Vanderdamp: More of the Same."

"As a rallying cry," one pundit put it, "it's not quite up there with 'Once more into the breach.'"

The Presidential Term Limit Amendment, meanwhile, was busily ratifying its way through various state legislatures. State senators were furious with Vanderdamp for years of having denied them pork. The people, on the other hand, seemed to find the President's breathtaking honesty refreshing, if not downright unique. According to the polls, many were rethinking their quondam odium. He was up by twelve points—or as they put it in Washington, "double digits."

In the midst of this howling gale, Pepper blew her nose, dried her tears, and tried to go about the business of interpreting the U.S. Constitution as best she could. But it wasn't much fun and she missed the view of Central Park. She missed lying in bed and looking out over it and eating hot bagels. Buddy had been wrong about there being no good restaurants in Washington, but she had yet to find New York–quality carbohydrates. Given other developments, this was a minor disappointment.

ONE LUNCH HOUR in the Court cafeteria, she found herself standing in line behind Crispus Galavanter.

"Why is it," he said in his plummy cello voice, "that you and I are always taking up the rear of the procession? When will we take our rightful places in the pageant of greatness? The world wonders."

Crispus bantered in these mock-heroic tones. His nickname among the clerks was "the Licorice Caesar." He quite liked it, even occasionally signed his memos "LC."

Pepper smiled, gathered up her Jell-O with embedded fruit, cottage cheese, and iced tea. Crispus's tray held a trencherman's portion of meat loaf, mashed potatoes, lima beans, onion rings, and two Dr Peppers.

"May I . . . join?" Crispus said. It was a mild breach of protocol, as Pepper had papers tucked under her arm, a signal she'd intended a reading lunch. But you couldn't say no to Crispus.

"How you making out," he said, "in the midst of all this Sturm und Drang?"

"Okay. No one's asked me to take a polygraph, anyway," Pepper said, forking up some cottage cheese.

"Disgraceful business. You shouldn't have been put through it. Makes us all look bad. I don't blame the CJ for being furious. But neither do I think that unleashing the FBI has enhanced the spirit of communality."

"I begged him not to do it on my account," Pepper said. "But he's running hot about it. Went on and on about what a disgrace, etc, etc. I think he's . . . he's not in a good way."

Crispus chewed his food pensively. "I *am* concerned for him. Either he is facing a periodontal crisis—he's awful

minty of late—or he is partaking of John Barleycorn in a vo-
luminous manner. Well," he said, "the man has been through
a crucible. I like Declan. I don't agree with him nine out of
ten times. I didn't agree with him on gay marriage. But that
cat is well out of the bag and it ain't going back in. No, it can't
have been easy. And now this *Swayle* business. Unfortunate.
Say, how is that Jell-O? Would you like some of this meat
loaf? It is . . . I have no words to describe its Platonic ideality.
Do you know whose recipe it is? Mrs. Frankfurter's. It lives
on after her. Now, *there's* a legacy. I would be well pleased to
have such a one myself. Perhaps my nachos *con everything in
el pantry*? Nachos Galavanter. Nachos *Crispus*. I will have the
recipe entered into the record. And to think that you were
present at the creation. Do you sense the historicity of the
moment?"

"Try the Jell-O." Pepper smiled.

"I demur," Crispus said. "Demur most strenuously. Jell-O
will not again pass these lips."

"You got enough saturated fats on that plate to kill a marathon runner."

"For your information, Miss Pritikin, that odious substance on your plate—intending no collateral disrespect to
the cottage cheese—was about all I could afford to eat back
in law school. That and those repellent Japanese noodles."
He shuddered. "No, neither Jell-O nor ramen shall frequent
these digestive organs in this lifetime. But," he said, "I do
worry about Declan. I try to avoid the water-cooler style of
discourse, but I confide to you here and now that I am *alarmed*
for him. So is Paige, dear, kind woman that she is. But she
can't get anywhere with him. Shuts her out. And when you're
shutting out Paige Plympton, you are denying yourself the
very quintessence of humanity. I saw him yesterday and he
had a look on him . . . like a character out of Edgar Allan

Poe. It gave me pause, I tell you. I said to him, in the most fraternal way, I said, 'Dec, remember that on the other side of the wall of humiliation lies liberation.' "

"What did he say?" Pepper said.

"He said, 'Did you find that in *Pilgrim's Progress* or in a fortune cookie in a not very good Chinese restaurant?' I laughed. He did not. Not even at his own bon mot. When you derive no joy from your own felicity, well, it's like dying of thirst in your own wine cellar."

"I feel like a fried green tomato about all this," Pepper said. "I . . ."

Crispus shrugged. "It's not your fault someone leaked *Swayle*. But I will say that your matriculation here has been"—he smiled companionably—"not uneventful."

Pepper stared forlornly at the remains of her fruit-dappled Jell-O. "Do you think I should . . ." She couldn't bring herself to finish the sentence.

"Eat any more of that ghastly substance? No. You need meat and potatoes, woman. So tell me, Justice Cartwright, what is it you like to do?

"Do?"

"Come on, this isn't oral argument. It's not a complicated question. *Do* you listen to music? *Do* you go to movies? *Do* you dance? Solve Sudoku puzzles in the bathtub while listening to Chopin's nocturnes? Maurizio Pollini is my preferred version. That man is touched by God. All due respect to Horowitz and Rubinstein, but next to him they sound like they're playing chopsticks. Do you climb mountains wearing lederhosen? Do you shoot elk with high-powered rifles and mount their horns? Do you keep tropical fish? Do you speak to your houseplants? Do you knit?"

"The only thing I've been doing," Pepper said, "is working my Texas butt off." She leaned forward and whispered across the table, "I'm drowning here, Crispus. I don't think I'm gonna make this whistle."

"What are you talking about?"

"Nothing. Bull-riding."

"Steady on," he said, wiping his mouth with his napkin, "steady on. For your information, *everyone* feels like they're drowning the first year. Except maybe Silvio." Crispus chuckled. "Silvio, you understand, was not appointed by the President, but from on *high*."

Pepper felt tears welling. "I'm a catty whompus."

Crispus stared. "What is a catty whompus? Something out of Lewis Carroll? It sounds . . . unpleasant."

"Something that's out of place. Something that doesn't fit. Something like me."

Crispus leaned back in his chair and patted his round belly pensively, as if posing for a nineteenth-century caricature. "Justice Cartwright, you disappoint me. I had not marked you for the self-pitying kind. You say you don't fit? You're here, aren't you? You're a Justice of the United States Supreme Court, aren't you? Suck it up, girl."

"Yeah," Pepper said, suddenly dry-eyed, "you're right."

Crispus stood and bussed his tray, a habit left over from working his way through college. "Meantime," he smiled, "I suppose the CJ could use a friendly word. Some bucking up. You're not to blame for the *Swayle* leak, but it squirted all over onto his lap and he's having a bad time with the mopping up. So, if you're not otherwise occupied writing landmark opinions legitimizing the grievances of bank robbers, drop him a note or something, tell him you appreciate his . . . oh, whatever. Now I must leave you. I've got to go see a man about a horse."

THAT NIGHT, a little after nine o'clock as Pepper was getting ready to leave, she thought of what Crispus had said and thought to stick her head in Hardwether's office on the way out and say . . . whatever.

His outer office was empty, the clerks and secretaries gone. But she saw light under the door to his inner office. She knocked softly. No answer. Knocked again. No answer. Opened the door. The lights were on, but no CJ. The door leading from his inner office to the justices' conference room was ajar. She walked over, opened it, and saw an arresting sight: the Chief Justice of the United States standing on the conference table, a rope around his neck, in the process of fastening the other end to an overhead light fixture. He turned and saw Pepper. The two Supreme Court justices stared at each other.

"Uh," Pepper said. "Am I interrupting?"

"As it happens," Hardwether said, "yes."

"I could come back. But . . ."

"Thank you. If you'd please close the door behind you?"

Pepper said, "Could I ask you a question?"

"If it's brief."

"Is this a cry for help or are you actually fixing to hang yourself?"

"Justice Cartwright," he said, "I don't mean to be rude, but if I could have the room? Thank you. As you can see, I'm occupied."

"I can see that," Pepper said. She turned and walked a few steps to the door, stopped. "I don't want to intrude."

"Then don't."

"Thing is, if I were to leave, I'd be guilty of aiding and abetting a felony. Suicide's a crime in DC. I'm already paying one lawyer to handle my divorce and another to handle a breach of contract suit. I can't afford a third one. Not on what this place pays."

"No," the Chief Justice replied. "You're perfectly in the clear. You've committed no act in support of the sui . . . of the deed.

Absent said support, you would be guilty only if there were a relational obligation. Absent relational obligation—there being none here—you're quite blameless. I would remind you that there is no 'duty to rescue.'"

"There's a moral duty, surely," Pepper said.

"We're not talking about moral duty, Justice. We're talking about law."

"Right," Pepper said. "Sorry."

"It's well established under case law that, for instance, even if you were an expert swimmer you would be blameless for failing to save a drowning person. While I am not aware of any case where the drowning person was attempting to commit su . . . was attempting to sink, the larger principle, developed in cases of accidental drownings, is equally applicable. So, you see. No problem. Good *night*, Justice."

Pepper said thoughtfully, "I disagree."

Chief Justice Hardwether said with annoyance, "On what grounds?"

"I believe," Pepper said, "that because of our employment relationship, that is as coworkers—if you will—that there is clear duty to care and that I am thus obligated to . . . well, do something."

"No, no, no." The Chief Justice shook his head. "Duty to care extends only to employer-*employee* relationships. As Chief Justice, I am your superior—if you will. The hierarchically subordinate individual is under no obligation to rescue the person in the hierarchically superior position. *Zerbo v. Fantelli*. The Court made it perfectly clear that it is only the hierarchically superior person who has the obligation to rescue the hierarchical inferior. So, if you would shut the door behind you?"

"There's a problem," Pepper said.

"For God's sake, Justice. *What* problem?"

"You're construing too narrowly."

"Pepper—I'm the Chief Justice of the United States!"

"Be that as it may, sir, duty to care runs both ways. See *Farquar v. Simpson*. And anyway, as a simple matter of constitutional law, the Chief Justice is most appropriately regarded as primus inter pares.* So," Pepper said brightly, "duty to care clearly obtains here. We're coworkers."

The Chief Justice's head sagged. "Could you just please . . . go?"

"All right," Pepper said, "okay. But you're going about this all wrong."

"We've been *through* all that, Justice."

"I'm talking about the knot. You call that a hangman's knot?"

"I . . . Pepper . . ."

"I know how to tie one, if you want. I was taught how when I was eight. By an actual hangman. Friend of my granddaddy's."

Hardwether stared. "All right," he grumbled. "Jesus. Whatever."

Pepper went over and took off her shoes.

"What are you doing?" he said.

"Trying not to scuff the table. Not that you cared. Look at those marks."

"Would you just proceed, please?"

"No need to get aggervated," Pepper said. She took the rope off his neck. "Where'd you get this? Looks like clothesline . . ."

Chief Justice Hardwether groaned. "If you'd please just *tie the knot*."

"All right. See, you take a length so, make your loop, then double it back—"

"I don't need to learn how. I'm not going to be doing this a second time."

"Didn't they teach this in Boy Scouts? Or were you get-

---

* First among equals. Not Juvenal.

ting your merit badge in library science or some wimpy thing? There . . ." She handed it to him, a perfect hangman's knot. "You better put it on yourself," she said. "Legal-wise."

He put it around his neck.

"You'd think a judge would know how to make a hangman's knot," she said.

"I'm against capital punishment," he said. "Perhaps you read any of my eight opinions?"

"I read 'em," Pepper said. "Now, you want the knot against the side, there, not the back. How much you weigh?"

"What?"

"Do you want to do this right, or you want to strangle to death slowly with your tongue sticking out black and blue and—"

"One seventy-five," Hardwether snapped.

"All right then," Pepper said. "Hm."

"What now?"

"We'd need at least a four-foot drop for a good clean snap."

"I'll work with what we have. *Thank* you, Justice."

"It's your funeral," Pepper shrugged, climbing down off the polished table. "Only now," she added pensively, "we got a definite problem."

"What?" the CJ said.

"Now I am an accessory. You die, I go to jail. That's not a satisfactory outcome from my point of view."

"For God's sake," the Chief Justice moaned.

"Tell you what," Pepper said. "Why don't you come down off there. We'll go over to the library, rustle us up a couple of real sharp clerks, see if maybe we can't find a loophole. If there is, then off you go and we're done."

Chief Justice Hardwether stepped forward as he raised his finger to gesture. As he did, his shoe slipped on the polished surface of the conference table. He pitched forward, the rope pulling taut against his throat. Pepper lunged forward as he crashed to the floor in a heap. He looked up at Pepper with a mixture of surprise, confusion, and betrayal, holding his abraded neck where the rope had been.

"Slipknot," she said half apologetically. "Escape clause. Hangman taught me that, too."

Hardwether made a hoarse sound.

"You want to go get some coffee or something? Valium? Crisis counseling? I believe it's covered under our health plan."

"*A drink*," the Chief Justice croaked.

THEY WALKED TO THE PORK BARREL, a bar on Capitol Hill frequented by congressional staffers, low-end lobbyists, and Vietnam veteran bikers. Hardwether ordered a double Scotch; Pepper tequila.

"So," she said when the drink came. "Seen any good movies lately?"

He stared glumly at the table.

"What was that all about?" she said.

"I apologize," Hardwether said hoarsely. "Can we just leave it at that? I haven't been thinking very clearly."

"Sure. But the *conference* room?"

"The ceiling in my office was too high."

"Oh. Would have made for one heck of a headline."

"Undoubtedly."

They sat in silence.

"Is it that bad?" Pepper said.

"I just tried to kill myself," he said. "*Res ipsa loquitur.*"*

"The wife thing?"

He stared into his drink. "The *life* thing. You won't mention this to anyone, will you?"

"I'm not the Court leaker."

---

* The thing speaks for itself.

"No, that's right. Oh, what a . . . mess."

Pepper said, "Reason I went to see you in the first place was Crispus gave me a whuppin' today in the cafeteria about feeling sorry for myself. I could recycle his lecture if you want."

"It's not self-pity. It's an admission of failure. Two different things entirely."

"We back on oral argument?"

"No." He rubbed the livid red line around his neck.

"You might consider a turtleneck tomorrow," Pepper said. "Or one of them high Edwardian collars. You'd look good in those. You've already got that stuffy owl sort of look."

"All I ever wanted to be was this," he said. "And now I'm in a bar, with abrasions around my neck. There's a Yiddish proverb. Want to make God laugh? Tell him your plans. 'Nother round?"

"Do you really need more depressants? Come on," she said. "I'll drive you home."

The Chief Justice was now living not in a multimillion-dollar mansion in McLean but in a nice-but-nothing-fancy apartment building in Kalorama, which means "beautiful view" in Greek, a name dreamt up by a nineteenth-century Washington developer.

Pepper pulled up in front of his apartment building. The Chief Justice stared vacantly through the windshield, making no move for the door handle. They sat in silence.

Pepper said, "You don't want to be alone tonight. Do you?"

"No. I suppose not."

"You got a couch?"

"I think so. Yes. I have a couch."

"Okay then," she said, "I'll take the bed."

"Fair enough," he said.

CHAPTER 23

It was a light day for Dexter on the set of *POTUS*. He had only a short scene in which the CIA would reveal that National Security Director Milton Swan had been poisoned by radioactive borscht at a Kremlin state banquet. Dexter hadn't convinced Buddy or Jerry to add the subplot about Swan being a Russian double agent.

A production assistant came to his dressing room with the word that his wife, Terry, was on the phone and that it was "extremely urgent." (Personal cell phones had to be turned off on the set, a strict rule.)

"Dexter," Terry said, "something very strange has happened."

Dexter's stomach tightened.

"Oh?" he said, trying to sound casual while looking over his lines. *"But Milton was like a son to me! At least until he started porking the First Lady."* Dexter made a mental note to ask Jerry if "porking" was presidential. These writers . . .

Terry said, "I gave Lee Tucker from the bank the go-ahead to wire the down payment to the broker. He called me back and said, quote, 'There's not enough in the account. Not nearly enough.' Do you know anything about this?"

Dexter took a deep breath. "I was going to call you."

A frosty silence befell. "About what, Dexter?"

make this other payment," Dexter said.

? For what? To whom?"

just . . . some people in DC."

"Dexter," said Terry, her temperature dropping like a Canadian cold front. "We're talking about five hundred thousand dollars. That's half a million dollars."

Dexter chuckled. "Yes. Yes. Like Ev Dirksen* used to say— God rest his soul—'A million here, a million there, pretty soon you're talking about real money.' Ha-ha. They don't make them like that anymore, do they?"

"Dexter. What have you done with our money?"

"Well, honey," he laughed, "technically *my* money. But sure, of course, ours . . ."

"Dexter."

"Terry, when I agreed to take on this new assignment, it was with the expectation, and the understanding that—"

"No, no, no, no. No speeches, Dexter. This isn't the Iowa caucus and it's not the New Hampshire primary. What. Have. You. Done. With. The. Money. Dexter? The money that was the down payment money for the maisonette."

"That must be, what, a French word?"

"Dexter."

"Terry, honey, lambie, listen to me for one minute, okay?"

"I am listening, Dexter. And I'm not liking what I'm hearing."

"That money *is* a down payment. But on a different residence." *Yes,* Dexter thought. *Good. Brilliant!*

There was a silence, as the Book of Revelation would say, for the space of about half an hour—the kind of silence that generally precedes rains of fire and blood and other unpleasant things, some of them on horseback.

---

* 1896–1969. Venerable senator of the kind now not in abundant supply.

"What," Terry said, "in God's good name are you ta
about?"

"The White House, Terry. The best housing in America.
Makes that maisonette or whatever the hell it's called look like a
mud hut. And no monthly maintenance charges, either. Terry?
Honey? Sweetie? Hello?"

There was the sound of a telephone being violently cradled.

Well, Dexter thought, *that was a success.* He returned to his
script.

*"We'll bury him at Arlington with full honors. In a lead-lined
coffin so the pallbearers won't get cancer. And once we've sounded
taps over the corpse, then I will deal with President Gennady Barra-
nikov. Get me the Russian translation for 'No more Mr. Nice Guy.'
And tell Admiral Murphy to signal the* Nimitz *to stand by."*

THE PRESIDENTIAL TERM LIMIT AMENDMENT was proceeding
toward ratification. Eight states, so far, had approved it—states
whose legislatures were peeved at "Don Veto" Vanderdamp
for having denied them federal spending monies for, variously:
a dam, a highway "enhancement," a wind farm, a Museum of
Gluten, an underground storage facility for used fast-food restaurant cooking grease, an Institute for the Study of Gravel, a
postoperative transgender counseling center, and an electric
eel farm "alternate energy source initiative." Eight states down,
twenty-four to go.

"Your campaign manager called again," Hayden Cork said to
the President in the Oval Office. "He wondered if he might actually meet with you sometime before Election Day next year."

"What else have you got for me?" the President said, barely
looking up from his desk.

"You might at least call him," Hayden said. "If only as a
courtesy."

at to do," Vanderdamp said, scribbling. It
er to the Russian prime minister suggesting
ssination of the prime minister of Ukraine,
-your-face blatancy by the Russian secret
have been in the best interests of international comity.

"Yes," Hayden said, "still, it might be nice for him to hear from you some, I don't know, message. 'A steady hand on the helm'? 'Putting people first'? Something . . ."

"He knows my message. 'More of the same.'"

"Well, I'm sure they'll find that invigorating at campaign headquarters. Mr. President, if I may—"

"No, Hayden, you may not."

"Very well, sir," Hayden said, a bit stiffly.

"Was there anything else?"

"Yes. I know how you hate foreign policy crises, but Elan Blutinger called and wants to brief you on developments in Colombia. At the earliest opportunity."

"Colombia? Crisis? Headache, maybe, crisis, I doubt. What is it?"

"Rather sensitive."

"Hayden," the President said, "we both know that he's already told you what it is. So why don't you just tell me and I'll promise to sound surprised when he tells me."

"President Urumbaga is going to announce that he's pegging the Colombian peso to the price of cocaine in Miami."

"And what am I supposed to do about that?" the President said.

"Essentially, the country is switching to what he calls an *economía blanca*. A white economy. He's in effect legalizing cocaine."

"He can't do that. Can he?"

"Well, I'm sure the National Assembly has to be consulted.

But you know how that goes down there. How it becomes our problem is that he's declaring it legal export."

"For God's sake," the President said. "We gave him a state visit last year. South Lawn ceremony, military band, testimonial speeches, dinner, entertainment by whatsername, Gloria Estefan and the Miami Noise Machine . . ."

"Sound Machine, I think."

"I'd say *that's* a matter of opinion. He swore—up, down, and sideways—he was committed to the drug war. 'We stand with you against this scourge.' His exact words. And now—this?"

"According to Elan's people, he doesn't really have much choice. The narcos kidnapped the last of his family last week. You'll recall his wife and mother-in-law were taken hostage right after they returned from the state visit here. So he's got the proverbial gun to the head."

The President stared out the Rose Garden window. "All right," he said, "send in the *Nimitz*. Maybe that'll get their attention."

Hayden pursed his lips. "Perhaps not the *Nimitz*, sir?"

"Why not? Is it in dry dock or something?"

"I know you don't watch much television, sir, but Dexter Mitchell, he's in a show now. It's doing rather well. He plays a president."

Vanderdamp snorted. "*Finally*. I know all about that. It's called *POTUS*. President Lovebucket or some such. My grandchildren watch. They like it. They tease me about it. Little Ann Marie told me, 'He's more handsomer than you are, Grampy.' Ha-ha. I said, 'Well, if that's the way you feel, I'm not going to name that new national park after you.' Ha-ha-*ha*! Darling thing. Looks just like her mother when she was that age . . ."

"Yes, well, President Love*storm*, his solution to every crisis is to send in the *Nimitz*."

"So?"

"I'm all for giving the Colombians the heebie-jeebies, sir, but why don't we suggest to the Joint Chiefs they send in the *George H. W. Bush* or the *Theodore Roosevelt* or . . ."

"I don't care what aircraft carrier we use," President Vanderdamp said. "But for God's sake, Hayden. What's it come to when you can't use an aircraft carrier because some *TV* president is using it."

"Let me check with Admiral Stavridis, see what we have on station down there."

"What's happening, Hayden?" the President said philosophically. "You can't tell anymore what's real and what isn't. Everything's all jumbled. The world has been reduced to a widescreen TV."

"Yes, sir. With respect to that, it appears President Lovebucket has engaged Buss Scrump to form an exploratory committee."

"For God's sake."

Would you know anything about this?" Buddy said.

He was standing, florid faced, in Dexter's dressing room, thrusting his BlackBerry at his star. Dexter, recoiling slightly, saw the headline on the little screen:

'POTUS' FOR PRESIDENT?
DEXTER MITCHELL
IN (REAL) PRESIDENTIAL BID

"Well, how about that," Dexter said airily. "Great publicity for the show, huh?"

"Yeah. Wonderful. So. Is this *true*?"

"It's true that there's a groundswell out there. You saw that poll in *USA Today*. Some folks down in DC thought, well, let's see how deep it is. It's just in the, you know, exploratory phase at this point."

Buddy stared. "Dexter, give it to me straight. Are you running for president?"

"It's a complicated process, Buddy. My gosh. First you have to file a thousand forms. Then you have to get thousands of signatures just to quality for—"

"Yeah, yeah. Just tell me: did you hire this guy Shrump—"

"Scrump."

"Whatever, to form this Mitchell for President Committee?"

"I wouldn't say *hire*. It's more of a—"

"This has your fingerprints all over it. O.J. Simpson left fewer fingerprints at the scene than you have here."

Dexter thought, *Goddamn Bussie. Asking a political consultant to keep his yap shut . . . might as well ask a nymphomaniac to keep her knees together.*

"I was going to discuss it with you today after we finished shooting."

Buddy was shaking his head and pacing and muttering. "What am I running here, a finishing school for Supreme Court justices and presidents?"

"I think you're missing the big picture here. This could be a tremendous boost for the show."

"Really? Is that what this is about? Funny. It's what my *last* star said as she was blowing her nose on her contract. Well, let me tell you something, Mr. President, I've already got the top contracts law firm on retainer, and I'm sure they'll cut me a discount for two lawsuits."

Dexter laughed. "You're going to sue me? For running for president?"

"In a word? You bet your ass."

An assistant director put his head in and said, "We're ready for you, Mr. President."

"Let's talk about this later, shall we?" Dexter said.

"Excuse me? I'm the fucking executive *producer* of this fucking charade."

"And a fucking good one," Dexter said. "Look, Buddy. Calm down. Don't you see? All this, everything—is a testimonial to you. To your vision. You created President Lovestorm. Sure, I play him. But you created him. The writers . . . okay, they did their bit, I suppose. But he's yours. *I'm* yours. You should be— my God—so proud of what you've done. Run with me, Buddy. Together, we can accomplish so much for this country. We can do what others have only—"

"Save it for the deposition," Buddy said, stomping out.

DEXTER'S ANNOUNCEMENT press conference three days later was heavily attended by the media, and somewhat unusual.

Normally the candidate's family clusters around, lending moral and visual support. But since Terry Mitchell was not at present speaking to her husband, her place was taken by Ramona Alvilar, wearing a quite fetching pantsuit that looked as though it might have been painted onto her.

Off to the side stood Buddy Bixby, producer of *POTUS*, trying with somewhat mixed success to look enthusiastic about this grotesque development. He had spent most of the previous days with contract attorneys, election law attorneys, and public relations advisers. The contract attorneys thought he had a very good breach of contract suit; the election attorneys said that airing *POTUS* in the midst of a presidential campaign would violate campaign finance laws. The public relations advisers thought that suing Dexter was definitely not the way to proceed. ("What if he wins?")

And so Buddy Bixby found himself once again betrayed by his own creation, grinding his back molars as Dexter Mitchell enunciated his Agenda for America, a lengthy manifesto the reader will be spared here, other than to note that it included a call for: a) change, b) a return to greatness, c) a brighter future for all, not just some, Americans, and d) a pledge to change the way Washington does business.

The sun did not stand still, nor did the earth tremble at these pronouncements, but the news that President Mitchell Lovestorm was in the race did lead the evening news that day.

CHAPTER 24

Pepper found it strange, sitting at the justices' conference table, thinking what had happened the last time she had been in this room—preventing the Chief Justice of the United States from hanging himself.

She and Declan exchanged brief knowing looks as they took their places along with the seven other justices. She caught the faint grin. Declan had been looking better than he had in a while. He no longer gave off a reek of mint.

His lightness of mood was not reciprocated by the other justices. He'd barely gotten off a cheery "Good morning" before Justice Haro bitterly complained that his clerks were being harassed by the FBI about the *Swayle* business.

"Could we discuss it after the conference, Mike?"

"No. I'd like to talk about it now. Calling in the gestapo is—"

Justice Santamaria groaned. "*Gestapo?* Did you actually say *gestapo?*"

"Call them whatever you want," Haro snapped. "But having them in here prowling the halls . . . it's infra dig."

"I don't like it any more than you do," Santamaria scowled. "But your language is inappropriate. No. That's not quite strong enough a word. *Vile . . .*"

"Gentlemen, gentlemen," Declan said. "Please. As to infra dig, let's all agree that leaking Court decisions *defines* infra dignitatem. Meanwhile we can discuss it all after conference. But as we're on the subject of the FBI, why don't we begin with *Peester*? You were the first to grant cert, Mike, as I recall. So, shall we begin?"

Peester v. Spendo-Max Corp was a knotty case. Security personnel at a Spendo-Max megastore outside Reno, Nevada, had noticed a female customer dressed head to toe in a Muslim *abaya* acting in a "suspicious manner." They called the Reno police, who discerned geometric-shaped bulges under her robes and deduced that she was a suicide bomber. They evacuated the store and called in the FBI, who arrived with a tactical unit, dogs, helicopters, and a robotic bomb disposal unit. They cornered her in the Bathroom Fixtures section. In due course the Muslim woman turned out to be one Dwight Robert Peester, neither female nor Muslim, but a career shoplifter. The suspicious bulges turned out to be CDs and DVDs secreted in pouches under the *abaya*. Mr. Peester was arrested and prosecuted but a jury acquitted him on the grounds that he had not yet exited the store and therefore had not yet technically shoplifted. A tsunami of lawyers rushed in. Mr. Peester sued Spendo-Max, the Reno Police Department, and the FBI agents on grounds of racial and religious profiling. He was asking for twenty million dollars for various psychic traumas, "plus dry cleaning costs." The nub of the issue—so far as Pepper, scratching her head as she read the brief, could discern—was whether you in fact had to actually belong to the particular race or religion in order to be a victim of discrimination against it.

The justices went around the table in order of seniority, splitting 4–4. Once again, all eyes turned to the juniormost justice. Pepper inwardly groaned. She daydreamed that she was back on *Courtroom Six*. Dwight Robert Peester stood before her, wearing bright orange, in chains. *Mr. Peester, it is the sentence of this court that you be taken from here to the place of execution.* . . .

"Justice Cartwright?" Declan said.

"Uh . . ." Pepper said.

"How do you vote?"

"I'm kind of . . . down the middle on this one," she said. "He was obviously planning to boost the stuff—"

"That's not the issue," Haro said.

"Well, it oughta be," Pepper said. "But there was prima facie evidence of profiling. . . . Still . . ."

The ticking of the grandfather clock in the corner sounded to Pepper like Big Ben striking noon.

"Anyone got a quarter?" she said.

"Sorry?" Declan said.

"Heads he wins, tails he loses?"

"That's an enlightened way of interpreting the Constitution," Justice Gotbaum muttered.

Justice Santamaria let out a sigh like a breaching humpback whale.

"All right," Pepper said. "Let's strike a blow for female Muslim-impersonating shoplifters. Vote to grant in favor of Peester."

As the justices left, Pepper overheard Santamaria saying to Jacoby in a voice calculatedly audible, "Pray God nothing critical comes before us in the next, say, thirty years." Haro, looking greatly peeved, followed Declan into his chambers.

That night over dinner at an Italian restaurant, Declan said to Pepper, "Haro's as hot as a tamale over the FBI investigation. 'Jackbooted thugs,' 'Storm troopers.' He made it sound like I've ushered in the Fourth Reich. Me—the Court's reliable liberal!"

"I always did suspect you were a closet fascist," Pepper said, forking up a bit of linguine alla vongole. "Look, if it's making everyone miserable, call it off. Let it go, Chiefy."

SUPREME COURTSHIP | 207

"I can't do that," Declan said. "It's beyond the pale. An impending Court ruling was leaked to the media. From within the Court. Incidentally, in no small part to embarrass you."

"I'm not asking for special protection," Pepper said. "I'm a big girl. I got a pistol. Know how to use it, too."

"That's certainly not the issue, either," he said sternly.

Pepper sipped her Chianti. "As for embarrassment, I am way beyond that. On the other side of the wall of humiliation is liberation."

Declan stared. "Kahlil Gibran or refrigerator magnet?"

Pepper got a good, close-up look at the Wall of Humiliation a few days later when an item appeared in the *Washington Post*'s Reliable Source column:

> Sightings: Supreme Court Justice Pepper Cartwright and Chief Justice Declan Hardwether enjoying a cozy dinner-for-two at Stare Decisis. Our source reports that the Supremes appeared to be in close agreement over whatever weighty legal issues were being discussed, and at various points held hands. Oyez, oyez! Both are in the midst of divorces. If their cases end up before the high court, look for a 2–0 vote. . . .

Within hours, hundreds of Web sites and legal blogs were fizzing with speculation over the question of whether a romantically linked pair of Supreme Court justices could be relied upon to render independent decisions. Outrage, calls for impeachment, an affront to the dignity of the Court . . .

Late that afternoon, Crispus knocked on the door of Pepper's chambers.

"I recall asking you to extend the CJ a friendly word," he said. "But dear me. . . ."

"Oh, hush," Pepper said.

"I *will* say," Crispus said, taking a seat, "he seems much more relaxed of late. Less minty. I congratulate you. You have saved a soul in distress. Have you considered a career in personal counseling?"

"I'm better at that than constitutional law, apparently."

Crispus pursed his lips. "Since you brought it up . . ."

"Go ahead," Pepper said.

"Your vote on *Peester*? Honestly, Justice Cartwright. Have you taken leave of your senses? Or have the senses taken leave of you?"

"Four other justices voted with me."

"Is that your rationale? Majority is the last refuge of scoundrels. Your poor sheriff grandfather must be spinning. And he not even *in* the grave."

"Did you come in here just to bitch-slap me?"

"Such elegant language. Are you familiar with the works of Mr. William Shakespeare?"

"I'm named for one of his characters."

"Pepper? I recall no Pepper in the bardic canon."

"Perdita. Let's see if you know your Shakespeare."

"*Winter's Tale.*"

"Two points. Very good."

"I was thinking more of Polonius."*

"Let me guess. 'To thine own self be true.' How original."

"My, but we're testy today. Did we sleep on a cactus last night? And here I thought love was an emollient."

"Who said anything about love? We had dinner."

"I was attempting, O Wicked Witch of the Wild West, to clarify something you yourself were on the verge of admitting,

---

* "To thine own self be true." Polonius's advice to his son, Laertes, who, by poisoning the tip of his sword in the climactic duel with Hamlet, does not *quite* live up to the paternal admonition.

but, being a *lawyer*, couldn't quite bring yourself to stipulate, namely that with these hyper-legalistic rulings you're handing down, you've been trying to *act* like a Supreme Court Justice, instead of just rendering your own best judgment. You used to be a pretty good judge, back when you stood astride the vast wasteland like a giant. At least in *Courtroom Six* your rulings had some heart."

As SHE WALKED up the redbrick steps of the Georgetown mansion, Pepper felt as though she were approaching the bench. Reflecting on it, she realized it had been a long time since she'd done that. For the last six years or so, it had been others who'd done the approaching, to her.

She rang the bell. The door opened with almost suspicious celerity. The butler ushered her into a study painted in deep, rich red, where a fire was laid. She had time while waiting to study the photographs. Every Washington mansion worth its mortgage has a Wall of Ego, but this one was truly impressive. There he was with—she counted—eight presidents, going back to Eisenhower. Most of them were signed, and not with an autopen. Off to the side in a space of its own was another photograph, of a young man in a military uniform. He was smiling at the camera, holding a machine gun, a cigar clamped jauntily in his bared teeth. Was it . . . no, it wasn't he. The uniform was of too recent vintage. On another wall, she found a picture, this one of him. He was in uniform, standing alongside a tall man with a large nose and a distinct kepi-style hat. Looking closer, she saw it was de Gaulle. The photo was signed. "*A G.C., avec les sentiments respectueux de son ami C de G.*" She remembered hearing at some point that he'd been in the OSS during the war; that he'd played a behind-the-lines role in advance of the Normandy invasion.

"Recognize anyone?" said Graydon Clenndennynn, standing in the open doorway.

"Impressive."

The old man smiled. "It's supposed to be. Sit, sit. What can we get you? You sounded distrait on the phone."

"Did you learn that word from your pal General de Gaulle?"

"No, from my French nanny. Want a drink? I'm dying for one, so even if you don't, be polite and keep an old man company. I'm not sure we have tequila."

"Whatever you're having."

"Good. Two martinis, George. And perhaps something to nibble on."

The butler returned with drinks and things made of hot cheese.

Graydon took a sip of his martini and emitted a soft purr of satisfaction. He was wearing a smoking jacket of the kind you see in old movies worn by Noël Coward or David Niven. As if reading Pepper's thoughts, he said, "I've always been shamelessly Anglophile in the wardrobe department. So, Justice, to what do I owe the pleasure? And it is one. It's good to see you again."

Pepper opened her mouth and—burst into tears.

"Oh, dear," Graydon said. He stood and came over and sat beside her on the couch. Held out his cocktail napkin. "Frette," he said. "*Hugely* expensive." He put a hand on her shoulder. "You don't have to talk. We could drink ourselves into a stupor."

Pepper laughed wetly. "Sorry, Mr. Clenndennynn. I didn't . . . I don't know what's come over me. I'll be fine." Whereupon she burst into tears again.

"You really might as well call me Graydon. Although I must say, I actually do like it when young people call me Mr. Clenndennynn. My Anglophilia extends—strictly *entre nous*, now—to embarrassing lengths. I secretly yearn to be called *Sir* Graydon

Clenndennynn. I was honorarily gartered by the Queen, for distinguished et ceteras. But you can't call yourself 'Sir' back here. A mistake, if you ask me. I've got the Medal of Freedom. *Nixon* gave that to me." He chuckled somewhat darkly. "Still, it's not quite the same as Sir Graydon, is it? But enough of my honorifics. Wherefore this torrent, this cataract of dolor?"

"I've screwed everything up. Everything," Pepper blubbered.

"It's not every day we get candor of this quality in Washington. Go on."

"Everyone hates me at the Court. There's an FBI investigation because of me. And that's made everyone hate the Chief Justice. Who's got enough problems. There's a *constitutional amendment* movement on account of me. And I'm voting on the side of criminals. . . ."

"Not to mention making goo-goo eyes with the Chief Justice over the pasta."

"I . . . You read about that?"

"Oh, yes. You've been a big topic of conversation. I was at Binky Slocum's last night and we talked of practically nothing else."

Pepper groaned.

"Well," he said, "remember what Oscar Wilde said. The only thing worse than being talked about is not being talked about. Most justices go through a period of adjustment. That's not so unusual. Though I will say, normally they aren't quite so . . . what's the word . . . ?"

"Tragic."

"Tragicomical, perhaps. Shakespeare."

"I *know*," Pepper said sharply. "Why does everyone here think a Texas accent means you're illiterate?"

"There are precedents. That's right—you're named for one of his characters, aren't you? No, I wouldn't say tragic. Though in this town, sometimes the tragedy can be comical, and vice versa. But did you come here for advice, or for my justly famous martinis? Or the cheese puffs? They are good, aren't they?"

"You're a wise man," Pepper said, blowing her nose into the Frette napkin. "I could use some wisdom."

"I've dispensed it all. I'm all out. But please don't tell the clients of Graydon Clenndennynn Corporation. It would ruin our bottom line and make the board of directors very unhappy. One does run out, you know. You have to replenish. It's been a long while since I've had the chance to do that. I've been . . . coasting for years. Lucrative years. Though I wonder to what end? No family to leave it to. Why does one work so hard at this age? To leave it to my foundation? I suppose it beats boredom and golf. Look now"—he patted her hand—"you'll sort all this out. I wouldn't have gone along with it, you know, if I hadn't thought you'd make the whistle. I liked you from the start. But I did warn you that the bull was an arm-jerker."

"You did, and it is."

Pepper, eyes now dry as the martini, sipped and let the gin do its thing. They talked for a while of politics and elections. Feeling relaxed, she pointed at the photograph of the young man in uniform and said, "Who is that?"

"My son."

"What does he do?"

"He was killed in Vietnam. Not long after that was taken."

"I'm sorry. I didn't . . ."

"No reason you should have known. His name was Everett. His mother wanted to name him Graydon, but I said, 'No, let's give *that* a rest for a generation.' The other soldiers in his unit— he was with the Special Forces, the Green Berets—they teased him about it. Soldiers can be rather merciless. I don't suppose Everett was a common name in the army."

"His mother . . ."

"She died. *Not* in Vietnam," he sipped the last of his martini, "though it played its part. So now you've seen the family album. It's Sunday. Let's have another."

"I should go," Pepper said. "I've got a ton of work."

Graydon pressed a button, summoning the butler. "Oh, stay. Unless you and the Chief . . ."

"It's *not* that," Pepper said.

"Good. Anyway, if you went back to work, you'd only make another pig's breakfast of things."

"Well, kiss my . . ."

"Now you're getting the hang of it," he grinned. "Ah, George, another pair of these lovely see-throughs, if you would. And we'd better have some more of Annabelle's cheese puffs. They seem to be rather a success with Justice Cartwright."

Pepper, suddenly aware that she'd eaten the entire plate, blushed, and then laughed.

CHAPTER 25

Donald Vanderdamp found himself in the one-thousandth—or was it the two-thousandth?—greenroom of his political career, reflecting on the strange vicissitudes that had brought him here while wishing, with every fiber in his Ohioan being, that he was back at the Wapakoneta Lanes. He imagined the feel of the kidskin soft leather glove as he pulled it on, the shoes that fit like ballet slippers, the ambient rumble of balls going down polished lanes, the rattle of the pins being struck, of the pin setting machines, jubilant cries of "Strike!" and groans of despair, of the buttery aroma of popcorn, the mouthwatering tang of broiling hot dogs and sizzling burgers, of ice-cold beer, the huggy cluster of grandchildren as you explained how to score. . . . If there was an afterlife paradise, surely it looked something like this. Keep your heavenly choir of archangels. Meanwhile, here he was, very much *this* side of paradise, preparing to go onstage to debate former Senator Dexter Mitchell, President Lovebucket, for a prize that he, Donald Vanderdamp, did not even want. How, he wondered, had it come to—this?

His campaign manager was talking to him. Perhaps he should listen? Though why, really? Well, one had to be polite.

"Right," the President said. "Good point."

"Sorry, sir?" the campaign manager said.

"What you were saying. I agree. I'll hit that point hard."

"Right," the campaign manager said diffidently. "Probably best to stay off the *POTUS* thing. It could open us up to the, well, the Cartwright . . . you know. Now, on the border mining," he said. "The numbers are pretty clear there."

The President, suddenly alert, said, "Charley."

"I know sir, but—"

"I don't *care* what the numbers are."

"I'm only pointing out that—"

"Charley. I don't *care* if every citizen, man, woman, and child, of Texas, of New Mexico, Arizona, California, or Guam for that matter is in favor of mining the gosh-darn border with Mexico. The United States Constitution says, in blazing neon letters, that individual states may not engage in their own foreign policies. It's just not up for discussion."

"That may be, sir, but four states legislatures are about to—"

"Make fools of themselves."

"Agreed. All I'm just suggesting is that we . . . that a little tactical ambiguity would go a long way toward—"

" 'Tactical ambiguity'? Charley. Is that what you think of me?"

"No, sir. Never mind."

"I appreciate what you're doing for me, Charley. I do. I know it's an unusual campaign."

"When you go out onstage, you'll walk toward each other, meet midstage, shake hands, go to your respective podiums. Now, he may try to pat you on the back or the shoulder. We have made it clear to his people that we do not want any pitty-patting, but I don't trust them. So when you shake his hand, do it face on so he can't reach your shoulder."

"Why don't I give him a kiss," the President said. "Full, on the lips. Our tongues melting into each other's, our bodies touching, becoming as one, heaving . . ."

Charley stared.

"I read that in a book when I was fifteen years old," President Vanderdamp said. "It was a spy novel. Not a very good one. Pretty awful, actually. But at the time I thought it was the sexiest, steamiest thing I could ever imagine. Now, my Lord, you can't turn on a television without seeing bodies writhing. I love this country, Charley, but I worry for it. What young people today see. . . . Well," he smiled, "I'll try to restrain myself from making mad, passionate love to President Lovebucket."

"Sir?"

"Yes?"

"This campaign, honestly? It's the most bass-ackward thing I've ever worked on. I don't get it. But however it turns out, I want to say, it's an honor working for you. You're a decent guy."

"Well, thank you, Charley," the President smiled. "In the unlikely event they ever give me a statue, I'll have that put on it. A decent guy."

An aide opened the door and said, "Ready, Mr. President."

President Vanderdamp stood, buttoned his jacket, patted his necktie.

"Battle stations. I used to say that in the navy. Course, those were only exercises, but it always gave me goose bumps. *Battle stations . . .*"

"Oh, on that . . ."

"Um?"

"The *Nimitz* thing? Maybe best to avoid . . ."

"*Yes*, Charley," the President said.

I KNEW THIS was going to lead to dessert," Pepper said. "Man does not live by entrée alone."

They were in a hotel. A nice one, in out-of-the-way Foggy Bottom. Pepper, having a net worth approximately twenty times Declan's, had made the reservation on her credit card. They had arrived half an hour apart so as to avoid being spotted together. If it had a furtive aspect—and it did—it was for a reason: photographers, alerted by the item about their cozy dinner at Stare Decisis, had begun staking out Declan's Kalorama apartment and Pepper's on Connecticut Avenue near the zoo, in hopes of getting a shot of the two of them emerging together early in the morning; perhaps holding hands or sharing a foamy latte.

"Does this feel at all . . . *dirty* to you?" Pepper said.

"I can't quite put my finger on it," Declan said. "But it certainly feels strange."

"Feels 'strange' to me, too. Well, shall we get out legal pads and analyze it?"

"It's not that I don't want to be here," Declan said, staring out the window. "I mean I'm practically bursting with intent."

"There's just nothing sexier than making love to a lawyer. Makes me all over quivery."

Declan blanched.

"What's wrong?" Pepper said.

"Tony said something like that to me once. And I couldn't"— his cheeks now filled with color: red—"perform."

"Honey, she was gay. I wouldn't be too hard on yourself."

"Maybe we should analyze it. Maybe a little discovery *is* in order."

"Maybe a little getting under the covers is in order. Baby?"

"Yes?"

"Are you going to take off your overcoat? Feels like making it with a flasher."

"Good point. Jesus, Pep," he sighed soulfully.

"Keep taking off the coat. That's it. Now how about the jacket? There you go. . . ."

"Six months ago I was happily married."

Pepper rolled her eyes. "Married, okay. Happily? Let's look at it. But could we maybe be in the now instead of the then?"

"Sorry, I'm so damned awkward sometimes. Do you like the top or the bottom?"

Pepper stared. "This ain't summer camp, and I ain't a bunk bed. Now look here, Chiefy, we are two grown adults, we are colleagues, we have discovered a mutual attraction. We are neither of us cheating on anyone, inasmuch as our spouses filed for divorce. We are both heterosexual—"

"What's that supposed to mean?"

"It's a statement of fact intended to differentiate myself from your prior partner for the purpose of putting you at ease so as to . . . oh, c'mere . . . initiate foreplay . . . um . . . yes . . . so as to stimulate the . . . mmmm . . . stim . . . u . . . late . . . the senses in such a manner as . . . oh, *yes* . . . yes . . . see, you haven't forgotten how to make a girl happy . . . oh . . . ohh . . . in such a . . . mmmm . . . lost my place . . . where was I . . . oh, yes . . . oh, yes . . . oyez . . ."

"Did you just say oyez?"

"Oh, yes."

CHAPTER 26

I felt good about that," Dexter said to Bussie Scrump and a half-dozen campaign operatives aboard the Freedom Express, the Mitchell campaign's official bus, on its way from Memphis to Little Rock.

"You should. You were great. But this is an unusual situation. Attacking a guy who who just stands there going, *Fine, don't vote for me.* You were good on defense, good on energy. On the Colombian situation, if it comes up again, and it will, maybe not do send-in-the-*Nimitz*. It felt a little flat. On border mining, I'm a little nervous about it. Maybe ease back on the throttle there."

Dexter shook his head. "No, no, no. No. The nums, Buss, the nums. Eighty percent. The vast majorities of the people in the border states *want* mines on the border. The federal government has failed them. A government that can't do *borders*? The people are frustrated. They're angry. They want to hear *boom-boom!* They want to see wetbacks flying into the air. Is it a perfect solution? No. Is democracy messy? Sure. But it's time to end the highfalutin philosophical discussions and come down off the Acropolis and get real. Texas, New Mexico, Arizona, California. Tot it up. Ninety electoral votes. Out of the two-seventy needed to win. Who am I to say to the good, hardworking, decent— *legal*—residents of these states, 'Uh-uh. Forget it. You're just going to have to live with *millions* of foreigners swarming across the border, tromping across your lawns, crapping in the flower beds, having babies in your hospitals, sending their kids to your schools for free English lessons, smashing into your car without insurance.' Oh, fuck it. Border-mining is never going to happen, so where's the harm in being for it? It's a freebie."

An aide came back and handed Dexter a printout. "Minnesota ratified the term limit amendment fifteen minutes ago!"

"Excellent. *Excellent* news. What are we up to now? Twenty-five?"

"Twenty-six. Eight to go."

Dexter considered. He asked for privacy with Bussie.

"Call Billy Begley," he said. "Tell him to call the senate majority leaders and the speakers of the house in Rhode Island, Delaware, Wyoming, Oregon. Hell with it—tell him to call all eight. Tell them: on day one of the Mitchell administration, the OPEN FOR BUSINESS sign is going back up on the White House. Whatever they want. Dams, eel farms, Institute for the Study of How Many Gerbils Fit Up a Hollywood Actor's Ass, a Museum of Lint, whatever. But Buss—tell Billy: we need the amendment now. Not after the election. *Now.* Tomorrow. Yesterday would be even better."

"I'm on it," Bussie said, flipping open his cell phone.

"Buss," Dexter said. "We're not the von Trapp family. Let's not yell this from the mountaintop. And this did *not* come from me. What's the most beautiful word in the English language?"

"Pussy?"

"The second most, then. Discretion, Buss. How do we spell it? D-i-s-c-r-e-t-i-o-n."

"*Dex.* It's my middle name."

"Your middle name is Ellrod, Buss. But make the call."

CHAPTER 27

SUPREME DISARRAY:
COURT BESET BY LEAKS, FBI INVESTIGATION,
AND NOW, INTERJUDICIAL ROMANCE

I ntra, surely," Declan said to Pepper. "Creeping illiteracy. And in the so-called 'newspaper of record.'"

As front-page headlines go, it was not what a Chief Justice desires to wake up to in the morning. The third paragraph noted that public confidence in the Supreme Court as an institution was "sharply" on the decline. The story ended predictably with a reference to *"quis custodiet."*

By noon, Justice Santamaria had dispatched to the Chief Justice's chambers a memo as blistering as one of his legendary opinions.

*Under the circumstances, I feel, nor am I alone in
this dolorous excogitation, that the Court would best be
served were you to resign as CJ, conceding frankly and
straightforwardly and for the good of all, not least the
country, that developments have overwhelmed your abilities
to cope with them.*

My feelings in this regard have nothing to do at all

with—let me speak directly—the depravity that your recent rulings have condoned, nay embraced, from gay marriage (enough said) to the abominations inherent in Swayle *and now* Peester. *But your insistence on calling in the FBI to deal with what should have been a family matter . . . this finally has shaken my confidence to the bone and cast a sickly-hued pall over this (once and pray, future) noble institution. And now this openly, flagrantly adulterous liaison with a colleague? What further degradations do you have planned for us? Orgies? Baccanales? Ecstasy raves in the Great Hall? Have you, Declan, finally, no shame?*

May God save the Honorable, the Supreme Court of the United States of America.

Yours sincerely,
Silvio Santamaria, Associate Justice

"I think Silvio missed his true calling," Declan said to Pepper. "Grand Inquisitor."

"My takeaway," she said, "aside from you and me being hell-bound adulterers, is that he's the one who must've leaked *Swayle*. Think about it. Silvio's idea of Utopia is the FBI banging down the door if they hear someone opening a pack of condoms on the other side. Why would he be so hot up about a legit FBI investigation? He's had it in for me from the git-go. Hated me for coming on the Court. Hated me for *Swayle*. Hated me for dissing him in the conference. Hadda be him."

"No," Declan said, "there's some undistributed middle here. I can't quite put my finger on it. Silvio's not the only one who's up in arms over the fact that I called in the 'gestapo.' The only one who hasn't harangued me is Paige, and that's only because Paige doesn't get upset about anything. It's that New England Yankee sangfroid. The end of the world could be at hand and they'd just look up at the sky and mutter, 'Looks like rain. . . .' " He stared at Silvio's letter. "I wonder how long before this ends up on the front page?"

"If it does," Pepper said, "that would seem to cinch it that he was behind the *Swayle* leak. Well, Chiefy, what's the next step here?"

"Well," the Chief Justice said, "my inclination is to sock him in his big fat Jesuit nose. But seeing as he worked his way through law school boxing professionally and has fifty pounds on me, I'm not certain that's the way to go. This term is going to be hard enough without having to wear a neck brace. Well, to work. Industry is the enemy of melancholy."

"Rochefoucauld or refrigerator magnet?"

"William F. Buckley Jr."

FOUR MONTHS BEFORE the November general election, and President Vanderdamp was in a funk because his poll numbers had been improving. He now trailed front-runner Dexter Mitchell by only eight points.

"Charley," the President said, "what in the name of heck is going on with these darn numbers?"

"Well, sir," Charley said, by now inured to these syllogistic conversations with his client, "apparently the people are responding to your clear signal that you don't want to be reelected. They understand that you're in it for the principle of the thing. They find it refreshing. Unusual."

"All right, but what do you suggest?" the President said with a touch of asperity.

"How do you mean, sir?"

"The numbers. How do we—there must be some way of . . . tamping them down. Surely."

Charley stared. "You want your poll numbers to go . . . down?"

"Well, I sure as heck don't want them going up. At this rate I'm going to be neck and neck with Lovebucket on Election Day."

It was a dilemma that had been keeping the normally sound-sleeping President awake nights. On the one hand, the thought of Dexter Mitchell ascending to an actual U.S. presidency was more than he could bear to contemplate. On the other hand, the thought of another four years . . . made him want to take the mother of all sleeping pills, but the National Security people had told him if he did, he was honor-bound to alert them so that they could summon the Vice President in the event they couldn't wake the President to cope with a critical situation.

Charley nodded sadly. The far-off look came into his eyes. "I don't know, sir. Maybe if you started sounding like you *wanted* to win? We could do a massive media buy on the theme of experience and steady hand on the tiller. Make it look like you actually—no." Charley brightened. "No. I've got it. Yes. Announce a shake-up of the campaign. Fire me. Fire all the top people."

"Why would I do that? You're doing a perfectly good job, especially considering what I've given you to deal with."

"It would send a signal of desperation!" Charley said, more animated than he had been in months. "A signal that you *want to win*. That you think the campaign isn't going the way it—"

"Forget it, Charley. Nice try, though."

Charley sighed. "We could always roll out a list of second-term initiatives. The usual hit-the-ground-running-on-day-one stuff. It might make them think you'd actually given some thought to a second term."

"Everyone already knows my second-term agenda."

"Yes. 'More of the Same.' It's on the bumper stickers. Stirring." Charley held up his palms. "Honestly, sir, I don't know what to tell you at this point. If you really want to lose this thing, well, I guess you're just going to have to stop being a leader and start being a politician."

President Vanderdamp looked out the window. "How many more states needed for ratification at this point?"

"Three. Tennessee, Nebraska, Texas."

The President nodded. "It does seem to have moved along briskly, this amendment."

"It's the professional pols, sir, on account of the pork. The people like you, at least according to these numbers. Maybe you won't have to worry after all. If it's ratified by Election Day, then you couldn't take office even if you did win. I'm not a constitutional scholar, but an amendment to the Constitution is an amendment to the Constitution. If you can't have a second term, then you can't have a second term."

President Vanderdamp sighed. "Yes. But it's not a very *elegant* solution."

DEXTER MITCHELL, TOO, was finding himself in an unusual situation.

His wife, Terry, had not gotten past her disappointment over the forfeited Park Avenue maisonette. Nor, at this point, was she oblivious to the fact that her husband now stood to become the next President of the United States. The Mitchell ménage was on the rocks, but through intermediaries, Terry had signaled her willingness to rejoin the campaign. The official reason for her absence up to now had been obscure "health reasons." She had not, in truth, been much missed: Ramona Alvilar had been campaigning at Dexter's side from day one as her surrogate and the people seemed quite happy to have this fetching bit of eye candy up onstage with the candidate. There had been some campaigning offstage as well; the *Nimitz*, as it were, had seen quite a bit of action. These things happen. The immediate problem for Dexter was how to explain to his life's companion, his childhood sweetheart, the mother of his children, that her presence was not especially desired on the hustings. It was, to be sure, a matter of some delicacy.

"What are you telling me, Dexter?" Terry said over the phone. "You don't *want* me with you?"

"No, honey. No, no. No. It's not that at all. Look it's—if it were up to me? But Buss and his people, they feel this is the way to go. Ramona's popular on account of the show. She's bringing in the Hispanics right and left. Our numbers there are way—"

"Dexter. I'm your *wife*."

"Valid point. Valid point. But Buss and his people, they say— the audiences have gotten used to seeing me with Ramona. And, honey, let's remember—it wasn't *my* idea for you not to show up for my announcement speech. But let's not go back. Point is, it's all going great, so let's not do anything to screw it up. It's all about ratings. And Ramona is helping us get ratings."

"Ramona is your TV wife. I'm your wife-wife."

"Again, valid point. *Valid point.* Stipulated. Look, baby, it's only until the election." He added in a stridently upbeat tone: "Honey, you *hate* campaigning. The last one I practically had to throw grappling hooks around you to get you out there with me. Think of it as a gift. How many political wives would kill to have a surrogate like Ramona to do all the heavy lifting? Listen, baby, I gotta go. I'm speaking to the NRA convention. You don't want to keep *them* waiting. No, no. Armed to the teeth! Ha-ha. Call you first chance I get. Oh, hey, by the way, use the Secret Service guys for whatever, picking up the dry cleaning, shopping. Nice benny, huh? Bye, honey. Love ya. Kiss the grandkids for me."

Dexter tossed the cell phone to an aide before it could ring again. *Minefield ahead,* he thought as he made his way toward the podium, inside a phalanx of aides and Secret Service agents, *and nothing to do with the U.S.-Mexican border.* But now, hearing the ambient sound of the 2,000 members of the National Rifle Association waiting for him to take the stage, he felt the sugar-rush of adrenaline in his veins. *Concentrate,* he told himself, *con-cen-trate. Let's just get this football into the end zone,* then *deal with the collateral stuff.* Maybe he'd been a little . . . yes . . . *incautious* with Ramona, promising her . . . *but, my God, what a fox. Could get tricky. . . . Well, she'd understand. Sure. Give her a nice—an ambassadorship! Perfect. Maybe even Mexico. She'd mollified some of the angrier Hispanics over the border-mining. . . . Yes, came in handy here . . . giving those interviews where she said she didn't really agree with me on it. Yes. Mexico. Or Nicaragua, or one of those places. Okay, Dex. Concentrate. Con-cen-trate. NRA. Jesus, wait a minute. . . . Texas. Texas is voting on the term limit amendment tomorrow.* Huge *gun state. THE gun state. Wonderful. And they've got me speaking to the NRA today? Great scheduling, guys. Okay. Concentrate. Guns. We like guns. They're so . . . American. But let's all agree, we have to be careful with guns. That little incident at the mall in Orlando . . . the media's calling it a massacre, that may be putting it a bit strongly, but okay, maybe a* little *more diligence on the background checks would be in order? The guy* had *spent the last six years in a psychiatric lockup ward. Should he really be able to buy a gun like that? I'll have a Big Mac, large fries, and a .38 caliber to go. Well, there are two sides to every issue. But the larger issue is . . . guns don't kill people. . . . Bullets kill people. . . . Yes. Without the bullets . . . Well, if you really want to get down to it,* people *kill people. Is it the fault of the guns, or the people aiming the . . . Right. Why don't we just ban* people *while we're at it?*

"Ladies and gentlemen, you've known him as Senator Dexter Mitchell, Chairman of the Senate Judiciary Committee. You've known him as President Mitchell Lovestorm of the hit series *POTUS*. Soon, you'll know him as President of the United States. Will you please welcome . . ."

Love this part.

Someone in the audience shouted, "Send in the *Nimitz!*"

You got it, pal.

PEPPER WAS IN HER CHAMBERS, GLUMLY watching television. Watching daytime TV was not the normal routine for a Supreme Court justice, but this did actually qualify as "must-see TV." She was following the voting in the Texas legislature.

Texas had cannily delayed its vote on the term limit amendment so that it would be the state that ratified it. Pepper's already keen interest in the voting was heightened by the fact that in the interim since she and JJ had stopped speaking over her *Swayle* vote, he'd been appointed to the state senate there by the governor—to fill out the term of a senator whose trucking company had been caught smuggling Mexicans over the border.

Much as the imminent passage of the Presidential Term Limit Amendment made for superheated discussion on the talk shows, the country was becoming alert to the possibility of an impending conundrum, namely: what if the amendment were ratified *and* President Vanderdamp won reelection? Could he—legally—take office?

That discussion now moved to the nation's front burner. Panels of experts and scholars were duly convened; also, panels of people who didn't really know much about it but who sounded as though they did.

One (actual) leading constitutional scholar wrote a much-discussed article for the Op-Ed page of the *New York Times,*

concluding that such an eventuality "might well prove insoluble—
the Perfect Constitutional Storm."

He wrote:

> The U.S. Constitution makes no provision for
> such an unprecedented, indeed, grotesque out-
> come. But nor should the Founders be held to ac-
> count for the persistent and adamant incontinence
> of the American people who, as always, want to
> have everything both ways: lower taxes and more
> government services; less reliance on foreign oil,
> and no domestic drilling; free health care, defined
> as someone else paying for it; reduced emissions,
> and enormous cars; wind power, but no windmills
> in our own backyards; a ban on waterboarding
> terrorists, but no terrorism; strict border controls,
> but we'll still need Manuel and Yolanda to mow
> the lawn and take care of the kids for $5 an hour
> and *(lo siento)* no benefits; and so on, ad nauseam
> and ad adsurdam. Meanwhile let us hope, let us,
> indeed, pray, that the state legislatures and the
> national electorate do not paint us into a corner
> from which escape is far from certain, and very
> certainly, messy.

Pepper perused these words while simultaneously watching
the voting in Austin. She was suddenly seized with a stomachache, for she understood, more acutely perhaps than anyone else
in the entire country, that this dilemma, this about-to-be-dead
mouse on the national living room floor, was going to end up
right here in the marble palace on her lap.

It was at this moment, as she sat clutching her cramped
tummy and watching C-SPAN (FOR: 43, AGAINST: 21) that her

secretary buzzed to say that her three o'clock appointment was here.

Presently the door opened, admitting two agents, the director of the Washington field office and—my, my—the assistant deputy director of the FBI. His presence, Pepper surmised, was a gesture of respect. This was after all, the Honorable, the Supreme Court.

The pleasantries made, coffee offered and politely declined, Pepper said, "With all respect, asking the FBI to become involved in all this—it wasn't my idea. I'd just as soon soak it up and move on."

The ADD nodded. "Understood and appreciated, Justice. But Chief Justice Hardwether officially requested that we become involved, so the train has left the station."

"Okay, then," Pepper said with a side-glance at the TV (FOR: 51, AGAINST: 25). "So, what can I do for you?"

One of the agents said, "Is there anyone here at the Court who might have some motive to embarrass you?"

Pepper smiled. "Yes. Everyone, more or less."

The agent nodded blankly.

"You read the papers," Pepper said. "It's no secret I'm a bit of a"—she almost said *catty whompus*—"kind of a polarizing figure here. In a divided Court, I might just be the only thing everyone agrees on."

"Have you had difficult relations with anyone in particular?"

Pepper said, "Not to sound rude, but that's really none of your business."

The agentry exchanged glances. "We're only trying to—"

"Boys," Pepper smiled, "I've been hanging around lawmen since I was in diapers. I know exactly what you're 'only trying to do.' And you can cut it out. I'm not going there with you. Now, was there anything else? I've got a heap of work to do."

The agents stared at her TV screen. "It's the Texas vote," she said. "Not Oprah."

The ADD said, "I appreciate what you're saying. Could I ask a direct question?"

"You can *ask*."

"Do you have any reason to believe that this leak might have originated within Justice Santamaria's chambers?"

"None whatsoever," Pepper said evenly. "Justice Santamaria is a man of integrity, honor, and reputation."

The ADD stared. "But you and he have had, I understand, a difficult relationship?"

"We're colleagues. Colleagues agree on things and disagree on things. We have had good, frank, vigorous exchanges on matters of law that sound, why, right out of Plato's *Republic*. Now come on, gents. This is a fishing trip. You're throwing out chum and it's smellin' up my chambers. Look—I don't know who leaked the damn thing and I don't give a damn. I got enough things on my desk to give me ulcers into the next millennium. I know you're doing your job, and I've got nothing but appreciation for that and nothing but respect for the FBI. But now, shoo. That's all I got to say other than good day to you."

The FBI rose. "Thank you for your time, Justice Cartwright."

"You're welcome. Thank you for *your* time, sir."

One of the agents hung back as the other left, and said, "Ma'am?"

"Yes?" Pepper said warily, this being when the detective typically says, *I was just wondering about that bloodstain on the carpet and this dented silver candlestick on your mantel. . . .*

"Just wanted to say, *Courtroom Six* was my all-time favorite show. Aces. Just aces."

Pepper said, "Well, thank you, Agent . . ."

"Lodato. Joe."

"Thank you, Agent Lodato."

He closed the door. Pepper looked over at the TV. FOR: 66, AGAINST 32. MEASURE APPROVED.

Well, she thought, Vanderdamp was still almost ten points behind Dexter. Maybe the situation would . . . self-clean. But the thought didn't do anything to help her stomachache.

PRESIDENT VANDERDAMP had insisted on spending election night at his home in Wapakoneta, where, indeed, he hoped to be spending the next four years and the four after that, verily unto the end of time.

Charley had informed him, "It's going to be a long night." The election was "too close to call." Pollsters, having called the last three presidential elections erroneously, were being uncharacteristically demure and refusing to predict the night's outcome other than to say it was going to be "a real nail-biter."

The President had told his doleful campaign manager, "I go to bed at ten most nights, Charley. Tonight will be no different." He had written out his concession speech, congratulating "President-elect Mitchell" on his victory and promising "the best transition in history." It had fallen to the speechwriter to draft an acceptance speech that *someone* would have to read if victory came after ten p.m. The speechwriter, morose over his principal's defiant hopes of losing, had typed the words, "Free at last. Free at last. Thank God Almighty, I am free at last," then deleted them in favor of some boilerplate about "a new beginning."

THE LAST WEEKS of the campaign had been peculiar even by American political standards. The ratification of the Twenty-eighth Amendment, limiting U.S. presidents to a single four-year term, had had the perverse—or inverse—effect of creating sympathy for President Vanderdamp. The day following the vote in Texas, Vanderdamp's poll numbers spiked to within two points of Dexter's.

This put the Mitchell campaign in the awkward position of having to say that even if President Vanderdamp *did* win, he would not be able legally to take office. The implicit message being: *So you might as well vote for us.* The trouble was, *So you might as well vote for us* is not the clarion cry the American political ear craves.

And so, that first Tuesday in November, an anxious nation took a deep breath, went to the polls, stared at the levers, check boxes, and chads, scratched its head and went, *Gee whiz.* . . .

FORMER SENATOR MITCHELL spent election night on the set of *POTUS*, with—as it were—both his First Ladies, Ramona and Terry. The two ladies had effected a temporary truce but looked as though they might, at any moment, go for each other's jugular with drawn nail files. This improbable yet iconic trio made for irresistible photo-opera. One TV commentator said it took President Clinton's 1992 quip —elect one, get one free—to "the next level."

President Vanderdamp, true to his word and athwart the implorings and protestations of his campaign staff, thanked everyone and went to bed shortly after ten o'clock. It was a testament to the man's peace of mind and strength of character that he actually fell asleep by eleven; as well as testament to the sleeping pill he took. He did not bother to notify his military aide to alert the Joint Chiefs of Staff to the commander in chief's somnambulance.

Shortly after one a.m., the President was awakened by the First Lady, gently nudging his shoulder.

"Um?"

"Donald?"

He knew—knew right away from the look on Matilda's face.

"I'm so sorry, honey," she said.

Donald Vanderdamp took another sleeping pill. Let the enemy attack. At this point, Armageddon would be a mercy.

CHAPTER 28

VANDERDAMP NARROWLY WINS REELECTION; POTENTIAL CHAOS OVER TERM-LIMIT AMENDMENT; *SUPREME COURT INTERVENTION SEEN AS 'INEVITABLE'*

President-unelect (as he was being rudely called in quarters of the blogosphere) Dexter Mitchell surveyed his options.

The important thing, he knew, was *Do not concede defeat.* As Winston Churchill had said, "Never, never, *ever* give in." Now that he had a mantra, he needed a strategy. Bussie Scrump said it was vital to keep his face out there in public, so Dexter, flailing, was trotted out for a press conference the day after the election. Adamant though he might be that he was the legitimate heir to the presidency, he decided not to start naming his new cabinet quite yet. Anyway, the press was interested in other aspects.

"Senator, are you planning to sue?"

Good question. But—whom, exactly?

"No. I mean . . . we're not . . . we're examining all aspects of

236 | christopher buckley

it. We're all . . . Look, everyone's doing their best . . . it's a confusing situation. Yes. Yes. But I've—"

"Senator, is it true that you've hired Blyster Forkmorgan?"

"No, no. No. Well, we've . . . there have been discussions but no—"

"Reuters reported ten minutes ago that you've hired him to fight your case."

"My case doesn't need fighting. Look, it's quite clear that President Vanderdamp is constitutionally prohibited from taking office next January. I don't need Mr. Forkmorgan to make that point."

"Then why have you hired him?"

"That's as far as I'll characterize it for the time being. Look, he's an authority on this sort of . . . a distinguished legal mind. Yes. Very distinguished. Why *wouldn't* I want to consult with him?"

Why not indeed? Blyster Forkmorgan, Esquire, was to the Washington legal establishment what the tiger shark is to the aquatic kingdom. The mere announcement by a corporation that it had hired (the ironically nicknamed) "Bliss" Forkmorgan was often enough to scare off a litigant, or even the Justice Department. He'd clerked at the Supreme Court (for Earl Warren), been state prosecutor, U.S. Attorney, U.S. Solicitor General, and Attorney General. In recent decades, he had been in hyper-lucrative private practice, occasionally lured forth to act as special prosecutor, an announcement generally made to the rumble of kettledrums. Over the years he had brought down: a vice president, twelve cabinet members, two governors, eighteen congressmen, four senators, fourteen Mafia dons, and twenty-eight CEOs. Federal penitentiaries teemed with his successes. He'd argued sixty-six cases before the Supreme Court and won fifty-four of them. He was the Man to See, if you could afford the $2,500 per hour fee.

If Dexter's answers at the press conference were ambiguous,

so, at this point, was everything. Even the Secret Service was at a loss whether to withdraw Dexter's protection, now that he had, technically, lost the election. President Vanderdamp quietly and graciously gave orders for it to be continued until the situation clarified. To that end, Hayden Cork picked up the phone the moment Ohio put its favorite son over the top on Election Night and, his voice barely above a croak, whispered, "Mr. Clenndennynn, please." Graydon, ensconced aboard the private 757 of the emir of Wasabia, had already heard the news and had instructed the pilot to turn around and fly back to the U.S.

His arrival at the White House was impossible to keep secret. It triggered a thousand camera shutters. A virtual computer game of questionable taste appeared on the Internet casting Clenndennynn ("White Knight") and Blyster Forkmorgan ("Dark Knight") in "Supreme Conflict." The White House press secretary calmly noted that Mr. Clenndennynn was a "trusted adviser" and that it was "perfectly natural" that he should "provide counsel at this"—she groped for the blandest possible word—"juncture." "Crisis" might have been more apt, technically. The country was in an uproar. The stock market had plunged nearly 2,000 points in three days, forcing a trading halt. When it reopened the next day, the bell was rung by the U.S. Vice President, a neutral enough entity, who gave a cheery little speech about "continuity," whereupon the market plunged another 700 points. Alarmingly, military blogs hinted that "various elements in the Pentagon" were "unhappy" about the developments.

"Hell of a mess, Donald," Graydon said, looking pale and hunched. He uncharacteristically waved away the offer of a martini. "*Hell* of a mess." He slumped into the fauteuil, looking for the first time—old.

"I wasn't trying to win," the President said defensively, holding his untouched and warming beer. "But there's no point wailing and gnashing our teeth and rending the garments. The question is where do we go from here?"

"I haven't the foggiest idea," Clenndennynn said. "We're in uncharted waters. You have a predilection for steering us into them. How *did* you manage in the navy?"

"We had radar."

"Well, it's going to take more than radar. He's hired Bliss Forkmorgan," Clenndennynn said.

"Do we know that?"

"Bliss called me in the car ten minutes ago," Clenndennynn said, wiping his brow.

"Oh. So it's on."

"Yes. It's on. Battle stations, gentlemen."

"I don't want a battle," the President moaned. "I just want to go home."

"Well, you should have thought about that before, shouldn't you have?" Graydon said irritably.

"Don't hand me that. You were the one who kept pressing me to run."

"And you did and now you've won. You did it for the *principle* of the thing. So now you can feel wonderful. Just don't look out the window, because the country is on fire over *your principle*. Meanwhile, once again, it's landed in my lap. Graydon Clenndennynn, presidential cleaner-upper. Every time you make a muck of things, I have to go forward to the cockpit and tell the pilot, 'Never mind, turn around, back to Washington. President Vanderdamp has made another gigantic caca. For the *principle*.'"

"Oh? Oh? Well, at least I *have* principles. I apologize if I'm keeping the chairman of the Graydon Clenndennynn Influence Peddling Corporation—an *offshore* corporation, I might add—from making another squintillion dollars for—"

"Will you both, please, just . . . *shut . . . up.*"

The President of the United States and Graydon Clennden-nynn fell instantly silent. They turned, stared at Hayden Cork, speaker of the harsh, imperative, unaccustomed syllables.

"I beg your pardon?" the President said.

"Sorry," Hayden said. "But shall we move on, or are you two going to bellow at each like a pair of old water buffalo?"

"I think I will have that martini," Clenndennynn said, mopping his forehead.

THE PROSPECT that *Mitchell v. Vanderdamp* or *Vanderdamp v. Mitchell* or *The People v. The U.S. Constitution* or whatever this judicial Frankenstein called itself was going to end up at the Court worked an eerie calm on the three hundred or so inhabitants of the marble palace.

A cloistral hush descended on the place. No one spoke in the corridors. The cafeteria was a funeral parlor. Even passersby on the sidewalk outside the building whispered, shot nervous sideways glances, and quickened their steps. Every hour brought another television satellite truck. Gradually, the building took on the look of an ancient, marmoreal Ground Zero—a temple in which furious gods were preparing to vie. Such was the atmosphere one afternoon when Pepper answered her cell phone, the very private one whose number was known only to a handful.

"Justice Cartwright?"

The voice sounded vaguely familiar, immediately annoying Pepper that it should be coming over this phone.

"Who is this?"

"Joe Lodato, ma'am. FBI. We met—that day, in your office? We spoke just as I was leaving?"

"How did you get this number?"

Soft chuckle. Was he laughing? Pepper felt her face reddening.

"No disrespect, ma'am. It's just a funny question to ask the FBI."

"What do you want?"

"I was wondering if I might see you. Off premises."

"Is this a professional matter?"

Another chuckle. "Ma'am, I may not be the smartest person at the Bureau, but I'm not stupid enough to hit on a Supreme Court justice."

"Why off campus?"

"This must be a tense time at the Court. Who needs a knuckle-dragger prowling the halls, right? There's a place on Capitol Hill called the Pork Barrel, it's . . ."

"I know it."

THEY SAT IN A BACK BOOTH and ordered coffee.

"I know this is sensitive for you," he began apologetically.

"Agent Lodato," Pepper said. "I can handle it. Now you've got me in a lobbyist bar at four o'clock on a school day. What's up?"

Agent Lodato produced a piece of paper that she immediately recognized as a page from her *Swayle* opinion, annotated.

Agent Lodato pointed to a spot on the page. Pepper saw the words—words that she herself had typed in block letters: "KISS MY ASS."

She froze. "No," she said. "No. Hold on. Something's wrong here. I *deleted* that."

Agent Lodato pointed to the lower right-hand of the page. "Do you recognize those initials and that handwriting?"

Pepper looked. "IH." Ishiguro Haro. The date was next to it.

"I'm told he initials every document he reads and dates it."

"I don't understand this," Pepper said. "I did write that, but

I deleted it." Her mind raced. "He'd sent me his comments on my *Peester* opinion. I thought they were a little patronizing and I got a little frosted and . . . I typed this. But then I went to the gym to cool off and came back and I deleted 'KISS MY ASS' and typed in . . ."

Agent Lodato was nodding metronomically.

". . . and typed in something like, OKAY, THANK YOU, GOT IT, GOOD POINT, OKAY, FAIR ENOUGH, and . . ." Pepper's voice trailed off. She looked at Lodato. "Aw, *shit*."

"Happens all the time," Agent Lodato shrugged. "You think you're closing a file. Instead you're hitting SEND and the next thing you know . . . I could tell you stories."

Pepper's heart was pounding. "How did you *get* this?"

"Ma'am," he smiled. "I'm an FBI agent. It's what I do."

"But you can't just . . . It's the Supreme Court."

"Off the record, Justice Haro appears not to be too popular among his own clerks."

"Well, okay," Pepper said, "but what does this prove?"

Agent Lodato took another piece of paper from his inside pocket, unfolded that, and laid it out in front of Pepper. It looked like a cell phone bill. One line had been yellow highlighted.

"This is a cell phone bill for someone named Aurora Fonacier," he said. "This number here that's highlighted, that's a cell phone belonging to a reporter at the *Washington Times* newspaper—the one who wrote the unsigned *Swayle* item in the paper. The article wasn't bylined so as to protect him from a subpoena, though I understand the AG is considering subpoenaing the editor and publisher and chairman of the board. See the date of this call? That's the day after Justice Haro read and initialed your 'kiss my' . . . rear-end comment note."

"Who's Aurora Fonacier?"

"Justice Haro's housekeeper."

Pepper stared.

"Filipino lady. Very nice person, from what I gather. Not a huge English speaker. Quiet worker. So you have to wonder what she's doing engaging in a twenty-two-minute phone call with a Supreme Court reporter for the *Washington Times.*"

Pepper slumped into the hard wooden back of the booth. After a moment or two she said, "What are you going to do with this?"

"Well, ma'am, I thought I'd ask you that."

"Who knows about this?"

"As of this moment, you and I."

"Aren't you required to share this?"

Agent Lodato smiled. "Yes, ma'am. However, you being a justice of the U.S. Supreme Court, I thought it would be permissible to exercise initiative. They like it when we do that. Up to a point. I appreciate that it comes at what seems to be shaping up as a challenging time for everyone at the Court. So," he slid the two pieces of paper toward Pepper, "that being the case, I thought I'd present this to *Courtroom Six.*" He stood. "I always liked the way Judge Cartwright handled things. To be honest, I'm not so sure about Justice Cartwright, especially after that *Swayle* vote. . . ." He let out a little whistle of amazement. "But I thought I'd take a chance on her. Thank you for your time, ma'am."

IF BLYSTER FORKMORGAN had imagined that he would be contending against the other gods of the bar in the rarified atmosphere at the summits of Olympus, he now found himself instead tramping about hip-deep in sheep turd and mud at its base. It was not exactly what Dexter Mitchell's plangent phone call to him at four a.m. on Election Night had promised.

His client sat across from him, crossing and uncrossing his legs, nervous, sweating, pallid.

"I never explicitly told her," Dexter jibbered, "at least I'm virtually sure I never . . . in so many words . . . Hell, I can't remember everything I said to everyone . . . every promise made to every group. . . ."

Forkmorgan stared through lidded eyes, a falcon watching a mole scrabbling across a field below.

He poured ice water into a cut crystal glass and handed it to Dexter, who took it and drank, as if more out of obedience than thirst.

"Campaigns," Forkmorgan ventured soothingly, "are promise-rich environments. The relevant question here is—did you in fact tell Ms. Alvilar that you were going to leave your wife and marry her?"

"No. No, no. No. Well . . . *aack.*" Dexter sighed. "Maybe . . . I don't . . . in the middle of . . . I . . . Look, you say things in the middle of . . . It just comes . . . out. . . . It doesn't necessarily *mean* anything. . . ."

To recap, then: you told your TV wife, probably during sexual intercourse in the midst of a presidential campaign, that you would divorce your actual wife in order to marry her and make her First Lady of the United States.

"Well," Forkmorgan said, "these things happen."

"Yes. Yes, they do. Yes," Dexter said. "She's, of course, *Latina.* . . ."

Forkmorgan raised one eyebrow questioningly.

"Emotionally they're, you know, all over the place. *Voluble.*"

Forkmorgan nodded. "They lack our Anglo-Saxon sense of reticence and decorum?"

Dexter frowned. "Something like that," he said uncertainly. "I explained to her, I said, 'Look, Ramona, for God's sake . . . now is not the time to worry about that. Let's take it step by step, okay?' What am I supposed to do—announce in the middle of a Supreme Court case that I'm tossing Terry over the side?"

"And how did she respond to that argument?"

"By going totally fucking bat-shit. By threatening to go public." Dexter shook his head at the iniquity of it all. "That's when she told me she had me on tape."

Blyster Forkmorgan's eyes widened. "*Does* she have you on tape?"

"*I* don't know," Dexter said. "I was in the middle of a *campaign*, for God's sake."

"Yes," Forkmorgan said, "I can see your mind might have been on . . . other things. Well, let's ascertain whether such a tape exists." He made a note on a pad. "Now, as to your wife. How do things stand with her at this point?"

Dexter sighed manfully once more at the unjustness of female wiles. "Terry? Well, now *she's* gone bat-shit. On the other hand, she's not some jalapeño like Ramona. She's bat-shit, but logical. She understands that there's no point in grabbing the wheel of this bus and driving it off the cliff."

"Have you told her that you are *not* going to divorce her in order to marry Ms. Alvilar?"

"In so many words."

"Tell me the actual words you used."

"I told her, 'Don't worry about it. We need to stick together here. Team Mitchell. *Team Mitchell.*'"

Forkmorgan nodded. "And did she give you reason to understand that she is in fact *on* Team Mitchell?"

Dexter shrugged. "Well, she was running kind of hot when we last spoke. But she wants to be First Lady, so she's not likely to do anything to screw that up."

"No," Forkmorgan said. "That would appear to be more on Ms. Alvilar's agenda."

"I was thinking," Dexter said, sounding suddenly the politician, "we could offer Ramona a nice ambassadorship. Somewhere warm, Spanish-speaking. She'd be a hero down there.

A queen. The Hispanics loved it when she disagreed with me about mining the border. . . ."

Forkmorgan shook his head. "No, I think we've made enough promises to Ms. Alvilar for the time being. Not to mention it would be illegal."

"I wasn't suggesting it was a perfect solution," Dexter sniffed.

CHAPTER 29

"Dear me, dear heavens, dear . . . *dear,*" Crispus said heavily after Pepper had recounted Agent Lodato's discovery. His eyeballs flickered side to side. "Why do you bring this fifty-five-gallon drumful of squirming worms to *me?*"

"Who else am I going to tell?" Pepper said.

"Who else? Who *else?* How about your boyfriend, for one? The Chief Justice. He's the one who called down the thunder in the first place. Why don't you tell him? Why is this my business? Re-*cu-use* me."

"I can't tell him," Pepper said.

"Why not?"

"He might *do* something about it. Something . . . injudicious."

"Whereas I'm just going to rub my fevered brow and ululate?"

"Look, Crispy, help me out here. What do I do?"

"Well, I wouldn't be hitting any more SEND buttons."

"Thank you. That's so helpful."

"Don't get your knickers in a twist." Crispus frowned and drummed his fingers on the surface of his desk. "What would Hammurabi do?"

"Cut off everyone's head, and call it a day. Is *that* your advice?"

"Let's just call it option B for now." He looked at her with what decoded for Pepper as a mixture of regret and rebuke. This made her, for the first time, think back on Mike Haro's awkward moment in her chambers, when he'd extended a tentative invitation to come on down to his wine cellar. It came rushing in on her in one, unwelcome wave, that whatever other talents she possessed, men was not one of them. Had she not, after all, accepted a marriage proposal prompted by the launch of a TV show? She stared back at Crispus, thinking, *Not you, too?* He was saying something to her.

"This seems as good a time as any to ask you, was it the best possible judgment, leaping into the sleeping bag with the Chief?"

"I didn't 'leap' into a sleeping bag with him. But okay. I stipulate maybe 'judgment' isn't the right word, either. Look, Crispy, these things happen."

"'These things happen' is, perhaps," Crispus said, "the biggest intellectual and philosophical cop-out since Pontius Pilate washed his hands."

"But practical, you have to admit."

"Oh—urrr."

"What was that?"

"*That* was a groan. They happen. Well," he sighed, "the Rubicon appears to have been crossed. And peed into."

"Stipulated."

"What would the Chief be likely to do if he found out about this unfortunate information? Leaving aside your computer skills, it doesn't appear to speak well of Brother Haro. On the other hand, he was under the understandable impression that you had petulantly instructed him to kiss your *behind*, which he doubtlessly viewed as poor recompense for having gone to the trouble of finding justification for your—may I say—deplorable vote in *Peester*."

"I don't give a church mouse fart about that. I understand why he was so pissed off. I don't think justices ought to be leaking all over each other, but I understand why he did it. Over and out. It's where we go from here. Chiefy'll go nuclear if he finds out what the FBI found out. He takes that kind of thing very seriously. He's an ethics wonk."

Crispus considered. "Well, I imagine the first thing he'll do is confront Brother Haro." He held up the incriminating pieces of paper and said, "I must say, I would dearly love to watch him try to explain *these* away. Thing is, he's so damn smart, he probably could. All right, so you present these to the Chief, the Chief goes through the ceiling like a helicopter, confronts the Last Samurai, and all this while a very large freight train is approaching our station." He looked at Pepper. "You have to ask yourself: is this, as your Mr. Shakespeare would say, a consummation devoutly to be wished?"

Pepper stared. She took the two pieces of paper, folded them, and slowly tore them into small pieces which she dropped into a wastebasket.

"For a moment there," Crispus said, "I thought you were going to make origami."

"Oh, shut up," she said, walking to the door.

"It's been most eventful here since you arrived," he said. "A strange energy seems to have descended upon our little temple and taken roost amid the pediments. You're not by any chance a witch, are you? A succubus, perhaps, sent by the Evil One to bring about the End of Days?"

Pepper shrugged. "I wouldn't rule it out at this point."

Thirty seconds, Mr. President."

"Thank you." For once, the President did not do his vocal exercises.

"Ten seconds . . ."

"Good evening. I . . ."

No further words issued from the presidential orifice. The pause continued, elongated, as everyone in the Oval Office, even the Secret Service agents, exchanged fraught glances. Given the tumult of the preceding days, anything was possible: a nervous breakdown, a stroke . . . ? A technician nervously examined the teleprompter. No malfunction was evident.

Seven seconds went by—an eternity when a U.S. president is going completely blank in front of a live TV audience estimated at a billion people worldwide. The lapse would quickly come to be called Seven Seconds in November.*

". . ."

The President's eyes were looking distantly off to the side, not at the teleprompter.

Hayden Cork, standing off to one side, looked on in something like frozen horror. He wondered, should he summon Dr. Hughes, the presidential physician?

Bringing eternity to a close, the President smiled gently and said, "Let me start over. This is one heck of a situation we find ourselves in, isn't it?"

At this moment, Hayden Cork realized, *God in heaven—he's improvising.*

"And I accept my share of the blame for it," the President was saying, words not found on the teleprompter.

Graydon Clenndennynn nudged Hayden: *What on earth is he doing?*

Hayden gave an exhausted shrug that seemed to say: *I don't know. I have no idea. But I'm going to kill myself after this, so it really doesn't matter.*

---

* A play on the book and film *Seven Days in May*, about an attempted military takeover of the U.S. government, an eventuality that might seem less dire given recent performances by civilian government.

"After the Congress passed this term limit amendment," the President said, "I got angry and decided to run, on the principle that I didn't think it was right to alter the U.S. Constitution just for petty political revenge. I thought a point needed to be made. I did not expect to win. But . . . now, here we are. For whatever reason, you elected me to a second term.

"At the same time, thirty-eight state legislatures ratified the amendment—with, I must say, impressive speed. That amendment, now having the force of law, bars me from taking office for a second term.

"And so we find ourselves in . . . a very American sort of situation. Darned if you do. Darned if you don't. The question is, where do we go from here? Where . . . *do* we go from here?

"Now, in the last few days, I have consulted with a lot of very smart people. Constitutional scholars, experts, professors, former attorney generals—you name 'em, I've probably heard from them. About the only thing they agree on is that it's all scr—it's a confused situation. So the question is how to *un*confuse it. At this point we need a little clarity. Clarity. As much clarity as we can lay our hands on.

"Now, the only other thing that all these wise folks agreed upon was that at this point, it probably makes sense to turn to the institution that was, in some ways, invented for just these situations. . . ."

Pepper, watching on TV, closed her eyes.

The President sighed. "The Supreme Court. It wouldn't be the first time that the highest Court got involved in deciding a presidential election. So it's not as though we haven't been there before.

"But I know, I know, somehow it doesn't seem a satisfactory way to deal with it . . . asking nine people to decide, when

more than a hundred forty million of you took the trouble
to vote.

"So," the President continued, "my inclination was to resign.
To resign the office of President, and go home to . . . Ohio," he
said longingly, "and to turn it over to Vice President Schmidtz,
who would, constitutionally, become President. That, at any
rate, *was* my plan.

"But as it turns out, that would not necessarily solve the
problem. Because when this proposal was made to Senator Mitchell, his representatives indicated that it was not a
satisfactory solution. I imagine you will be hearing from
him directly, but I think it is fair to summarize his position
as follows: he feels that the presidency ought to be his. By
default.

"And so the situation remains unresolved. Or at least not
solved by my saying good-bye and going home.

"So that's where we are as of now, my fellow Americans. I
just wanted to let you know where we stand. And to tell you
that I'm trying to do my best. I really am. But whatever happens,
don't give up on America. It's still a great country. It's just a little
confused at the moment.

"Good night. Sorry to interrupt your TV shows. God bless."

Motherfucker," Dexter said. "Cocksucking motherfucking
cocksucker . . ."

They had watched the President's televised address in a suite
purposefully and strategically situated in the Hay-Adams Hotel,
directly across from the White House. It was Bussie's idea. Send
the signal: *We're here, and we're moving in on January 20. Deal
with it.*

Bussie and Blyster Forkmorgan and the other lieutenantry
of Team Mitchell let the Senator continue with his frothing

expostulations. It reminded some in the room of the possession scenes in the movie *The Exorcist*. At one point it was feared the Senator might put his foot through the television, no doubt an expensive one.

". . . cocksucking . . ."

A few frozen moments after the President had indicated his willingness to resign, Bussie had murmured, "We're fucked, Dex." The language in the war room that night could hardly be called elevated.

Ignoring Dexter's ongoing spasms, Blyster looked over at Bussie and said mildly, "Was it your impression that he was improvising? He didn't seem to me to be reading from a text."

"Whatever it was," Bussie said, "we got problems."

"Yes. But a case, still." He looked at his watch. Right about now a courier would be arriving at the Clerk of the Court's office at the Supreme Court to file the petition for *Mitchell v. Vanderdamp.*

". . . mother*fucking* . . ."

"How long," Blyster said, "does he go on like this?"

"Dex?" Bussie interjected. *"Dex? Senator?"*

"What?" Dexter said in midfoam.

"You want to get back to work? We need to respond. They're waiting on the roof." The television networks had permanent tents on the hotel roof, the White House serving as backdrop; especially apt here.

"Oh, I'll *respond. Cocksucker!"* Dexter glowered at the now-muted TV. An anchorman was talking to a coanchor. Both had moist eyes.

"They're crying! Look at them! *You pussies!* Don't you see? It was an act! That whole fucking thing was an *act!"*

"Perhaps a sedative?" Blyster said to Bussie.

"I need him awake. It's great energy. Just needs harnessing."

"He's putting out enough energy to light Cleveland," Blyster said, rising and putting on his coat. "Well, I have to be in court tomorrow. Bussie?"

"Yeah?"

"Don't let him call the President of the United States a cock-sucker on national television."

Bussie nodded wearily.

CHAPTER 30

S o," Chief Justice Hardwether smiled wryly, "are we granting cert?"

The remark drew a rare collective laugh from the justices around the conference table.

"I'm not going to give a speech," he went on. "But let me just say aloud what is probably on everyone's mind. Back in the sixties—a period some of you actually remember—I was, of course, too young, or too intellectual, to pay attention. . . ."

Another ripple of laughter. Pepper was struck by how relaxed Declan seemed; her own stomach was in knots. She'd lost eight pounds. Maybe there was a book in it: *Supreme Weight Loss?* Declan continued: ". . . the antiwar demonstrators used to chant, 'The whole world's watching' as the police advanced with truncheons."

This elicited a low groan from Justice Santamaria. "Truncheons?"

Declan went on: "All right, nightsticks. Batons. Clubs. Whatever, Silvio. What I am attempting to say is that I promise you all I will do my best. These last few months, I have not given you that, and I apologize to you. You deserved better. This institution deserved better. But as Chief, I have responsibilities, and one of them, it seems to me, is to remind us all that any further leaks, especially pertaining to *Mitchell v. Vanderdamp*, could have a terribly deleterious impact. Disastrous impact. This is the Supreme Court. So," he smiled wanly, "let us act supremely."

"Thank you, Coach Hardwether," Crispus said.

"Anyone want to add anything?" the Chief Justice said.

"Yes," Silvio said with a mischievous look. "I think we should start with a prayer. Why don't *you* lead us, Mo?"

Justice Gotbaum smiled. "I tried prayer, Sil. Prayed for the Skins over Miami.* Looks like God *is* dead, after all."

"Funny, I prayed for Miami," Silvio said. "Won twenty bucks. I'd say God is great."

"That sounds familiar. That's right—it's what they say as they're flying planes into our buildings and stoning women to death. 'God is great.' Knew I'd heard it before. How does it go in the original? *Allahu*—"

"Won't it be nice to have Bliss Forkmorgan back with us," Paige Plympton interjected before Silvio's and Mo's badinage escalated, as it usually did, into full-blown jihad.

"He's got his work cut out for him," Justice Jacoby said a bit provocatively.

Justice Haro said, "So does Clenndennynn."

"*Okay* then," Declan said, in an cheery but emphatically peremptory tone, "I guess that's it, unless anyone else has anything? Thank you, honorables."

Walking out with Pepper, he whispered, "*Quis* . . ."

"Good luck," Pepper said. "This is gonna be awful."

"I'm not a believer, but I may ask Silvio to pray for me."

"Say, Dec, about the leaks," Pepper said.

"Um?"

"I was wondering—did you ever hear back from the FBI?"

Declan pursed his lips. "Not a peep. Our vaunted Federal

---

* A sports reference, apparently.

Bureau of Investigation seems to have drawn a big fat blank. Disappointing, especially after all that abuse I got from everyone here for requesting an investigation in the first place. You'd think—how hard can it be to . . . Incompetence. Everywhere you turn, these days, *incompetence*."

"I'm sure they did their best," Pepper said, avoiding eye contact.

"Let's hope they're better at catching terrorists. Say, Pep?"

He had an embarrassed, boyish look. "Yes, Dec?"

"I . . ."

"Go on. Not going to bite ya."

"I was thinking . . . until this is over, it might be better if . . ."

"If we don't make violent love to each other?"

"There must have been thirty photographers and reporters outside my apartment this morning. Madness. Who's to say they're not tailing us."

"I understand. This is going to be tough enough."

Declan said sheepishly, "I'm certainly going to miss our . . . our . . . little . . ."

"You're going to miss getting laid, is what you're trying to say."

He blushed. "I didn't mean it that way."

"Yeah, you did." She gave him a chaste peck on the cheek. "I'll try to channel my frustrated lust into oral argument. See you in Court, Chiefy." She said after him, "If you get desperate, come on by my chambers. You can mount up, see if you can stay on for eight seconds and make the whistle."

Pepper had never seen a human being turn that shade of red before. The Chief Justice scuttled off like a frantic crab. She laughed, feeling light, almost flighty, for the first time in a long while. It was short-lived. There was a message waiting for her: "Buddy—please call ASAP."

She waited until "ASAP" no longer applied before return-ing the call. Would she meet him for a drink? He didn't want to discuss it over the phone. He sounded subdued, not at all his blustery, cigar-smoke-blowing self.

"All right," she said. "There's a place called the Pork Barrel." She couldn't resist adding, "You'll feel right at home."

He was waiting for her, in the same booth, oddly, where she had conversed with Agent Lodato. As she slid in opposite, a waiter came over and said merrily, "Justice Cartwright! Good to see you again."

"I see you're a regular," Buddy said when the waiter had gone to get Buddy's beer and Pepper's coffee.

"Yes," Pepper said. "I do all my drinking here. We're all major boozers on the Court."

"You look fantastic."

"Buddy?"

"Yeah?"

"Cut the crap."

He nodded. "Okay."

"What did you want to talk about? I'm a little busy these days."

"Yeah. Boy," he laughed nervously. "Must be some kind of pressure, huh?"

"It is, yes."

"Good luck with it."

"Thank you." She waited for him to get to the point. He didn't. She said, "Is this about our divorce or your breach of con-tract suit? Because if it is, I'm not going to discuss either. It's been so much fun paying someone six-fifty an hour to discuss it with that I've gotten used to it."

He said heavily, as if each word were a cinder block, "I wanted to apologize to you."

Pepper stared.

"Well?" Buddy said.

"Don't quite know what to say. I don't think I've ever heard you say those words all in one sentence."

"I mean it," he said gravely.

"You seem of late, but wherefore I know not, to have lost all your mirth."

"No Shakespeare, Pepper, please, I'm not in the mood."

"What's going on?" She looked at him with sudden concern. "You're not—did you just get a cancer diagnosis or something?"

"No, nothing like that."

"Did you just come here to apologize, or is there some hidden agenda here?"

"Why would there be?"

"Because I know you, Buddy."

"I'm willing to drop the breach of contract suit."

"I told you I'm not going to discuss it."

"I'm also willing to drop the divorce suit."

Pepper looked at him. "What's that supposed to mean?"

"It means I'm prepared to forgive and forget."

"I don't even know how to begin to process that statement," Pepper said after a pause so lengthy it was measurable in geologic time.

"I've done a lot of thinking," Buddy said. "Maybe you have, too."

"Not really. I've been too busy to think."

"That's good. That would be a good line."

"For what?"

"I don't know, if we ever did another show, say."

"Buddy," Pepper laughed, "do you have any idea how transparent you are? A doctor wouldn't even have to give you a CAT scan."

"Okay, maybe I reacted perhaps not perfectly."

"*That's* a good line. 'Maybe I reacted perhaps not perfectly.' Are you sure you didn't study law? Talk to me, Bud man. What are you trying to say to me?"

"I want you back, Pep."

Pepper stared. "Why? It's not a trick question. You never really wanted me in the first place. Marrying me was just a way of sealing the business deal."

"No way."

Pepper reached across the table and took his hands and held his wrists with her thumbs and forefingers. "Look into my eyes and tell me that you loved me. I mean, *loved* me."

"Sure I did."

Pepper released his wrists. She laughed. "That was a home-made lie detector test, darling, and *boy* did you flunk."

"I'll learn. Whatever. I want you back."

"No, you don't, baby. I think—and this isn't a criticism, honest, we're past that—but I think the only way you can *be* real is on TV. I don't think reality measures up for you as well as whatever's on a fifty-two-inch plasma-gel screen at eight o'clock on Monday nights. What's the matter?"

"That's a horrible thought."

"Maybe. But I figured it out the night you locked me out of our apartment. Which, by the way, wasn't very nice."

"It wasn't 'very nice' of you to sic the FBI on me."

"We've been through that, Buddy."

"Well, let's go through it again."

"What would that accomplish, other than mutual annoyance?"

"Objection. Evasion."

"Honestly, I don't care whether you believe me or not. But it remains a fact. I've got to go, baby. I'm in the middle of a constitutional crisis. This job," she smiled. "Remind me—why *did* I take it?"

"Don't look at me."

Pepper stood. Buddy said, "I'm still dropping the breach of contract suit."

"Your call." Pepper shrugged. "But I think we might as well see the other one through." She held out her hand. "Either way, I'd still like to go on calling you buddy."

Buddy looked at her for a moment, smiled, said, "Motion granted," and took her hand.

As she headed off, he said after her, "Hey, Pep?"

She turned. "Um?"

"*Supreme Court*. Make a hell of a show."

" 'Nine old farts sending footnotes to each other'? I don't know," Pepper said. "Sounds kind of dull to me."

CHAPTER 31

"Are you sure you're up to this?" President Vanderdamp said.

The thin, wintry morning light was slanting through the French windows into the Oval Office. Graydon was on his way to the Court for oral argument in *Mitchell v. Vanderdamp*. He looked to the President quite splendid in his London suit, but Vanderdamp saw traces of exhaustion in the old man's face. The eyes, normally vivid blue, seemed pale and watery. He had a stoop and dabbed at his nose with a monogrammed handkerchief.

"No, I'm not," Graydon said, "but it's too late now. *Alea jacta est.*"*

The President smiled. "Save the Latin for them. You may need it."

"I was trying to think when I last argued up there, and it took that story in the *Post* today to remind me. 'Clenndennynn's Last Stand.' I'd have preferred 'The Return of the King' or something more Augustan. Less *Custerish*, at any rate. Well, I need to review my notes and put something in my stomach. Do you know—unpleasant but not unrelevant detail—the first time

---

* Still more Latin. "The die is cast." What Caesar reportedly said after crossing the Rubicon.

I argued, I threw up. Not *during* argument—thank God. Well, Donald, aren't you going to wish me luck?"

"I'm not sure," the President said. "Do we really *want* to win this one?"

"I feel your conundrum. But the prospect of the Republic falling into Dexter Mitchell's hands?"

"Good luck."

"Did you see in the paper," Graydon said, "about that woman, Señorita Cha-Cha or whatever her name is? What *could* he have been thinking? Rather good timing from our perspective. But yes, I think we do want to win this one and keep Dexter Mitchell's mitts off an actual nuclear button."

"Thank you, old friend."

"Not at all. Not at all. It's been an honor to clean up after your messes. If you *do* get another term, promise you won't call me."

I T HAD NOT BEEN A GOOD WEEK, PR-wise, for Team Mitchell. Ramona, despite silky handling by Blyster Forkmorgan, had correctly smelled a *raton**** and, making good on her threat, had ventilated her grievance on national television.

"Ramona," said the interviewer, "is it true Dexter Mitchell asked you to marry him?"

"*Many* times," Ramona said, looking suspiciously chaste in a Marc Jacobs that looked like it might have been designed as a convent school graduation dress. "*Many* times. The first time, after he win the Iowa cow-kus . . ."

"Iowa caucus?"

"That. Then after the New Hampshire primary. And the South Carolina primary. Every time he wins a primary, he says

---

* Spanish: rat.

to me, 'Ramona, I am divorcing my wife to make you Primera Dama.'"

"First Lady. The role you played so memorably on *POTUS?*"

Ramona dabbed at her eyes with a tissue—a beautiful television moment.

"Ramona, I have to ask you—why are you telling us this now?"

"Because Dexter Mitchell is a *horrible* person and he should *never* be President of the United States. I love this country too much. You know?"

D EXTER WATCHED the grotesque spectacle with his eyes closed, in the company of a somewhat somber Team Mitchell at the Hay-Adams suite which, though on the eighth floor, had of late taken on the feel of a subterranean war-bunker.

Ramona's lurid revelations did nothing to enhance Dexter's postelection ratings, which had been in free fall following President Vanderdamp's public offer to resign—his Finest Hour, it was being called, to Dexter's great vexation. But *Mitchell v. Vanderdamp* having been granted cert, Dexter went before the cameras and manfully announced his intention to see it through, that being, as he put it somewhat opaquely, "the only honorable course." Blyster Forkmorgan, his warrior instincts aroused, and Ms. Alvilar's claims of affection—*or* alienation—being extraneous to his client's arguments, nodded, strapped on buckler and sword, mounted, and rode to battle.

O YEZ! OYEZ! OYEZ! . . ."

"It just came to me," Crispus whispered to Pepper as they filed in, "it's Old French for *oy vey.*"

Any other day, Pepper might have giggled. Not today. She was too nervous.

Taking her seat at the bench, Pepper, trying to appear calm and collected, briefly let her eyes wander over the assembled. She and Graydon's eyes instantly locked. It was the first time she had ever viewed him from above. He looked small but formidable; peregrine-nosed, impeccable in three-piece suit and gold watch chain. He gave her the briefest smile and nod. Pepper glanced over and got her first live look at the famous Blyster Forkmorgan: grave, knife-lean, eyes like beads of mercury.

Mitchell v. Vanderdamp boiled down to two arguments, the first technical, the second more philosophical. The first was that President Vanderdamp's election was invalid because the term limit amendment took legal effect the moment it was ratified by Texas, two days before the election. Mitchell's second argument centered on the larger issue of governance, that is, whether the Court should recognize a validly adopted amendment, or the People's decision in the election. Forkmorgan's brief asserted that the validly adopted amendment took precedence over "metaphysical, however admirably intentioned, considerations," i.e., the will of the people as expressed in the popular vote.

Chief Justice Hardwether managed to make the preliminaries sound so mundane it might have been another routine day in traffic court. (Which was, indeed, his intention.) And began.

"Mr. Forkmorgan, in your brief, you make two separate arguments." He smiled. "Does that signify that one argument is stronger than the other? Or are you just piling on?"

"Either argument should be sufficient to carry the day, Mr. Chief Justice," Forkmorgan said. "As to 'piling on,' perhaps I am attempting to overwhelm the Court with a veritable feast of reason."

A ripple of laughter went through the Great Hall: the sound of hundreds of buttock cheeks unclenching.

"Which argument do *you* find more compelling?" the Chief Justice asked.

"Ah, you lay an elegant trap for me," Forkmorgan replied. "Both arguments are equally compelling, albeit admittedly distinct in terms of texture. Call it juridical dimity."

Dimity? Pepper thought. *What in hell is dimity?**

"It seems clear enough to me," Justice Santamaria said in a gruff, enough-already tone, "that you're putting most of your eggs in the *Dillon v. Gloss* basket. Or am I missing something here?"

"I doubt very much that you've ever missed anything, Justice Santamaria," Forkmorgan said.

"I was being sardonic."

Laughter.

"We cite *Dillon* for a very straightforward reason. There, the Court, construing the Eighteenth Amendment—Prohibition—found that the critical date was the date of ratification, not the date of certification by the Secretary of State. It goes without saying that certification takes place *after* any election. At the time, of course, the statute vested certification authority in the Secretary of State, rather than—as now—in the National Archivist."

"Isn't that a somewhat narrow interpretation?"

"Even if certification—and not ratification—were the key determinative moment," Forkmorgan said, "the amendment was in effect *prior to* certification by the Vice President of the vote of the Electoral College. Thus the term limit amendment clearly prevented the President from being chosen by the Electoral College."

"'Clearly' is the issue here. But nice try, Counselor."

"You clearly see through me, Mr. Justice." Forkmorgan smiled.

As the elegant swordplay proceeded, Pepper found her eyes

---

* Two interwoven cloths of different texture.

wandering again, toward the back of the hall. A recognizable visage came into view: walrus mustache, a beef-jerky face beneath a pale forehead. *Well, who let* you *in?* The leathery face creased into a wink. Pepper turned back to the proceedings. Forkmorgan and Silvio were still going at it. She wanted to get a word in. The clock was ticking. Each side got an hour to present its case. Then there would be five minutes each for rebuttal.

No one, perhaps, had grasped better than she the CJ's admonition that the whole world would be watching.

Yards, furlongs, miles of print, on paper and online, had been expended on feverish speculation as to which way Justice Cartwright would swing in *Mitchell v. Vanderdamp*. Editorials and TV commentators demanded she recuse herself. How could she possibly be unbiased? She owed Vanderdamp her seat! Dexter Mitchell's loathing of her was a universally known fact, despite his shameless tactical pretense of enthusiasm for her at the hearings. (His fellow committee members had amply ventilated their anger at him to the media.)

Listening to these demands that she walk away from the case, Pepper's reaction was a (silent) reiteration of the comment in *Swayle* that had created so much bother: *kiss my ass.* This time, she would be careful not to hit the SEND button. After some three a.m. tossing and turning she had come to the conclusion that she was perfectly capable of rendering judgment. And that was that. It was one advantage to being a Supreme Justice: they could beller and holler as long as they wanted, but you didn't have to explain or account for yourself. Meanwhile, the boys were still going at it.

"The operative words, Justice Gotbaum, are 'when ratified by the Legislatures of three fourths of the several states,' which indicates that ratification is the critical moment. Post-election certification by the Archivist is a ministerial act that has no legal significance."

"I'm well aware of that, Mr. Forkmorgan. But under 18 USC 106b—to which you yourself allude on page twelve— the Congress has entrusted the Archivist with the final step necessary to complete enactment of the amendment. He or she must determine that the states have officially adopted the amendment. So it would seem to me that until he or she does so, the amendment is not effective."

Pepper took a deep breath—*no Latin,* she warned herself— and leapt in.

"Mr. Forkmorgan, as I understand it, the Court held in 1939, in *Coleman v. Miller,* that the efficacy of ratifications by state legislatures is a political question left to political departments, not the courts. Doesn't the rule of *Coleman* then apply here? Aren't you, in effect, asking us to second-guess the congressional judgment reflected in the statute?" *Whew* . . .

"Not at all, Justice Cartwright, though I thank you for highlighting this very aspect. We dispute the notion that *Dillon* should be overturned in light of *Coleman* . . ."

Suddenly the Chief Justice interrupted the attorney in the middle of a string of citations. "Thank you, Mr. Forkmorgan. Mr. Clenndennynn?"

Graydon rose. The spectators stirred at the sight of the President's attorney.

"You seem to put quite a bit of emphasis on *Opinion of the Justices, 362 Mass. 907,*" Hardwether began.

"Indeed, but no more than it is capable of sustaining, Mr. Chief Justice. It is a hardy opinion, I would say. But we also cite *City of Duluth; State v. Kyle; Real v. People;* and *Torres v. State.* At the risk of putting the Court to sleep."

A ripple of laughter.

"Oh, no," the Chief Justice smiled. "I'm wide awake."

"If I may, Mr. Chief Justice," Graydon said, slipping his right hand into his vest pocket, imparting a faint Churchillian aspect, "despite all our—I freely admit—rather busy citing, we are making, or trying to make, a simple and straightforward argument that to the extent there is ambiguity here, this amendment should not be deemed to apply to a *sitting* president. The Twenty-second Amendment was explicitly *prospective*. It didn't bar President Truman from running for reelection in 1952. The people did. So the Twenty-second Amendment's prospective reach can hardly be read as a background principle."

A little purr of appreciation went through the Hall. Paige Plympton, always on the lookout for the high ground in any argument, asked the President's attorney if the Framers had envisioned such a "conundrum as the one we seem to find ourselves in." Graydon, hand still tucked in his vest pocket, arched an eyebrow in bemusement.

"Justice Plympton, it has long been my impression, though I have never given voice to it publicly until now, that the Framers, had they known the procedural contortions and abominations to which their descendants would put their sublime efforts, might well have thrown up their hands in the air and begged the British to take us back."

A wave of laughter went through the Great Hall. The old man was about to continue when he suddenly turned gray. His hand moved from his pocket to his chest. He stood, gasping. Pepper thought, *Sweet Jesus.* And then he fell forward.

News that the President's attorney had collapsed during oral argument was received, in evangelical America, as a sign that the End of Days might, indeed, be at hand.

FIFTEEN MINUTES LATER, Pepper was in her chambers, stunned and teary-eyed. Crispus was keeping vigil with her at the TV set, handing her serial tissues. They watched.

Graydon Clenndennynn had been ambulanced to George

Washington Hospital, where an enormity of media were now swarming. Almost all of the stand-up reporters were calling him *"Mr.* Clenndennynn," as if in premonition of mortality. He was alive, but barely. Words crawled across the bottom of the screen: . . . PRESIDENT'S ATTORNEY SUFFERS 'MASSIVE' HEART ATTACK DURING SUPREME COURT ORAL ARGUMENT OVER DISPUTED ELECTION . . .

Declan was in his own chambers, manning a sort of command post, though it was anything but clear what its precise function was at this point, Court being—obviously—adjourned.

Pepper reached for the phone and called the Marshall of the Court's office. "I need a car. Right away."

Crispus stirred from his own lugubrious meditations—in fact, he had been offering silent prayers for Mr. Clenndennynn; doubtless Silvio was phoning the Vatican in Rome and exhorting the Holy Father to convene the College of Cardinals and put them to collective flash-priority orisons.

"Hm? Where are you going?" Crispus said.

"To the hospital."

This took a moment to sink in. "No," he said, "you can't do that."

"Got to."

"You *can't.*"

"Shut up, Crispy."

"Darling child—you'll be crucified. . . ."

"Screw that."

"But—"

"I'll call you from the hospital."

"At least let your boyfriend know," he called after her, but she was already out the door.

Twenty minutes later, Crispus, watching on the television in his own chambers, saw the commotion at the hospital's entrance as her town car arrived, the swarm of media turning on it like a wave as she emerged and was shouldered through the horde by Court marshals.

"Justice Cartwright . . . Supreme Court Justice Pepper Cartwright has just arrived at the hospital. . . . Justice Cartwright has arrived at George Washington Hospital where Graydon Clenndennynn is in critical condition following a heart attack during oral argument. That's all we know at the moment, but it would appear that she has come to the bedside of the lawyer who just an hour ago was arguing the President's case before the Supreme Court. Jeff, does that complicate matters any?"

"Well, yes, it could. Judges and attorneys are proscribed— prohibited—from discussing a case outside of court. The term for it is ex parte discussion. While it's obvious—at least I would think—that Justice Cartwright hasn't come to the hospital to discuss *Mitchell v. Vanderdamp* with Clenndennynn, there is so much tension surrounding this case that her presence here could play into the hands of those who have been insisting that she recuse herself. So the short answer to your question would be, yes, it could be a complicating factor in an already hypercomplicated matter."

Crispus closed his eyes and shook his head. Less than a minute later, his phone rang. It was the CJ.

"Jesus Christ, Crispus."

"She's your girlfriend, Dec, not mine."

"Does she have any idea . . ."

"Declan. Why don't you just breathe into a bag and calm down. She didn't go down there to get his views on *Coleman v. Miller*, for God's sake. She cares for the old goat."

"That's not the point!"

"Well, it's going to have to be 'the point.' Look, he's probably not even going to regain consciousness, so it's moot."

"Let's hope he doesn't."

"A fine sentiment."

"I didn't mean it that way."

"Steady hand on the tiller, Declan. Steady hand. Dec? Hello?"

Pepper had reached the ICU when her cell phone began twittering. She pulled it out and flipped it open when an intercepting nurse said, "You need to turn that off, ma'am." She looked ready to pluck it out of Pepper's hand before it could compromise life-sustaining telemetry.

JUSTICE'S CELL CALL FINISHES OFF GRAYDON CLENNDENNYNN— MURDER CHARGES BROUGHT

Pepper looked at the phone as she was pressing the OFF button and saw DEC.

She paused, then did a 180 and walked briskly to an area where cell phones were not considered lethal weapons.

"I'm at the hospital—"

"I *know* you're at the hospital," he said. "It's on TV. You need to not be at the hospital."

"Dec, for Pete's sake, I didn't come here to discuss the damn case with him."

"I don't care. I want you to leave the hospital now, Pep."

People were staring at her. She said in a whisper, "He doesn't have family. I'm just going to hold his hand is all."

"No, no, no. That is not your role, Justice Cartwright. Now leave. And make sure everyone *sees* you leaving. I want to watch you leave on TV. Tell the reporters you didn't talk to him, you just came to . . . talk to the doctors and see how he was doing."

"Jesus, Dec. I don't want him to die alone."

"You're not a hospice worker. You're a Supreme Court justice."

"And you're a supreme jerk." She pressed END and turned back to the ICU. Normally, visitors were not admitted, but apparently they made exceptions for the Supreme Court.

SHE'D BEEN BY HIS BED for a half hour, sitting, hovering, pacing. She counted the machines he was hooked up to and stopped at nine. From her conversations with the chief of cardiology, the head of the unit, and the head of the hospital, he was being well looked after, Mr. Clenndennynn. She grasped that the end was near for the old man. She pulled a rolling stool up to the bed and, finding a part of his hand that didn't have an IV or O_2 saturation sensor attached, held it.

She whispered to him, "Don't you dare leave me alone with this mess you got me into."

Suddenly, behind her there was a commotion and she became aware of men in suits with earpieces. She heard someone saying to her, in commanding terms, "Ma'am?" She looked up. There were several men, all large, grave-looking. One was saying to her, "Ma'am? You need to vacate the room."

She ignored him and turned back to Clenndennynn.

"*Ma'am.*"

She heard her name being uttered, murmurs, then no more barking at her. A few moments later there was another commotion, louder, the room filled. She looked up and there was the President. He looked stricken and his eyes were red. Hayden Cork was there, too, looking pale and drawn. She stood. She and the President stared at each other awkwardly and then embraced. The imminence of death forces intimacy. Even Hayden Cork, who gave the impression of someone who'd gone unhugged even by his own mother, embraced her.

The President's arrival at the hospital was duly reported. At the Supreme Court, Chief Justice Hardwether, watching on TV, muttered, "Oh, *great.*"

Graydon Clenndennynn died at 5:42 p.m. that afternoon. He regained consciousness briefly. He opened his eyes, took in Pepper, the President of the United States, the White House Chief of Staff, and smiled as if satisfied by this bedside concentration of eminence.

"Did we win?" he whispered. Poignant, as last words go, but in this instance, far from ideal. Pepper was trying to formulate some answer when the old man closed his eyes.

CHAPTER 32

CARTWRIGHT DEATHBED VISIT TO CLENNDENNYNN CASTS PALL OVER CASE AMID CALLS FOR RECUSAL

It was one of the milder headlines of the days following.

The burial at Arlington took on the aspect of a state occasion. In attendance were the President, the entire cabinet (minus the obligatory nonattendee in case of sneak nuclear attack), and—Declan had insisted—all nine justices of the Supreme Court.

Dexter Mitchell was in conspicuous attendance. One TV commentator whispered that it reminded him of the funeral scene in *The Godfather*. Would Blyster Forkmorgan approach Hayden Cork as taps was sounding to arrange "a meet on neutral turf"?

Pepper had not spoken with Declan since Graydon's death. It would be more accurate to say that Declan had not spoken to her. Crispus acted as go-between.

With the clock ticking toward Inauguration Day, there was no time for a cease-fire between the Mitchell and Vanderdamp camps. A replacement for Graydon Clenndennynn was engaged, Philip "Flip" Soyer, a much-garlanded appellate lawyer who had once practiced law with Graydon, a former Solicitor General universally acknowledged to be a Matterhorn of probity. His only public statement was to say that he saw no need to file a new brief and would endeavor to pick up where Mr. Clenndennynn had left off.

Team Mitchell also issued bland statements, meanwhile maneuvering furiously in the dark. Graydon Clenndennynn's body was still on its way to Gawler's Funeral Home on Wisconsin Avenue when Blyster Forkmorgan filed a motion for delay. He did this banking on Vanderdamp's sense of orderliness; as the days went by, the mounting chaos, anathema to his Ohio soul, might impel him to throw up his hands and resign, taking VP Schmidtz down with him in the higher interests of the nation. Forkmorgan also subpoenaed a) President Vanderdamp, b) Hayden Cork, c) Justice Pepper Cartwright, d) the Secret Service agents present at Graydon's deathbed, and e) the entire staff of the Intensive Care Unit, with the objective of finding out—as he put it—"the full extent of the ex parte discussions pertaining to *Mitchell v. Vanderdamp*." Hearing of this, President Vanderdamp said to Hayden, "Could you look up in the Constitution whether I'm allowed to order summary executions?"

At the press conference announcing these developments, Blyster Forkmorgan asserted that, regrettable as it might seem, these measures were essential, "given Justice Cartwright's continued refusal to recuse herself in the matter of *Mitchell v. Vanderdamp*." Here his straightforward object was to impute as much bias to Pepper as he could. And it worked. According to almost daily polls, 80 percent expected Justice Cartwright to vote for Vanderdamp. Mitchell's apparatchiks seized on this and dispatched their agents to appear on various TV shows to issue strident demands for her impeachment.

Meanwhile, Forkmorgan continued, "It is critical that discovery go forward so as to ascertain the extent and substance of the inappropriate discussions that were held between defendant and judge." The President was in no sense technically a "defendant," but the word had a nice criminal ring to it.

Adding gasoline to the flames, an ICU nurse who'd witnessed the embraces between Pepper and the President and his Chief of Staff revealed them to a reporter. It was—Pepper, the President, and Hayden silently and separately reflected—probably a matter of time before someone got hold of Graydon's last words, and retailed those.

THERE WAS A CHILL in the justices' conference room air just short of visible breath-vapor.

Pepper, as the juniormost justice, closed the door and stood ready to serve coffee, if asked. Normally, Silvio delighted in making her undertake this menial office, but not today. As Pepper took her seat, she passed Declan's, and caught a faint whiff of mintiness. *Oh, dear*, she thought, but then who could blame him? She could use a stiff one herself.

The CJ began with a few anodyne housekeeping notes. At length he seemed to take a deep breath and said, "I thought it might be appropriate, before we dive in, to ask if anyone had any . . . general comments."

No one spoke. Most justices stared at the table, as if a good movie were playing on its surface.

"I think maybe we ought . . . at least . . ." Mo Gotbaum said slowly as if each word were being drawn up by bucket one by one from a deep well, ". . . *discuss* the matter of recusal."

The statement hovered in the air for a moment or two. He added, in a cheery tone of voice, "I stipulate it's an entirely personal decision. I'm not for a minute suggesting compulsion. But all things being equal it might make sense at least for us all to . . . discuss it as an issue . . . qua issue."

"Anyone see the piece in *Legal Times?*" Silvio ventured.

This brought a palpably awkward silence, for they had all indeed read the article by the Dean of Fordham Law—Pepper's own alma mater. (Oh, dear.) It was entitled "Recusal Now, or Impeachment Later?"

Pepper said, "*I* read it."

"Oh?" Silvio said, uncharacteristically reticent. "Ah. Well . . ."

Excruciating silence. Pepper said to Declan, "Chief, may I say something?"

"Of course."

"First," she said, "I want to apologize to all of you. I did what I did because I felt I had to be there. As to the hugs, anyone here who's been at a deathbed knows that just . . . happens. It wasn't any celebration among plotters."

"But this wasn't just any deathbed," Justice Haro sniffed.

"I'm aware of that, Mike," Pepper said. "There's something else you should all know. Just before he expired, Mr. Clenndennynn said, " 'Did we win?' "

Justices stared. No one spoke. Finally, Paige Plympton said, "Did anyone make a *reply* to Mr. Clenndennynn?"

"I was trying to figure out something to say when he died."

There was a rumble, a low rumble that at first sounded like bronchitic lungs gasping for air, but which shortly revealed itself as—laughter. It was coming from Crispus, from very deep within him, as magma from an erupting volcano. His shoulders shook, his eyes teared, his hands gripped the edge of the conference table.

"I . . . aha . . . ahaaaa . . . sorry, sorry. It's not in the least . . . *haaaa-haaa-haaaaaa*. It's just too . . . *haaaaaa*." Ruthless stared at him with pursed lips, like a church lady confronting a bishop who had just farted in the middle of the Sermon on the Mount. Crispus gave a few final shudders, dabbed his eyes. "I'm sorry. Sorry," he said. "It's just . . ." This was followed by another few eruptions. After which he said, "Sorry. Sorry."

There was silence and the ticking of the grandfather clock.

"I think—" the Chief Justice said.

"If I might?" Pepper said.

Declan waved her on.

"I know it's my decision whether to recuse myself, and I thank Mo for pointing that out. There was no ex parte discussion. But under the circumstances, I'm going to let you all decide whether I should have a vote in *Mitchell*." She stood. "I'll abide by whatever your decision is."

"No. No," Declan said, bringing his hand down on the table with an angry thump. "That's is not how we do things."

"You got a better idea?"

"It's your decision. Don't ask us to make it for you. Take responsibility. It's your conscience. Your integrity. Don't ask for a proxy vote on it."

Pepper was formulating a response to this outburst when Justice Haro said, in a lowered but distinctly audible voice, "Is 'integrity' applicable here?"

Pepper wheeled. "You know, Mike," she said in a measured tone, "there's something I've been wanting to say to you for a while now. Kiss my ass."

To everyone's knowledge, it was the first time in history those three words had been uttered in the justices' conference room. No one moved. The Chief Justice stared at Pepper with icy contempt.

"I'll be in my chambers," Pepper said, gathering up her papers. "Let me know how the vote goes."

PEPPER BURIED HERSELF in mind-numbing minutiae, redrafting an overdue opinion, poring over footnotes, even paying bills, until she'd managed to put herself into a sort of zombielike state. When finally she looked up at the clock she saw that nearly two hours had gone by. It was taking them a long time to vote. Or did the delay portend some graver development? Were they drafting a petition asking her to resign? Articles of impeachment? No, she recalled from Introductory Con Law—*that* was up to the Congress.

Eventually there was a knock on her door. She looked up, expecting Crispus on some lugubrious ambassadorial mission— *For what it's worth, darlin' child, I took your side, but they all felt it would be best if you did the decent thing and resigned. . . .* But no, it was Declan, looking either drunk or like someone had smacked him across the face.

"You look like shit," Pepper said.

He sat in a chair facing her.

"You okay?" she said.

"You just said I look like shit."

"Sorry. You been . . . ?"

"No. I had a little snort before the conference. I could drain an entire bottle right now, but I don't think that would help."

Silence.

"So, you all want me out of here?" Pepper said.

"No. It's not that."

"Well, what is it? You look like an armadillo just crawled up your butt."

"Crispus told me."

"Told you what?"

"About the FBI. About Haro."

"Aw, he wasn't supposed to do that."

"I'm not sure where to begin. So I'll start with the apology."

"No one here owes me any apology."

"I confronted Mike. *Not* in front of the others."

"Was that smart, in the middle of this shit storm?"

"There's a principle at stake here, Pepper."

"I'm sick of principles. Vanderdamp ran on principle, and look what that accomplished. This country's ready to explode. And we're the detonators. Principles. Nothing but trouble. I don't want to hear any more about principles."

Declan seemed unsure how to process this declaration.

"So what did Mr. Justice Integrity have to say?" Pepper said.

"Not much."

"He could always just deny it. I destroyed the evidence."

"You're about as adept at destroying evidence as you are at using our Intranet. Crispus dug the pieces of paper out of the wastebasket and taped them together."

"That sneaky . . ."

"I showed it to Mike. I enjoyed *that* part. He went appropriately pale. Started blathering about gestapo tactics and criminal procedure. I was tempted to ask for his resignation."

"Kind of draconian, isn't it?"

"Draco is on the frieze in the Great Hall. You may have noticed."

"I did. Along with Moses and the Ten Commandments, with his beard covering the Thou Shalt Not parts. You ought to do something about that, by the way. So where was it left?"

"It was left that he is going to apologize to you at conference, starting fifteen minutes from now. For impugning your integrity. Further, he is going to propose that you not recuse yourself. My sense is that the others will accede. As for the leak and the FBI, nothing more will be said, by anyone, to anyone. You might apologize to *him* for telling him to kiss your ass."

"Slick, Chiefy," Pepper said. "Real slick."

"Yes," Declan said. "It was, rather."

THE VOTE on *Mitchell v. Vanderdamp* was 4–4. It fell to the junior-most justice to cast the deciding vote.

There had been vigorous discussion around the table. Normally, the Chief Justice did not encourage "debate," preferring that these contentions be waged on the cooler battleground of written opinions and footnotes. *Nine old farts sending footnotes to each other.* But this was an unusual case, and sensing that a certain amount of face-to-face combat might be cathartic, he allowed it.

The four justices in favor of granting Mitchell's motion clove to the (technical) argument that the term-limit amendment was in effect prior to the election, and that Vanderdamp's election was thus null and void. The four justices in favor of denying the motion, and allowing President Vanderdamp to take office for a second term, made their stand on grounds of the larger issue, namely that the people—as in "We the People"—had elected him, amendment or no. They viewed with approval, too, Graydon Clenndennynn's final (in so many ways) point that the Twenty-second Amendment was not "prospective."

It got pretty heated. The word "goddammit" was uttered several times; the table was thumped; motivations subtly questioned; the Chief Justice had to interject, "Come on, now," or "Please." At one point, Crispus leaned over to Pepper and whispered, "This is better than Friday Night Smackdown."

"Silvio," said Justice Gotbaum, "you're completely twisting what Bernstein said."*

---

* Richard Bernstein's *Fordham Law Review* article, "The Sleeper Awakes," a study of the Twenty-seventh Amendment: "Article V sets forth only one limitation on the types of amendments that may be proposed: 'that no State, without its Consent, shall be deprived of it's [sic] equal Suffrage in the Senate.'"

"I goddamn well am not. I do not 'twist.'"

"Well, for your information, it's a valid *goddamn* constitutional amendment. The Congress is the ultimate expression of the will of 'the People.' It has the superior claim to legitimacy—and therefore trumps—even the results of an election."

"I'm with Mo," Ruthless Richter said. "The principle here is precisely the same as in judicial review. We're back to *Marbury*. And if you want to bring in law review articles, I'd refer you to Bill Treanor's in *Stanford Law Review*.* As Justice Marshall observed in *Marbury*, 'Ours is a government of laws, and not men.' The amendment, adopted by 'We the People,' through the constitutional process, has a superior claim to legitimacy over an election result."

"You make 'election result' sound like an abstraction!"

"I do not."

"You do, too."

"All right," the Chief Justice finally said. "I think we've covered the ground."

"Some of us covered it," Silvio snorted. "Others stamped their little feet on it."

"Bullshit!"

"All right," Declan re-interjected. "Thank you, all."

A heavy silence fell, like the one that hangs over a battlefield after the firing has stopped.

"Justice Cartwright?" he said. "How say you?"

---

* "Judicial Review Before *Marbury*," *Stan. L Rev* 58 (2005): 455.

CHAPTER 33

5–4, SUPREME COURT DENIES MITCHELL'S MOTION, CLEARING WAY FOR VANDERDAMP SECOND TERM

Justice Cartwright, writing for the majority in denying *Mitchell v. Vanderdamp*, noted, "In finding for the President, we simply give effect to the principle of popular sovereignty that lies at the heart of our *real* founding document: 'We hold these truths to be self-evident . . . that whenever any Form of Government becomes destructive to these ends, it is the Right of the People to alter or to abolish it, and to institute new Government, laying its foundations on such principles and organizing its powers in such form, as to them shall seem most likely to effect their Safety and Happiness.'"

She said to Declan, "When the going gets tough, the scared-shitless quote from the Declaration of Independence."

"It's not a bad place to take cover," Declan said. He had voted in favor of Mitchell (albeit holding his nose), thus Pepper was spared a public racking for having taken the side of her "main squeeze," as the Chief Justice of the United States was now often referred to in the media. Declan added, "I think in some ways, Pep, it's your own declaration of independence."

There were demonstrations calling for Pepper's impeachment outside the Court, and a cascade of death threats. She and Ruthless Richter (who had voted for Mitchell) bonded over this aspect. They started making dollar bets as to whose daily mail would contain more threats and whose security detail was bigger.

Controversial though the ruling was, it was generally conceded that *any* ruling would have been controversial. There was, too, a sense of relief that the crisis was finally over. Though several senators stood on the floor to denounce the "Imperial Judiciary," Congress as a body did not take up impeachment.

Less than an hour after the Court issued its ruling, President Vanderdamp appeared on television from the Oval Office. He thanked the Court and resigned the office of the presidency, "effective January nineteenth"—that is, one day before the inauguration. Vice President Schmidtz would become president. The very next day, he would be sworn in again, in front of the whole nation, to serve the term of office that had been granted President Vanderdamp by the Court; becoming, in the process, the first president in history to be sworn in twice on consecutive days.

Within hours of Vanderdamp's announcement, the Speaker of the House of Representatives and the Majority Leader of the United States Senate—members of different political parties, moreover—appeared together on television to announce that they would introduce legislation calling for a repeal of the Twenty-eighth Amendment. The move was immediately hailed by a majority of the Congress; the bills were expected to pass and go on to the states for ratification. There was a practical reason: the Majority Leader was planning to run for president in four years, and did not relish the idea of going to the trouble only to be barred from having a second term. Democracy has its flaws, but it is (often) self-corrective.

On January 19, Vice President Schmidtz was sworn in, the oath of office administered by Associate Justice Crispus Galavanter, an old friend and golfing buddy. Crispus was a busy man these days. A few weeks later he married Pepper Cartwright and Chief Justice Declan Hardwether in a private ceremony at an "undisclosed location." The bride was given away by her grandfather.

Terry Mitchell divorced Dexter and married a New York real estate broker specializing in Park Avenue properties. Dexter went to work at a K Street firm lobbying his former colleagues for railroad subsidies.

In the spring, Buddy Bixby debuted his new television prime-time drama, *Primera Dama Desesperada*, starring Ramona Alvilar. It received mixed reviews but monster ratings.

ACKNOWLEDGMENTS

Thank you, my very dear Justice Jonathan Karp for this, our eighth collaboration. Others who greatly pleased the court: Amanda Urban of ICM; Cary Goldstein of Twelve; Lucy Buckley; John Tierney; Gregory Zorthian; Steve Umin; E. Barrett Prettyman Jr.; Harvey-Jane Kowal and Christine Valentine; Professors Thane Rosenbaum and Ben Zipursky of Fordham Law School. A large debt of thanks and a hearty oyez to Dean William Treanor of Fordham Law School, constitutional scholar and gentleman par excellence. And a large Milk-Bone to the Faithful Hound Jake who chased away the squirrels and secured the cone of silence.

ABOUT THE AUTHOR

Christopher Buckley is the author of thirteen books, including *Boomsday, Thank You for Smoking, Little Green Men, Remembrance of Things Past,* and *The Aeneid of Virgil.* He received the Thurber Prize for American Humor and the Washington Irving Prize for Literary Excellence. He lives on the Acela train between Washington, DC, and New York City.

ABOUT TWELVE

TWELVE was established in August 2005 with the objective of publishing no more than one book per month. We strive to publish the singular book, by authors who have a unique perspective and compelling authority. Works that explain our culture, that illuminate, inspire, provoke, and entertain. We seek to establish communities of conversation surrounding our books. Talented authors deserve attention not only from publishers, but from readers as well. To sell the book is only the beginning of our mission. To build avid audiences of readers who are enriched by these works—that is our ultimate purpose.

For more information about forthcoming TWELVE books, you can visit us at www.TwelveBooks.com.